Until Depths Do Us Part

Until Depths Do Us Part

Cruising Sisters Mystery

K.B. Jackson

Until Depths Do Us Part

Tule Publishing First Printing, April 2024

The Tule Publishing, Inc.

First Publication by Tule Publishing 2024

Cover design by ebooklaunch.com

ISBN: 978-1-964703-68-8

Dedication

To the real Charlotte and Jane, two sisters who loved each other fiercely and laughed the whole way.

Room Assignments:

701: Charlotte McLaughlin and Jane Cobb (Aunts of Groom)
750: Andy Cobb (Groom) Plus 2 Groomsmen
601: Phoebe Braithwaite (Bride)
703: Rhonda Cobb (Mother of Groom)
607: Dale and Susan Braithwaite (Parents of Bride)
615: Frank and Elaine Braithwaite (Uncle of Bride and Spouse)
668: Lily and Neal Alcorn (Sister of Bride and Spouse)
663: Ivy and Clyde Evans (Sister of Bride and Spouse)
600: Sawyer Braithwaite (Brother of Bride) Plus 1
612: Bridesmaid Suite

Chapter One

I STARED AT my naked reflection in the chrome overflow plate of the bathtub. Those rolls were hard-earned. Maybe not the calories I'd consumed that helped to create them, but the grief which had fueled the consumption of those calories.

My neighbor, Inga, after observing me hauling a box of donuts into my house last week, had told me the Germans had a word for what I was experiencing. *Kummerspeck*. The literal translation was grief-bacon, but it could apply to any emotional eating. My personal weakness happened to be tacos from the truck down the street from my house, but, since the funeral, my freezer had been stocked with baked goods and casseroles each made to serve a dozen people. I lived alone now, so it was on me to make use of them.

And I had.

I pressed play on the stereo remote and sank into the warm water. Some might have thought it odd, submerging myself in a bubble bath while listening to songs about money from a playlist comprised of artists like Pink Floyd, Dire Straits, even the Flying Lizards, but music was how I processed my emotions, and I had a lot to process when it came to the subject of money.

I'd had no idea of our net worth until six weeks ago when I sat, shell-shocked, in the law offices of Bacon, Volks, and Bettencourt listening to attorney Richard Volks read my husband's lengthy will.

Money was never something Gabe and I talked about. He was neither stingy nor overly flashy. When we'd gotten married, he told me his income alone could support us, but I loved my job at the library, so I'd continued to work part-time.

I knew we had a financial cushion, but it turned out to be more of a *Princess and the Pea* situation, with mattress stacked upon mattress. I'd been stunned as Richard listed Gabe's considerable assets, including several banking and investment accounts and the sizable numbers they held.

Of course, I'd sensed the pea, the vague notion something wasn't quite right. You couldn't live with a person that long without noticing they weren't mentally or emotionally present even while sitting across from you at the dinner table. As one often did when they loved someone, I tried to explain it away, making excuses for the disquiet that had unsettled me for more than two years.

At night I'd lay in bed, restless, wondering why I couldn't sleep. It felt like that nagging sensation you got when you left home in a hurry and were certain you'd forgotten to pack an item or unplug the iron. Did I turn off the bathroom faucet? The coffeepot? Was the front door locked?

Then I discovered the pea underneath all those layers of the life we shared.

More accurately, the police and paramedics on the scene of the accident did.

A heart attack, they'd said, standing on my front porch about two months ago. Instantaneous. He was gone before his car wrapped itself around the light pole.

My knees had buckled, and I'd gripped the doorjamb. "Heart attack?"

The woman in the passenger seat had suffered moderate injuries, they'd informed me, including a broken right leg, but otherwise she was in good shape. The infant in the back was without a scratch, despite his blanket covered in broken window glass.

"Infant?" Darkness crept into the corners of my eyes. "What infant? What woman?" I parroted his words back to him in the form of questions, hoping that hearing them come out of my own mouth might make sense of it all.

The pea? Well, that was the double life my husband of twenty years had been living.

Officer Wyatt—who I'd taken to be the boss, as he'd done the bulk of the talking—grimaced. "A young woman, in her early thirties. Blonde hair. The child, a boy, is about a year old. She said they were on a family outing when Mr. McLaughlin gripped his chest and lost consciousness."

When a sixty-five-year-old man with a penchant for red meat and cheesecake dallied with a woman less than half his age, I suppose he took the risk of his heart failing him.

In many ways, his heart had failed both of us.

Perhaps I'd have sympathized with him if I hadn't been so busy dealing with my own humiliation, I thought, as "Money,

Money, Money" by Abba echoed off the marble surround of the tub.

I sank deeper into the bath until my ears were fully submerged under the water, as if it were remotely possible to shield myself from the pity thrown my way over the past few weeks with a fortress of soapy bubbles. I snorted at the absurdity and accidentally inhaled a bit of the peony-scented foam. The lower I sank, the more muffled the music became, but the chorus was unrelenting in its chanting message about money and the world of the rich man.

I knew very little about the world of the rich man.

While I'd dutifully clipped coupons and ate leftovers, my husband had been living in the rich man's world. While I spent gloomy winter days shelving books in a library, he'd been basking on beaches with another woman.

I fixated on a water stain in the ceiling above me. Gabe had said he'd deal with it, but he never did. I'd have to hire someone to fix it before it became a bigger problem. I knew we had a handyman who could do it, but I didn't know how to get in touch with him. Peter. Peter, uh…I didn't even know his last name.

The one thing that had been made clear to me throughout the past couple months was I knew very little about my own life. Next to nothing, as a matter of fact.

I didn't know about the money.

The woman.

The baby.

The lies.

When I died, it should be etched on my tombstone:

HERE LIES CHARLOTTE MCLAUGHLIN
SHE DIDN'T KNOW

Richard Volks had known. Gabe had Richard change his will the previous August shortly after his son, Quinton, was born. Accommodation had also been made for Quinton's mother, Kyrie Dawn. Between the two of them, they'd been given twenty-five percent of Gabe's assets.

I couldn't help but wonder who else had known. Staff from Gabe's office? His friends? The barista at his favorite coffee shop? And yet they all were still able to look me in the eye at his funeral. Perhaps they were the same people huddled together at the reception afterward in whispering conclaves as they drank from the open bar and filled their bellies full of crudités and charcuterie trays.

I grabbed the wineglass from the table next to the tub and swigged. The wine probably wasn't helping my figure any more than the nine-by-nine pan of brownies I'd defrosted that afternoon and finished in one sitting while watching *Charade* for the zillionth time.

I'd always loved the movie, but since the revelation of the pea, it resonated with me in a viscerally familiar way. Newly widowed Audrey Hepburn discovered her husband wasn't the man she'd thought. Unfortunately, I was still waiting for my Cary Grant to show up and make me feel better about the deception of my marriage.

My cell phone rang from the counter.

I heaved a sigh. Time to climb out of my refuge and back into reality. My joints groaned as I hoisted myself from the tub and over to the vanity. Without looking at the screen, I knew it was my older sister, Jane. No one else called me anymore. None of them knew what to say.

"I was taking a bath." I wrapped a towel around my damp body with my free hand.

"At four thirty in the afternoon?"

"It's already dark." I shrugged my shoulders, despite her not being able to see me.

"If we were sipping margaritas poolside in Puerto Vallarta, it would still be light outside. Instead, we're in gloomy Seattle trying to ward off seasonal affective disorder. It's only November ninth. We've got four more months of this. I'll never make it to spring."

"I buried my husband six weeks ago. Cut me some slack. We can plan a trip. I just wasn't ready when you brought it up at the wake."

"Yeah. Sorry about that. Probably should've waited until after the bast—" She paused and cleared her throat. "Until *Gabe* was cold in the ground for more than five minutes." His name dripped off Jane's tongue like the venom she felt toward him.

It was understandable. She was, after all, my protective older sister, so of course she was angry at him. I was, too, but my anger was muddled with the betrayal I felt in the deepest parts of my wounded soul.

There was something else. Something shameful I'd yet been able to voice to anyone: I blamed myself as much as I blamed him.

It took two people to have a terrible marriage.

"How about now?" Jane said.

"How about now what?" I pulled the drain plug and the bathwater gurgled.

"Are you up for a trip?"

"What are you talking about?"

I waddled into the bedroom and flopped onto the left side of the bed. I still wasn't used to sleeping alone and had yet to venture to the right side. Gabe's side.

"Andy called. He and Phoebe have run into an issue with the wedding."

"What kind of issue? Other than interrupting everyone else's family traditions because they insisted on scheduling the ceremony at a farm in the boonies on Thanksgiving Day, I mean. Who does that?"

I knew very well who did that. The boy who'd always been the center of our family's universe, who, along with strong prompting from his bride, knew we'd move mountains for him.

Andy, a fourth-grade teacher, was the only child of our older brother Bernard. Since neither Jane nor I ever had any children, Andy was the last of the family line. When Andy was only three, his father was diagnosed with terminal brain cancer. Bernie died less than two years later, and raising Andy became a group project.

"What's the problem? Did they break up?" I tried to keep my optimism at the thought, out of my voice. It wasn't that I didn't like Phoebe, exactly, but she and Andy had dated only eight months, and during that time I'd witnessed several red flags in her behavior toward him.

The private remote wedding was understandable, considering Phoebe was trying to stay out of the spotlight. Two years ago, Phoebe Braithwaite was a globally known YouTube personality who'd let her viewers observe her every waking moment from the time she made avocado toast for breakfast to the application of her bedtime skincare routine. All that had come to an abrupt end when she began receiving threatening messages and packages at her home from an obsessed fan. It had spooked her enough to shut down the whole channel. Her resulting paranoia affected everything in her life, including her mercurial relationship with Andy.

"No. The farm flooded in the rainstorm last night. There's at least a foot of standing water everywhere. Even if it drains by the day of the wedding, the barn and the furniture are too damaged to be repaired and or replaced in time."

"What does that have to do with taking a trip?"

"I've been looking into it, and I believe that surprise you found in Gabe's will might be just the ticket."

"Which surprise? The millions of dollars he had stashed away or the previously unknown infant heir and his"—I swallowed the pejorative term I wanted to use—"*mother* to whom Gabe left one quarter of his estate?"

"The other one. The cruise ship condo."

"Ah. His lover's lair on international waters." My nostrils flared at the thought of Gabe and Kyrie Dawn clinking champagne glasses as they watched the sun set over Ibiza or Sydney Harbor.

"I did some research after Andy called in a panic. Phoebe's a blubbering mess, and he's desperate to fix it, of course.

The ship is due to dock at the Port of Seattle the weekend before Thanksgiving. They've got tons of open berths for rent because a large portion of the owners are visiting family on land for the holiday. We—and by we, I mean you with your newly discovered fortune—we could rent several of them and have the wedding onboard. It's scheduled for a weeklong tour through the waters of Alaska, arriving back in Seattle the following Sunday. It's the perfect solution."

"How is that the perfect solution?" I grunted. "Alaska in November sounds awful. Isn't the ocean frozen up there at this time of year? I swear I saw once on *Deadliest Catch*, there are chunks of ice floating around, waiting to tear a hole in the hull."

"It's called the *Thalassophile of the Seas*, not the *Titanic*, and the itinerary doesn't have us docking for a land excursion until the last full day. The rest of the time will be spent floating around looking at the beautiful scenery from within the warmth and comfort of a luxury residential cruise ship."

"You know Thalassophile means lover of the seas in Greek, right? So, basically, the boat is called the lover of the seas of the seas."

"Is that a yes?"

I released the deep exhalation of the emotionally exhausted. "Fine. But Phoebe's uncle Frank's room needs to be far away from mine. Every time I encounter him, he's got a glass of scotch in one hairy hand and my buttocks in the other."

Chapter Two

I STOOD AT the entrance to the gangplank and stared up at the *Thalassophile of the Seas*. It wasn't as large as the cruise ship Gabe and I had taken to the Caribbean for our honeymoon, but it was still quite impressive.

I'd done a little research, so I had a general idea what to expect. The website boasted a hundred luxury residences ranging in size from studios to three bedrooms, along with five restaurants, two bars, a handful of boutiques, a casino/gaming room, a cigar lounge, a spa and hair salon, a grocery store, a fitness center, a full-sized tennis court, two swimming pools, two hot tubs, a theater, and a library.

Unbeknownst to me, Gabe had purchased a two-bedroom unit in both of our names for his trysts. I suspected my signature was not the one on the contract, although it was possible. I didn't always pay attention to documents he shoved in front of me. I probably should have. I also should have noticed his so-called business trips always seemed to be in port cities, but, honestly, who would suspect anyone of traveling to Galveston to have an affair?

While full-time residency on the *Thalassophile* was an option, most owners spent an average of four months a year onboard and the remaining months at one (or more) of their other homes while their units either sat empty or were rented out by the week like a timeshare.

For Andy and Phoebe's wedding, we'd rented nine additional staterooms for the week. Andy and his groomsmen would take one, Phoebe would have her own, and her two bridesmaids would take another. After the wedding, Andy and Phoebe would share his room, and his groomsmen would move into Phoebe's vacated room. Phoebe's parents, Dale and Susan Braithwaite, Andy's mom Rhonda, Phoebe's uncle Frank and his wife Elaine, Phoebe's brother Sawyer and his girlfriend Macy, and Phoebe's two sisters, identical twins Lily and Ivy, along with their husbands took up six of the condos.

"You look as though you're not certain where you are going or if this is where you are supposed to be."

Never a truer statement was spoken.

I whirled around to face the man who owned the baritone voice with the French accent and wasn't disappointed by what I found.

He seemed to be about my age, perhaps as old as his mid-to-late fifties. It was hard to tell. The laugh lines were an anomaly on his otherwise smooth olive skin, and the minimal gray that peppered his black hair was predominantly concentrated in his temples and goatee. His eyes were brown, but not dark. They reminded me of the chai tea I used to make lattes.

He wore white pants, white shoes, and a white short-sleeved button-up shirt with black and gold stripes and patches. He held his white cap under his arm. He had the look of a captain but gave off a different vibe. In my experience, limited to a handful of cruises with my lying, cheating husband, ship captains tended to have high levels of swagger and bravado. This man struck me as more enigmatic and subdued.

"This is a private ship. Perhaps you are looking for the sunset dinner party boat?"

Did my khaki pants and navy sweater say I was headed for a booze cruise by myself?

"No, this is me."

"Forgive me, but I am the head of security here on the *Thalassophile*, and I do not know you. Are you on the manifest?"

I reached into the tote bag slung over my shoulder. I'd printed out the information, even though everything was on the app. I handed him the papers.

"I'm Charlotte McLaughlin."

His thick brows arched as he scanned the page. His forehead wrinkled, his head slanted, and then realization visibly dawned across his face.

My heart sank.

He knew.

I hadn't known, but he had. I could see it in his pitying expression. I'd seen it too many times over the past two months not to recognize it.

He cleared his throat. "Forgive me, Madame McLaughlin. We have never met." He held out his hand. "I am Xavier Mesnier. As I said, I am head of onboard security. I was acquainted with your husband. I was sorry to hear of his passing."

"Thank you." I didn't want to go further down that conversation road. "Has anyone else in the Cobb-Braithwaite wedding party arrived?"

"I believe the groom and his mother are settling into their staterooms, as well as the bride's aunt and uncle."

Frank. My nostrils flared.

"In which room are Frank and Elaine staying?"

Xavier glanced at his manifest again. "Stateroom 615 on the Aegean deck."

"And which one has been assigned to me?"

He squinted at me and tilted his head. "Your own, of course."

"Oh, I… uh, I guess I hadn't realized it was a set location. I figured it was a membership that gave access to a certain class of berth, not a specific one. Did he…does one choose the furnishings and décor, or is it preselected?"

"Each owner has the option to select how their suite is furnished, but there are specific designs from which to choose."

"And, uh, my…Mr. McLaughlin? Which did he choose?"

"It does not say here, madame. It only says the number. I have not been inside the suite."

I closed my eyes for a brief moment, willing my nerves and humiliation to subside. "What unit is that again?"

"It's 701, madame. On the Odyssey deck."

I nodded vigorously, as if it could shake the humiliation

off me. "Thank you."

As I rushed up the gangplank, he called out to me.

"I do hope you're able to enjoy your trip, Madame McLaughlin."

I whirled to face him, my cheeks warm and my lungs already winded. "Thank you, Mr. Mesnier. You as well."

Immediately, I felt foolish. He wasn't there for vacation. But he merely smiled.

After checking in at the reception desk and getting the spare key—apparently, Gabe had kept the original somewhere in his office, car, or home study—I trudged to suite 701. I opened the door just enough to poke my head inside.

I had to give it to Kyrie Dawn: she had great taste. I knew it wasn't Gabe, since his style tended more toward old English library rather than the sleek and sophisticated look of the condo. I hadn't been sure what to expect, considering Kyrie Dawn had arrived at the graveside service wearing a black leather skirt and a blouse so sheer her bra was visible, but apparently her interior design style was less risqué than her clothing.

Thankfully, the living room showed no signs of personalization. I wasn't sure my tattered heart could take the sight of a family portrait featuring my husband, his mistress, and their baby.

Stepping foot into this suite was my first attempt at reclaiming my life and my dignity. If I could exorcise the ghost of Gabe's betrayal from this place, perhaps I could rid myself of the embarrassment that hung over me like an outdated set of drapes.

I wheeled my suitcase into the bedroom, but before I could even get to the closet, the doorbell rang, followed by a desperate pounding.

"Char! You in there? Hurry! I'm in the middle of a hot flash and I gotta use the toilet."

My sister, Jane, ever the classy woman.

I opened the door, and she pushed past me.

"Where is it? I left Turd-lock at six thirty this morning for the long drive to Oakland airport with one of those giant tumblers of coffee, and I've had to pee since I got on the plane. With all that turbulence, they never let us up to use the toilet. Don't they know how bad turbulence affects a full bladder?"

Jane often made derogatory comments about Turlock, the central California town where she'd resided for twelve years. She'd been in a graduate program at UC Berkeley when Bernard got sick. After he died, she moved back to the Seattle area and stayed until Andy graduated high school. Not long after that, she was recruited to run the library in Turlock and had complained about it ever since. I suspected she loved the town as much as it loved her, whether she'd ever admit it or not.

"Why didn't you use the restroom when you landed?" I asked.

"Couldn't. My driver was waiting. I thought I'd be smart and book it prior to takeoff to make sure he'd be there on time. I was worried about missing the boat. Didn't anticipate flying into a satellite terminal and having to take the tram."

"Your bathroom is through that door." I indicated where

to go, and she hustled down the hallway as there was another knock on the door.

"It's like Grand Central around here!" Jane called from the head, where she'd left the door ajar. "Is it Andy? I told him to come find us as soon as he was settled."

I opened the door to find my nephew Andy standing on the other side.

"It's Andy," I called over my shoulder before turning my attention back to him with a critical eye. "You look thin. Is she feeding you?"

He drew me in for a hug. "It's good to see you, Aunt Char." He pulled back and scanned my face. "How have you been holding up since the funeral?"

I swatted the air. "No talking about dead people. This is your wedding."

He followed me into the living room. "Thanks again for making this happen. I didn't know what we were gonna do."

He sat on one of the white armchairs, and I sat on the dark gray lounge chair across from him.

"I'm the one who made it happen." Jane appeared in the doorway, tucking her shirt into her high-waisted jeans. "She just happened to have the resources."

"Aunt Jane." Andy stood and gave her a hug.

Jane flopped herself onto the sofa. "Isn't this place to die for?" She made a gurgling sound. "No pun intended."

"Jane!" I scolded.

"Aunt Char's been through a lot."

Jane bobbed her head. "I'm just sayin'. Money helps heal many wounds."

I rolled my eyes at Andy. "It's fine. I'm used to her after fifty-three years being her sister. Has Phoebe arrived yet? I know the captain wants to leave by four."

Andy checked his watch. "It's two forty-five. She planned to leave work by two, and it should have only taken about fifteen minutes to get here from Ballard. I'll go check on her in a bit."

"She worked today?" I shifted in my seat.

"She said she had something to take care of before she got on the boat for a week but didn't say what."

I clucked. "Frank was one of the first onboard. I can't believe he'd risk his niece missing her wedding cruise by making her work until the last minute."

After quitting public life, Phoebe went to work as the office manager for her family's business, Braithwaite Industrial Storage. They leased lockers, shipping containers, and space in their warehouses. Their main clients were local and deep-sea fishing companies based in the Lake Washington Ship Canal near the Ballard Locks, but they also rented space to other types of businesses. Technically, Phoebe's father, Dale, and his brother, Frank, co-owned the company, but Dale had abdicated the daily running of things to Frank shortly after they'd inherited it from their father.

"I don't think Frank told her to go into the office." Andy turned serious. "She said something about odd happenings around the lot, and she was going to check on something while Frank wasn't there."

Jane sat straight. "Odd happenings. Did she say what?"

"No. She was vague about it. She mentioned Frank had

recently met with a couple guys she described as shifty looking. I don't know if they were clients or what." Andy ran a hand through his hair and blew out a long breath. "I really wish she'd quit that job. I don't like her working there. Something in my gut says it's unsafe."

"Have you told her that?" I asked.

"We've had a few arguments about it. She says I'm being ridiculous and if I don't stop acting like a controlling Neanderthal—her words, not mine—she won't marry me."

Jane gasped and placed her fingertips against her throat. "She wouldn't call off the wedding over something so silly, would she? I can't believe she called you, of all people, controlling. It's clear to anyone with eyeballs who wears the pants in that relationship."

Andy shrugged and then slumped his shoulders. "I don't know how to convince her. She won't listen to me."

I kept quiet and attempted to tamp down the flutter I felt over the prospect of the wedding being canceled. It wasn't that I didn't want Andy to be happy. It wasn't that I didn't like Phoebe in a general sense. I simply didn't think she was the right woman for him. She was shortsighted, hardheaded, and tended to roll over Andy like a construction vehicle flattening freshly paved asphalt. Despite that, I'd offered my great-grandmother's sapphire and diamond ring to Andy for his proposal.

Andy's phone rang in his hand. The ringtone was a song I vaguely recognized, one of those female empowerment anthems. I suspected Phoebe had set it herself.

Andy breathed his relief. "Babe. Did you make it on the

boat?"

Phoebe's side of the conversation was unintelligible, but her tone sounded abnormally subdued. Typically, her voice was high-pitched and worked up about something.

Andy's smile was strained. "Good. Dinner is at five thirty in the main restaurant. Don't forget, tonight is Roaring Twenties night."

This time her tone was more animated.

"Don't be like this, Pheebs. It'll be fun, I promise." Andy sighed. "I hung your flapper dress in your closet." He paused. "No, you don't have to wear the headpiece. I just thought it would be cute on you." He closed his eyes and pinched the bridge of his nose. "I'm sure you'll feel better after a shower and something to eat." He opened his eyes, his lids heavy. "Alright. Alright. Okay, see you in a bit." He disconnected the call. He didn't make eye contact with either Jane or me. Instead, he stared at his hands, clasping the phone in his lap. "She's here."

"Oh…good?" Jane queried.

Andy slapped his thighs and stood. "I've gotta go put on my gangster costume. I found a real three-piece pinstripe suit at the thrift store for twelve dollars. Who knows, maybe it once belonged to an actual criminal. Anyway, don't forget to do the digital muster drill. I already did mine. It's all set up on your TV, and then you've just gotta pop over quickly and check in with the crewmember at your assigned station."

"Andy…" I hesitated when I saw the pained look on his face. "See you at dinner."

Once he'd shut the door behind him, Jane turned to

look at me with wide eyes. "Should we stop this wedding?"

"We can't keep coddling him like we've always done. He's thirty. He gets to make his own decisions, and he must live with the consequences of his choices."

Jane glanced in the direction of the door. "I sure hope those consequences aren't an unhappy marriage and a life filled with regret."

AFTER WE'D UNPACKED our suitcases and watched the safety videos on the smart TV in the living room, we headed over to our muster station on the sixth floor to check in with the safety officer assigned to us. As we made our way past rows of lifeboats and wooden paddles painted bright orange, I spotted the bride up ahead, having a heated conversation. I couldn't see who she was talking to, as they were in the shadows of an alcove blocked by a six-foot Ficus, and, by the time we reached Phoebe, she was alone.

"Phoebe?"

She wiped tears from her pale cheeks. "Charlotte. Jane. Hello."

"Are you all right, dear?" Jane put on her most friendly librarian voice. She also had in her repertoire, among others, *stern librarian*, *helpful librarian*, and *hissing librarian*.

Phoebe waved her hand dismissively. "Oh, yeah, uh, just a minor pre-wedding breakdown."

"Whoever you were just talking to seems to have really upset you," I said.

Her eyes flashed briefly before being replaced with a façade of nonchalance. "You must have misunderstood what you saw. I've been standing here by myself all along. Maybe you saw me talking to myself. I do that sometimes."

I opened my mouth to refute what she'd said but stopped when the overhead speaker beeped, followed by man with a Scandinavian accent.

"Ladies and gentlemen, last call for checking in at your muster station. In ten minutes, we will begin calling you out by name, and nobody wants that, do we?"

Jane grabbed me by the arm. "We'd better go. See you at dinner, Phoebe."

As Jane pulled me away, I glanced back at Phoebe, who stood stone-faced. She'd been talking with someone. It had upset her, and she'd lied about it. What could she be hiding? A secret lover? A secret identity? Whatever it was, it didn't bode well for our nephew's happily-ever-after.

Was his marriage a sinking ship before it even left the docks?

Chapter Three

"IS THAT CHARLOTTE McLaughlin or Clara Bow?" Frank's voice boomed across the dining room, causing several diners to look my way. His smirk was only partially hidden by his fake mustache and the shadow of the oversized white fedora he wore tilted to one side. He held up his customary glass of scotch in salutation. A gold link chain dangled from his wrist and a gold medallion hung from his neck. "Come on over. We're just getting seated."

Frank was dressed as a prohibition-era gangster. That figured.

Standing next to him, his wife, Elaine, tittered, pretending his open flirtation didn't bother her. Elaine had teased her strawberry blonde curls into some sort of helmet with a bouquet of black feathers jutting out at an angle dangerous to anyone standing near her. Her diamond chandelier earrings hung down three inches at least. She wore a boxy black fringed dress, which appeared at least two sizes too big everywhere but in her cleavage area, where her surgically enhanced ample bosom was on full display.

"I'm gonna kill him," I said to Jane through gritted teeth. My cheeks grew warm under the scrutiny of our fellow passengers.

From the corner of the room, I spotted Xavier Mesnier observing me with an unreadable expression.

Jane tucked her dark bob (courtesy of Mr. Alfredo's House of Wigs) behind her ears. "Take it as a compliment. Clara Bow was the most famous flapper in the world."

"She was also five-three and about a hundred pounds. I look like a linebacker compared to her."

The formal dining room was on the ninth floor of the ship, also known as the Mykonos level. There were no passenger cabins on this level, only the dining hall, a bar, a live music stage, and an outdoor observation deck. The room we were in featured high ceilings, elegant light fixtures dimmed for ambiance, and tall windows on both sides for optimal views.

In the corner, a jazz band played "West End Blues" by Louis Armstrong.

Each table's centerpiece was a vase containing white roses and black ostrich feathers. Scattered throughout the room were floating bouquets of black, white, and gold balloons.

As Andy waved us over to the large round table, I noticed his forehead was creased and his mouth was pulled taut.

Phoebe paired her beaded champagne-colored dress with a sullen pout. The achromatic outfit didn't do much for her fair skin, highlighting her gaunt cheekbones and shadowed under eye. She'd chosen not to wear the hairband and had twisted her platinum hair into a chignon, which wasn't exactly era-appropriate but, based on her attitude, I thought it best to keep that fact to myself. She fidgeted with the *too big for her* sapphire ring on her left finger, rolling it with her thumb.

I'd have thought Phoebe's parents had gotten the nights mixed up, but I knew Dale's open-collared shirt under a Patagonia vest and Susan's floral kaftan weren't costumes for hippie night—they were standard attire. Now in their late sixties, Dale and Susan had met and fallen in love as teenagers while serving in the Peace Corps in 1971, and their style had remained in a time warp ever since. They were both Deadheads and Parrotheads.

"Evening, everyone." I smiled as I pulled out my chair, grateful Frank was on the opposite side of the table.

Jane took the seat to the left of me, leaving one open chair.

An older gentleman, in his mid- to late-sixties, with gray hair, a protuberant nose, and sagging jowls appeared out of nowhere. He wore a double-breasted pinstripe suit and a white tie.

"Good evening, ladies and gentlemen." His accent sounded German. "My name is Ulfric Anton, and I am your maître d'. How are you all doing tonight?"

Everyone murmured something along the lines of "fine."

"Good to hear. I believe you are celebrating a wedding?"

"Yes, I'm marrying this beautiful woman." Andy cradled the back of Phoebe's neck. "Thursday."

"Thanksgiving Day. Very nice."

"Can I get another scotch, my good man?" Frank's request sounded less like a question and more like an order.

Ulfric gave a quarter-bow. "Let me get your server,

Haimi."

"Jaime?" Frank said. "He Mexican?"

While Ulfric had pronounced the server's name as hi-my, Frank had pronounced it hi-may, with a guttural emphasis on the first syllable like it was a combination of Spanish, Hebrew, and phlegm.

Ulfric's cheeks reddened. "Uh, no, sir. Haimi Dara is female. She joined us last year from London."

Ulfric shuffled over to a petite woman with dark hair, medium-toned skin, and dark eyes fringed with long black eyelashes. Her eyes grew wide as she listened to Ulfric's recap of the goings on at our table. I watched as she squared her shoulders, took a deep breath, and marched over to the table.

"Hello, my name is Haimi, and I will be your server for the duration of this voyage. I am told someone here requested a scotch. Can I get anyone anything else?"

We took turns giving her our drink orders, and then she hustled over to the bartender.

I leaned forward. "Andy, where's your mom? She's booked for the room next to us, but I have yet to run into her."

Phoebe emitted a disgruntled gurgle.

Andy's mouth formed a tight smile. "She wasn't feeling well. She says she'll join us for breakfast."

Phoebe muttered something about Xanax.

Andy grabbed his steak knife and used it to butter a piece of bread. It occurred to me, Jane and I might have dropped the ball on his table etiquette training.

Jane craned her neck and scanned the room. "I see Phoebe's siblings, but what about the rest of the bridal party? Did everyone make it onboard? It would be tragic if someone missed the boat, so to speak." She chuckled to herself. "You, know, because it's both a literal boat and also a metaphor."

Andy groaned. "Aunt Jane, please, let's limit the puns this week. Everyone's accounted for. Phoebe's bridesmaids Serena and Nikki, my groomsmen Vance and Duncan."

The table next to ours was empty. "So, where are they?"

Phoebe pursed her lips. "They all decided to skip dinner and head straight for the bar."

"So tacky," Susan murmured.

"I wish I could join them." Phoebe's pout deepened as she crossed her arms.

Andy shifted in his seat.

"He looks miserable," Jane whispered in my ear.

I had to agree with her.

"Speaking of," Dale began. "New earrings, Elaine?"

I suspected he meant speaking of things that are tacky, but I couldn't be certain.

Elaine reached up to touch the bottom of her right earring with her fingertips. "Yes, Frank bought them for me for our anniversary. It's hard to find clip-ons that can hold diamond pieces this heavy."

Dale rolled his eyes.

"She's worn them every day since I gave them to her." Frank preened and puffed up his chest.

"They make me feel glamorous, even when I'm wearing yoga pants."

"My girl is worth every penny."

Dale guffawed.

Frank narrowed his eyes at his brother. "Jealousy doesn't become you, brother."

Dale opened his mouth to protest, but Andy leaned forward and dramatically put his elbows on the table. "I heard there might be karaoke at the lounge. Maybe we can head over later." He gestured toward the table a few feet away from us. "I've heard Ivy and Clyde do a mean 'Islands in the Stream.'"

I observed the group at the other table. Phoebe's sisters, two identical waiflike thirty-something blondes, sat next to each other, flanked on each side by their very different-looking husbands. I knew from talking with Phoebe that Ivy and Lily's disparate taste in men indicated they weren't identical in every way.

Ivy's husband, Clyde Evans, was a short, stocky Black man. Lily's husband, Neal Alcorn, was a tall, thin, white guy who looked every part the banker he was. I couldn't help but wonder if they'd ever attempted the old twin switcheroo on their husbands, just for giggles.

Also at the table were Phoebe's brother, Sawyer, and a young woman I'd never seen before. She had medium-brown hair and dark eyes. Her long nose came to a sharp point, which tilted up like a tapir. She wore a black fringed dress and a silver locket around her neck.

"Who's next to Sawyer? Is that his girlfriend?" I asked.

Andy craned his head to look around Phoebe. "Yeah, that's Macy."

"How did they meet again? I think you mentioned it

once, but I can't recall," I said.

"She's a barista at his favorite coffee shop," Andy said.

"Only until she graduates from her coding program," Susan interjected. "She has goals."

"Their idea of a fun night out is parkour." Phoebe rotated her wineglass on the table. "Sawyer's annoyed with me for not putting her in my wedding. In fact, last week he threatened not to even come at all. What, you're gonna not come watch your sister get married because your baby girlfriend got her feelings hurt?"

"Give the girl a break," Andy said. "You know she's had a rough go in life, Pheebs. He just wanted her to feel part of the family."

"They've only been dating a few months!" Phoebe took a swig of wine.

I chased my swallowed comment on her hypocrisy with my own quaff of merlot. Had she forgotten she and Andy had only been together eight months?

I observed Sawyer and Macy as she absentmindedly played with her locket and gazed adoringly at Sawyer. He kissed her on the tip of her nose.

"So, Dale and Susan, Phoebe mentioned you just got back from vacation?" I knew it was a thinly veiled attempt to change the subject, but I was hoping to ease the palpable tension that permeated the table.

No such luck.

Frank snorted. "Following aging rock stars around isn't a vacation. It's called stalking."

Elaine swatted Frank with her napkin. "Frank, that's unkind and unnecessary. Let people have their hobbies."

Dale cocked his head to the left. "Not everyone worships at the altar of the almighty dollar like you, Frank."

"Oh, sure. Easy to say when you don't have to do anything to earn it. But go ahead. You two keep up your groupie lifestyle, and I'll keep running the business that funds it."

Dale closed his eyes, inhaling and exhaling three times while humming in a low register.

"What is this, some new-age technique to keep you from punching me in the mouth, little brother?" Frank thumped the table with his fist, and Dale's eyes shot open. "I'd like to see you do it. I think it'd be good for you. Grow some hair on that chest. If you still can, after all that soy Susan's been shoving down your throat."

Dale leveled a steely gaze at Frank. "Violence is never the answer."

Frank chuckled and swigged his scotch. "Don't knock it 'til you try it."

Phoebe stood and threw her napkin onto the table. "I'm tired. I'm going to bed."

"But you haven't even eaten yet!" Susan said.

"Not hungry."

She marched out of the dining room. Andy glanced around the table in a panic, and then jumped up and followed her.

"Was it something I said?" Frank sipped his scotch, but neither the glass nor the fake mustache he wore could hide his smirk this time.

His disingenuous bewilderment at what he could have

possibly done to cause offense while knowing full well he was the antagonist in the encounter was familiar to me, reminiscent of conversations I'd had over the years with Gabe. They'd increased in the past couple years; gaslighting had been his way of deflecting attention from his double life.

Which begged the question, from what was Frank deflecting?

IN MY SLEEPY haze, I wasn't sure what had woken me until I heard the noise again. At the sound of the second thump, I popped one eye open. It seemed to have come from the cabin next door, the one Andy's mom had been assigned. I picked up my phone to check the time. It was just after midnight. I listened for quite a while, but when there were no other noises, other than the low hum of the ship, I closed my eyes and rolled back onto my side.

The next time I woke, the sound was louder and more persistent. I grabbed my phone from the nightstand and tried to focus my vision.

"Does that say six twenty-three?" I groaned. "For the love of—"

The pounding continued, intensifying to a frenetic pace.

"I'm coming." My irritated voice echoed as I stumbled down the hall, trying to yank on my robe at the same time.

Jane's door opened, and she toddled out in her robe, rubbing her eyes like a sleepy child. "What's all the racket?"

"No clue." I got to the door and deepened my voice.

"Can I help you?"

"Aunt Char! Aunt Jane! Open the door!"

I unlocked the door and opened it to find a disheveled and wild-eyed Andy.

"Andy, what is it? What's happened?" I asked.

"I need your help." He was winded and fidgety.

"Of course, darlin'." Jane reached to pull him into the room. "But first you gotta tell us what's going on."

"It's Phoebe." His chest heaved and his gaze darted around the room, like he was searching for something.

"Did you two have a fight?"

"No—I mean yes, we did, but that's not it. Phoebe's missing. I feel like I've scoured this entire boat, and I can't find her anywhere!"

"Sit down, honey. Tell us what's going on." Jane used her calmest librarian voice as she led him to the sofa.

I followed, and as I eased myself onto the chair, I realized I was trembling with adrenaline.

We both stared at him as he tried to pull himself together enough to speak.

"Now, what's this about a fight?" I leaned forward and clasped my hands in my lap to keep them from visibly shaking.

Andy rocked forward and back as he spoke in a rushed tone. "As you know, last night at dinner when she stormed off, I followed her. I thought she was mad at *me,* because she wouldn't stop to tell me what was wrong. When I finally caught up with her out on the observation deck, she was crying. I asked her what I'd done. She said it wasn't about me at all. She said it was her uncle. She discovered something yesterday before she got on the ship, and she wasn't sure what to do about it. She was either going to confront him and demand an explanation for what she saw, or she was going to keep quiet and do some snooping when we got back to shore. I told her I didn't like either of those options and she needed to just quit her job immediately. Tell him whatever he was wrapped up in, she wasn't going to be part of it. That did *not* go over well."

"I can't imagine it would," Jane said dryly. "Phoebe doesn't strike me as the type who appreciates ultimatums."

"She lost it. She started screaming I had no idea the enormity of what she was dealing with, and I didn't trust she could handle it, as if those two statements didn't completely contradict each other. Then she stomped off again. That's when I realized the whole bar was watching through the wall of windows, including most of our wedding party. It was humiliating."

"Then what happened?" I asked.

"I tried to catch up to her, but she was gone. I figured she went to go blow off some steam at the gym or something. She likes her space when she's upset, so I tried to give it to her, even though I hate leaving things unresolved like that."

"Can we skip to the part where you discover Phoebe's missing?"

I gave Jane a pointed look, but Andy was too caught up in his emotions to notice her lack of couth.

"When I got up this morning, I decided to bring her an

apology smoothie. She's an early riser, so I figured she'd be up by six, but she didn't answer the door. I used the spare key they gave me at check-in yesterday so I could hang her dresses in the closet, but when I went inside, her bed hadn't been slept in. There was a pillow and blanket on the sofa like someone had slept there, but why wouldn't she sleep in the bed? I'm starting to wonder if she ever made it back to her suite after our fight."

"Maybe she bunked with her bridesmaids," I offered.

"I checked. And I checked with her parents. They said they hadn't heard from her since she left dinner last night." He wrung his hands.

"Lily or Ivy?" Jane asked.

"I checked with her sisters and her brother. Nobody's seen her."

"What about your mom?" Jane placed a hand on his arm. "She's right next door, you know."

I had a vague recollection of noise coming from Rhonda's room during the night. "You should definitely check with her."

Andy heaved a sigh. "I doubt Phoebe would have gone to see her. They aren't exactly close. They've only met once, at our engagement party, and talked on the phone a handful of times. Heck, when I called to tell her about the wedding and set up a dinner to have her meet Phoebe, it was the first time I'd spoken to her in more than a year. Frankly, I'm surprised she even showed. As you know, she's not exactly the most reliable...*mother*." He spat the word out of his mouth like it tasted foul.

"Still, I think it's worth asking her." My voice was soft but firm. I rose to my feet. "Up, up, up." I waved my hands. "If Rhonda doesn't know anything, then we should go report Phoebe's disappearance to the head of security."

As the three of us headed for the door, there was a knock. Andy's and Jane's expressions mirrored my surprise and confusion.

"Who in the world would be knocking at this early hour?" I said.

I opened the door to find handsome Xavier Mesnier, head of security, and two uniformed security officers with him.

"Oh! Hello." I jerked at the sight of them. "We were just coming to see you."

Xavier slanted his head and raised one dark eyebrow. "Oh really? Why is that?"

"We"—I indicated Jane and Andy behind me—"would like to report a missing person."

He tilted his head the opposite direction. "I see. Who is this missing person?"

Andy moved forward. "My fiancée, Phoebe Braithwaite. Her bed hasn't been slept in. I'm really worried about her."

"Madame Braithwaite is not missing."

Andy heaved a sigh of relief. "Where is she?"

"On the fifth floor, Capri. In the medical."

"Medical? Is she sick? I need to see her!" He moved to go out the door, but Mesnier held up a hand to stop him.

"I am sorry, Monsieur Cobb. She is not sick. I regret to inform you, she is dead. Murdered, in fact."

Andy's knees gave way, and he gripped the door to steady himself. Jane squawked and draped herself across my back. My breath caught in my lungs. I still held the doorknob; my knuckles had turned white.

"No!" Andy's voice was barely audible. "It's a mistake. It has to be."

"I am sorry. It is not."

"Wh-what? How? What happened?" I wanted to pound on his chest over how coldly he'd dropped this horrific truth into our lives.

Andy bent over, wheezing like he'd just finished a marathon. "I kept calling her, texting her, she didn't answer. I thought she was ignoring me because she was angry." He looked up at Mesnier. "Why didn't she answer?"

"I cannot speak to her frame of mind, but I can tell you no phone was located...nearby."

"Nearby? Nearby where?" My voice rose several octaves.

"On the Capri level."

"What?" Andy's voice cracked. "Why would she be down there?"

The commotion must have woken Rhonda, because her door squeaked open and her timid voice called out, "Is everything okay out here?"

"Monsieur Cobb, come with us, *s'il vous plaît.* We would like to ask you a few questions."

In a daze, Andy began to lean forward, but I threw my arm out to block him.

"Wait. Questions? What kind of questions? Surely, you don't mean to imply he's a suspect. They loved each other.

They came on this cruise to get married!"

"Madame McLaughlin, the victim and her fiancé were seen arguing last night. We have multiple witnesses who can speak to that. So, yes, he is not only a suspect, but he is, in fact, the primary person of interest in the murder of Phoebe Braithwaite."

Chapter Four

"ANDY, DON'T SAY a word. You have the right to remain silent." Jane had read way too many crime novels to let our nephew incriminate himself in the murder of his fiancée.

"Where are you taking him? How did you even know he was here?" I asked.

I stood between Xavier Mesnier and my precious nephew. He said nothing but pointed up toward the ceiling and the security camera positioned above us.

Rhonda came into the hallway. She had a dazed look and dilated pupils. She was still in a flannel nightgown. "I don't...understand." Her words were slurred. "Is Andy in trouble? He's a good boy. He's always been a good boy."

Xavier glanced over his shoulder at Rhonda, did a double take at her disheveled appearance, and returned his attention to Andy.

"Monsieur Cobb, I have full authority on this ship, as does Captain Knutson, to investigate this crime, and I have both the intention and duty to do so. You can come with us willingly or...not."

A lump formed in my throat, and I struggled to swallow.

"He has rights." My assertion was less theatrical than Jane's.

Andy placed his hand on my shoulder and stared at me with red-rimmed eyes and a sagging mouth. "I have nothing to hide." He slid past me and into the hallway. As Xavier began to lead him away, Andy called over his shoulder. "Ivy's husband, Clyde, is an attorney. I'm not sure what kind, but maybe he can help."

"We'll let you know when we're through with the questions." Xavier's eyes filled with the same pity as when we first met.

He placed a firm hand on Andy's back, and the four men began to walk solemnly toward the elevators. I leaned farther out the doorway, with Jane still leaning against me. Her soft cries sounded like the mews of a kitten, and her tears dampened my back.

Andy's shoulders slumped as they disappeared around the corner, and I felt a piece of my heart break.

Rhonda, still in her daze, regarded at us with curiosity, like she'd just noticed us for the first time. "Char? Jane? What are you doing here?"

Jane gasped and waved her hands in the air. "Rhonda! Your son was just taken away for questioning as a murder suspect! Pull yourself together!"

I walked over and put my arm around Rhonda's shoulders. "Come on in. We'll make some coffee and try to get those sleeping pills to wear off. Then we can go talk to Clyde. I'm sure Phoebe's family is a total wreck right now."

The three of us shuffled into our stateroom. I helped ease Rhonda onto the sofa, and Jane dropped onto the lounge chair facing her.

Jane fanned her face. "Oh Lord, I'm having the hot flash of all hot flashes."

"Sugar or cream?" I walked into the kitchen.

"You know I like my coffee like I like my men. Rich, sweet, and from somewhere in the vicinity of the equator." Jane grabbed a magazine off the coffee table to act as a fan.

Rhonda mumbled something about milk not agreeing with her digestive system. I didn't probe further.

"I can't find the coffeemaker." I opened every cabinet and drawer to no avail.

"Call the butler." Jane said this like it wasn't an absurd thing to come out of her mouth.

"What do you mean, *call the butler*?"

"Didn't you read the information on the website about what comes with this place?"

"No. I mean, I checked out the website to get the gist, but I figured we'd do the wedding, and then we'd be off the boat, and I'd sell the unit. No point in getting into the details of the thing."

Jane clucked her tongue. "Selling would be a darn shame. I hope you reconsider, 'cause I could get used to this. There's a butler assigned to each stateroom. I think if you pick up the phone and ask, they'll connect you."

I picked up the receiver and pressed zero.

After two buzzing rings, a man with a thick British accent answered. "Good morning, Mrs. McLaughlin. How may I be of service?"

"Oh, hello. I'd like to be connected to the, uh, butler

please?"

"Mrs. McLaughlin, this is your butler, Windsor Hadwin. Is there something you need?"

"Oh! Yes, I can't find the coffeemaker."

"Would you like me to bring you coffee?"

"No. I can make it. I just don't know where it is."

"It should be right on the counter, ma'am. Would you like me to come locate it?"

"Normally, I'd say no, but I'm looking at the counter, and all I see is a toaster, a teapot, and some glass vase thingy."

"Ah, that glass vase *thingy* is your coffeemaker. Perhaps I can come show you how to use it. It's a pour over."

"I don't know what that means, and I don't have time for a lesson. In that case, if it wouldn't be too much of a bother, we could use coffee service for three. No, make that six."

I had a feeling I was going to need a lot of coffee to get through the day.

"My pleasure, ma'am. I'll be there in approximately fifteen minutes."

I hung up the phone and walked back into the living room. "The butler is bringing coffee." I stopped mid-step. "I can't believe I just said that. His name is Windsor."

"Like the castle?" Jane asked.

"I guess."

Rhonda watched our exchange with a slow-blinking stare, only a half-step above catatonic.

I snapped my fingers twice. "Rhonda, what medication

did you take?"

She fumbled with her hands in her lap. "Just a couple sleeping pills. Oh, and an anti-anxiety pill. I got nervous, all those people. If my own kid doesn't like me, why would judgy Phoebe's rich and snooty family want to meet me?"

"Andy loves you. He does, no matter the complications of your relationship. And as for Phoebe's family, most of them seem down-to-earth." I leaned against the dining table. "Totally unrelated, Rhonda, I wanted to ask you about something. I thought I heard some noises coming from your room last night."

She blinked. "Noises?" She smoothed the fabric of her nightgown across her lap.

Jane narrowed her gaze and arched her brow.

"Yes. I could have sworn I heard a couple of loud thumps. It woke me up, but then nothing after that so I went to sleep."

"You must have dreamed it." Rhonda's face was placid, but her fidgeting fingers told another story.

"I didn't hear anything, but I sleep with earbuds while my phone app plays recordings of dolphins talking to whales." Jane turned to Rhonda. "Maybe in your drug-induced state, you stumbled into the wall trying to get to the bathroom."

Rhonda's gaze darted around the room like it somehow held the answer. "Maybe."

The doorbell rang, so I left to answer it. On the other side stood a man who could only be Windsor Hadwin. His white hair, what was left of it anyway, formed a fluffy ring around his head. His bulbous nose crooked to the right, and his dark blue eyes were hooded under sagging eyelids and bushy white brows. He wore gray slacks, a robin's egg blue vest, a pressed white button-up with a matching light-blue handkerchief, and a silver and black striped tie fashioned in—what else—a Windsor knot. Balanced upon his left palm was a pewter tray, matching coffee carafe, and three porcelain cups and saucers.

"Hello, Mrs. McLaughlin. Lovely to meet you."

We stared at each other for a moment.

"May I bring this inside?"

"Oh! Oh, yes. Sorry, I just…I've never had a butler before. I don't even know what to do." I ushered him inside, but he waited for me.

"After you, ma'am."

"Oh, silly me. Sorry."

I hustled into the living room, where Jane watched with amusement. Even Rhonda was starting to perk up a bit.

I pointed to the middle of the seating area. "Right here on the coffee table?"

"Yes, ma'am." He set the tray in front of Rhonda. "Shall I pour it for you, or would you like to do it yourself?"

I waved my hand. "No, thank you. This is great."

Jane reached for a cup and stopped. "Windsor, is it?"

"Yes, ma'am."

"Did you know Mr. McLaughlin?"

My breath caught in my lungs. What was she doing?

Windsor cleared his throat. "Yes, ma'am. I have been assigned to this stateroom since the ship launched two years ago."

I tried to give Jane the eye, but she ignored me.

"Was he alone?"

"Jane!" Her name came out of me like a bark. I took a long, slow breath. "Thank you for the coffee, Windsor."

"Will there be anything else?" His face was grim, and he shifted his weight from foot to foot.

"No. That will be all."

"If you need anything else, please do not hesitate to call."

That man hustled out of the cabin faster than I could say *will do.*

"Why did you do that?" I glared at my sister.

Jane eyed me from just above the brim of her cup. "You know you want to know."

"I don't, actually."

My cell phone rang on the counter, but after two rings, it stopped.

There were two missed text messages on the lock screen. One from my local taco truck, letting me know where they'd be that afternoon, and one from Susan Braithwaite. She was also the one who'd called. I called her back.

"Hello?"

"Susan, I saw a missed a call from you."

Susan's voice was ragged. "Charlotte?"

"Yes. Hi."

Susan began to cry. "Charlotte, it's Phoebe. My Phoebe." Her cries became heaving sobs.

Tears pooled in my eyes and streamed down my face at the sound of her grief. My own grief was still so fresh and close to the surface. "I know. I'm so sorry. I'm so very sorry."

Jane's face mirrored my own sorrow, but Rhonda's expression was one of confused consternation.

"Susan, where are you? Jane and I will come to you."

Rhonda furrowed her brows further and mumbled to herself. "Am I not invited?"

"I'm in the captain's lounge, Char. The others are here, too," Susan said.

"We'll be right there."

RHONDA WENT BACK to her room while Jane and I got cleaned up and changed in record time. Fifteen minutes later she knocked on our door, wearing jeans and a long gray cardigan. She'd brushed most of her hair.

We rode the elevator up one level to the eighth floor—Santorini—and the captain's lounge where the Cobb-Braithwaite wedding party had gathered. We entered the room, and all gazes turned to us.

In the overstuffed chairs near the fireplace, teary-eyed Ivy and Lily were being comforted by their husbands. Dale and Susan sat shell-shocked at the round table in the middle of the room. Sawyer and Macy huddled close to them. Macy held Susan's hand and rubbed her back. Frank paced, while Elaine followed behind him in impractical stiletto heels, waiting for an opportunity to give him solace from his grief. He appeared oblivious to her presence. A handful of twenty-somethings, friends of the bride and groom, sat forlornly at the long captain's table next to the window.

It was the first time since we'd left the port in Seattle that I'd taken the time to look outside. All I saw were storm clouds and gray seas. Not a bit of land to be seen anywhere. The ominous sight felt appropriate, given the circumstances, but it also filled me with dread.

Dale rocked back and forth, side to side, with the rolling of the waves. He kept shaking his head, as if denial could change reality instead of the other way around. I knew this feeling well.

Rhonda rushed over to Susan. "Oh, Susan, I know we don't know each other, but I want to say I'm here for you. And there's no way my boy could have hurt her."

Susan jerked her head up sharply. "What do you mean?"

Rhonda sputtered. "Andy loved Phoebe. He would never kill her. You must believe me."

Every sound, every murmur in the room ceased. Rhonda froze under the glaring spotlight.

Frank stopped pacing. "What do you mean Andy wouldn't kill her? Is that who they think did it?" He surveyed the room. "Where is he, anyway? Is he hiding? If he hurt that girl, I'll kill him with my own bare hands."

Elaine rushed to his side, but he shook her off.

"Is this true Charlotte? Have they arrested Andy?" Susan asked.

Sawyer stared at his mom then at me. He got to his feet. "Where is he?"

I tried to remain calm, even though the whole scene was freaking me out. "I don't know, exactly. We were on our way to report Phoebe missing when the head of security arrived at my cabin to ask Andy some questions."

Clyde got up from the arm of the recliner and joined me. "Andy showed up at our room looking for her this morning. I never heard or maybe he never said...how did he know she was missing?"

"Clyde." I held out my hand. "We didn't get formally introduced last night. My name is Charlotte McLaughlin. Jane here"—I indicated Jane next to me—"Jane and I are Andy's aunts. And this is Rhonda, his mother."

Clyde didn't shake my hand but instead folded his burly arms across his chest. "I know who you are. Please answer my question."

I retracted my hand. "Andy went to bring Phoebe a smoothie around six. She didn't answer, so he used his key to get in and found she hadn't slept in her bed. You're the attorney, aren't you? He's hoping you can help him."

Clyde relaxed his pose and held up his hands. "I can't help him."

"Didn't you take some sort of lawyer oath to help people?" Rhonda's voice held a pleading tone.

"Please, Clyde. Andy didn't do this." I glanced at Susan, who chewed on her lip. "Susan, you know he didn't. He couldn't." I turned to Dale, who held clenched fists against his cheeks. "Dale, you know him."

Neither of them made eye contact, much less answered me.

Clyde slowly shook his head. "It's not that I don't want to help him—although I still haven't made up my mind about that—but I'm in mergers and acquisitions. I could write him an ironclad contract blindfolded with one hand behind my back, but I'm not sure I'll be much help against a charge of murder one."

Chapter Five

WHEN JANE, CLYDE, and I arrived at the security office, Andy was nowhere to be found. One of the men who'd shown up at my door with Xavier Mesnier sat at one of two utilitarian desks that faced each other. His buddy wasn't in his seat. Hopefully, he was scouring the boat for Phoebe's actual killer.

The officer appraised our group without emotion. He gave a head bob to Clyde, who responded in kind. He wore a nametag just below the ship's logo on his black polo shirt that I hadn't noticed earlier. Pike Taylor. It was an unusual name, evocative of a fish. However, nothing about this man's appearance was piscatorial. He was tall and muscular with broad shoulders. His head was round, but his jaw was square. He was dark-skinned with dark eyes and close-cropped dark curly hair. If I had to guess, I'd put his age somewhere between twenty-three and thirty-five. It was kind of hard to tell.

He gave off a serious vibe, but the tattoo of Grogu—a.k.a. Baby Yoda—that peeked out from under his shirtsleeve on his left bicep indicated he had a lighter side.

"Mrs. McLaughlin, right?" He folded his hands and rested them on the desktop. "How can I help you?"

I touched Clyde's shoulder. "This is Clyde Evans. Phoebe was his sister-in-law."

Officer Taylor's mouth, set into a line, deepened, and his furrowed brows arched closer together. "I'm sorry for your loss."

"Thank you." Clyde leaned forward, planting his splayed fingertips on the desk.

Was this an intentional intimidation tactic or a power move that came second nature to him after years of battling corporate attorneys in mediation and the courtroom?

"Would it be possible for me to meet with Mr. Cobb?" Clyde's question landed more like a statement.

Officer Taylor leaned forward himself. He wasn't easily intimidated. "He's currently being interviewed by our head of security."

"You wouldn't be violating my client's Miranda rights, would you? He's entitled to representation under the terms of the Athens Convention."

I tried to read Clyde's face to determine if that was a real thing or he'd made it up, but if it was fake, he was selling it.

Officer Taylor narrowed his gaze. "You're his attorney? I thought you said you were his brother-in-law."

"One can be both."

Clever. He didn't claim he was Andy's attorney, only that it was possible.

Officer Taylor glanced at the closed door behind him. The frosted glass panel was etched with the words CHIEF SECURITY OFFICER.

"Let me go talk to my boss. Wait here."

Jane leaned toward Clyde and whispered in his ear loud enough for me to hear. "The Athens Convention?"

He gave a slight nod. "I Googled it on our walk over here."

Apparently, Clyde had decided to go all in on the *fake it 'til you make it* strategy of defense.

The door opened and Officer Taylor peeked his head out. "Chief Officer Mesnier says the attorney can come in. You two ladies can wait out here if you'd like, but there's no telling how long this will take."

I had the distinct impression it was preferred we not wait in the security office.

Clyde turned to Jane and me. "Let me see where things stand. I'll come find you when I'm done."

"Let me give you my number."

He pulled out his phone and handed it to me to store my contact information. I gave it back to him, hoping my eyes communicated the depth of my earnestness. "I promise you; Andy would never hurt Phoebe. You must make them understand. You have to help him."

He placed the phone in his jacket pocket. "I'll do what I can, but I can't promise anything."

Just as the door shut behind Clyde, a hulking man burst into the office from the hallway. Both Jane and I gasped at the sight of him. It wasn't the urgent and unexpected nature of his arrival that left us breathless but the looming magnificence of his entire being, from his physical appearance to the way the air changed in the room merely from his presence.

He came to a screeching halt when he spotted Jane and me, our mouths agape.

At least six foot two or three, he was fit but not as bulky as Officer Taylor. His hair was dark blond with specks of gray to indicate he was likely in his forties, shaved on the sides but long and combed back on top. His beard was of similar color to his hair, maybe a shade or two darker but still with hints of blond. His suntanned skin highlighted his eyes, which were a color of blue typically only found in a tube of toothpaste or the feathers of a peacock. He wore a thick wool navy-blue sweater with four gold stripes on each shoulder over a white collared shirt and a matching pair of navy slacks.

"Oh!" The word escaped my lips before I had a chance to stop it.

He cocked one perfectly formed brow. "Hello. I am Captain Knutson. Are you ladies in need of assistance?" There was a hint of a Scandinavian accent in his voice.

Jane blinked at him a couple times, clearly at a loss for words.

I shook my head to snap out of my stupor caused by his beauty. "Oh, um, we were just leaving. Our nephew is here." I pointed toward Mesnier's office. "I mean there." I held out my hand. "I'm Charlotte McLaughlin. This is my sister, Jane."

As he reached for my hand to shake, that all-too-familiar dawning recognition and subsequent pity I'd come to both expect and loathe crossed his face.

"Yes, Mrs. McLaughlin. On behalf of myself, my cohort,

Captain Bellucci, and all the crewmembers of the *Thalassophile of the Seas*, I offer my deepest condolences on your husband's untimely death."

I swallowed the rage I felt toward Gabe for how many times of late I'd been put in a similar situation. It was bad enough to lose my husband, but to lose my dignity in the process was infuriating.

"Mmm. Thank you."

"Is there anything I can do for you?"

Jane bobbed her head. "Well, you can start by telling your head of security to release our nephew."

Captain Knutson's brows furrowed. "Is this the fiancé of the murdered woman?"

"Yes, and he absolutely would not, could not, and did not do this." I shifted my jaw to the right to indicate my adamancy.

He beheld the two of us, ostensibly gauging how much of a thorn in his side we might become. "You do understand why it is necessary for Chief Officer Mesnier to interview your nephew, do you not?"

"Of course, we do. However, I've seen enough true-crime documentaries to understand the importance of the first forty-eight hours following a murder and how myopic investigations can be if the investigators decide who the perpetrator is before all the evidence is gathered. Have you even checked the security tapes?" Jane crossed her arms. "I hope you would agree the last thing any of us want is for the real killer to get away with murder while you persecute an innocent man."

Captain Knutson inhaled a deep breath and slowly exhaled. "As captain, it is my duty to oversee any investigations regarding criminal activity on the ship. You have my word that I will ensure the investigation is thorough and fair."

"I hope that's true." A thought occurred to me. "We're not even twenty-four hours into this cruise. What happens next? Do we go on to our scheduled destinations, or do we go back to Seattle?"

Once again, the captain sighed. "I have not decided that quite yet. We are at sea today, currently out of any jurisdiction. We are scheduled to enter the Tracy Arm Fjord sometime tomorrow, but there is currently no plan to dock anywhere. Typically, in situations like these—not that this situation is typical in any way or indicative of how I run my ship—we might partner with local authorities or even the FBI to conduct an investigation.

"However, on this ship we have our own highly trained enforcement and investigative team. I have every confidence they will be able to solve this case before we enter—or reenter—any other jurisdiction. No need to veer off course, literally or metaphorically. I have a ship full of fractional owners and VIP clientele who will not be very happy with me if this voyage does not adhere to its original itinerary."

"You consider solving a murder on your ship less of a priority than preempting the complaints of a bunch of rich folks inconvenienced by an unscheduled stop?" Jane scowled.

"Jane. No need to be rude." I was embarrassed by her accusation, even though I agreed with her assessment.

Captain Knutson held up his hand. "I am not offended

by her tone. I am, however, offended by her assertion I cannot manage to serve the wants and needs of the residents of this ship and their guests while also overseeing this investigation. It is not my place to discuss his previous operations, many of which are highly classified, but I assure you, Xavier Mesnier is more qualified to conduct this investigation than any small-town sheriff, big city police officer, or FBI agent. Combined."

JANE CLOSED THE door of the security office. "That was...interesting."

"Yeah." I chewed my lower lip.

"So, the captain of the ship is Leif Eriksson, and his head of security is James Bond?"

I laughed. "I was thinking Mesnier is more like Chief Inspector Armand Gamache."

Jane and I were big fans of Louise Penny's Three Pines mystery series, set in Quebec, and especially fond of her brooding protagonist.

"I can see that, especially with that French accent. Armand is supposed to have a British accent when he speaks English, but in my head his voice sounds like Celine Dion, only deeper."

"Interesting." I slanted my chin. "You know what's bothering me?"

"Are we talking bothered, as in hot and bothered by the Viking and the Frenchman?" Jane fanned her face with her hand. "Oh wait, maybe it's just a hot flash."

"I keep thinking about what you said to the captain, and I'm realizing he never answered you."

"Which part?"

"That with the high level of security on this ship, wouldn't they be able to check the cameras to see who did this?"

Jane stopped and threw her arm in front of me to get me to stop as well. "You don't think that's why they've got Andy in there, do you? What if they saw footage of him doing something?"

"That's ridiculous. We both know he didn't do this." We did, right? He couldn't possibly have done this.

"That's not what I mean. What if they have security footage that looks incriminating, even if he didn't do it? They did have a fight. Maybe they saw the interaction, and it doesn't look good for him."

"Everyone knows they had a fight. There are multiple witnesses. They don't need videotape for that."

"Yes, but what if there was more? Didn't he say she stormed away from the observation deck, and he followed her?"

"I think he said he tried, but—"

"Maybe he wasn't telling the whole story because he knows it will incriminate him."

"Jane, what are you getting at?"

"Only that we need to be prepared for the possibility there's evidence that may point to Andy. That doesn't mean he'd hurt her, but us assuming they have no reason to question him won't do him any good. We need to assume things look bad so we don't get blindsided."

"I see your point. Hopefully, Clyde will have those answers when he's done talking to Mesnier. Let's go back to the captain's lounge and see if anyone saw or heard anything."

"Divide and conquer?"

"I'm thinking a subtle approach would be more effective. Nuance, not the Spanish Inquisition." I pursed my lips and cocked my left eyebrow.

"Charlotte Anne, are you saying you don't believe I'm capable of being subtle?"

"Not at all. I'm merely reminding you our goal is to gently elicit information, not conduct hostile interrogations."

Chapter Six

THE VIBE HAD dramatically shifted in the captain's lounge. The crying had stopped for the most part, replaced with the buzzing energy of angry grief that had no outlet.

I understood this phenomenon.

Andy and Phoebe's friends were gone, likely commiserating in the bar. Only family remained.

Lily and Ivy had moved to the table with Susan and Dale, their eyes red-rimmed. Macy, still posted up next to Susan, might have also had red-rimmed eyes, but they were too heavily underlined in blue makeup to know for certain. I couldn't see Sawyer's eyes at all. He held his head in his hands, his fingers embedded in his floppy blond hair.

Rhonda sat crisscross on the rug in front of the fireplace, stoking the burning logs with an ornate iron poker and wearing a glazed expression. I wondered why anyone had thought that was a reasonable thing to allow, but no one seemed to be paying much attention to her.

Neal stared out the porthole at the back of the room.

When the door shut behind us, everyone turned to look except Neal and Rhonda, who gently rocked and hummed an unrecognizable tune.

"Well?" Dale said. "What's the update?"

I scanned the room. Frank and Elaine were nowhere to be seen.

"Should we wait for Frank?" I asked.

Dale grunted. "My brother is probably attempting to boink his wife right now. No need to wait. It'll be a while before the little blue pill takes effect."

Jane made some sort of gurgling noise.

"We spoke with Captain Knutson, who informed us he has full confidence that Xavier Mesnier, the ship's head of security, is capable of handling the investigation at this time."

Susan squinted at me. "What does that mean?"

Dale sat back in his chair. "What that means is, he doesn't plan on bringing in outside law enforcement. He's more concerned with keeping this quiet than catching our daughter's killer."

"I think he believes he can serve both interests at the same time," I said.

Sawyer peeked through his shaggy bangs. "What about Andy?"

Jane cleared her throat. "Clyde is with him now. He's finding out the status, and he promised to let us know as soon as Mesnier is done questioning Andy."

"My boy didn't do this." Rhonda continued to stoke the fire, causing embers to crackle and a plume of smoke to rise.

"Jane and I are compiling a list of questions for Mesnier. It occurred to us there are security cameras all over the ship.

One of them must have caught something."

Neal jerked his head my direction. "What?"

"This ship has high-level security monitoring. It's one of the selling features since the residents tend to be people with high net worth."

"Of course. Right." He turned back to the window.

Neal's reaction to the idea of security cameras was strange, not only that he wouldn't have expected it, but also that he seemed to be panicked about it. What had he done that might have been captured on a recording that he didn't want anyone to see?

"What about Phoebe's phone?" Macy asked. "If someone lured her to that area with a late-night text or phone call, wouldn't there be record of it on her phone?"

Both Neal and Rhonda jerked their attention to Macy.

Dale glowered. "Why would you assume it's someone she knew? Everyone loved Phoebe. No, if it wasn't a lover's quarrel with Andy, it must have been a stranger."

Macy opened her mouth, then shut it just as quickly.

"I want to see the ship's manifest. There's got to be some psycho living on here," said Dale.

"Or one of the staff. Someone who got a job on the ship because they found out where we were having the wedding." Susan gasped and her fingertips flew to her lips. "Maybe her stalker followed her here!"

"Jane and I will be sure to bring all these things up with Officer Mesnier when we have the chance. As far as I know, her phone hasn't been located."

Lily raised her hand, a surprising response from an adult

amid a family conversation.

"Yes, Lily?" I felt like a kindergarten teacher addressing a shy student.

"What are they going to do with Phoebe?"

"What do you mean?"

"What will they do with her body? Can we see her?"

Neal rushed over to his wife's side. "Oh, honey, I don't think you want to do that."

Ivy frowned at her twin. "Why the hell would you want to see her now? We should wait until we get home, and then the funeral director will make her nice and pretty."

Where Lily's voice has been soft and timid, Ivy's tone was coarse and raspy, like a seasoned barfly at a smoky trucker bar.

"She wanted to be cremated." Macy was so quiet I barely heard her.

Susan pulled away from Macy and gawked at her. "What? Who told you that?"

"Phoebe did. She wanted her ashes to be sprinkled through the Montlake Cut where she raced crew for U-Dub."

I'd forgotten that Phoebe had been on the rowing team when she attended the University of Washington. The Montlake Cut was a narrow passageway between Lake Washington and Portage Bay where the boat races took place.

"I never heard her say that." Susan turned to Dale. "Did she ever mention that to you?"

"I'm not even sure that's legal." Dale scowled.

"Under what circumstances did that topic of conversation come up, anyway?" Susan rubbed her neck. "We're Presbyterian. We don't do cremation."

Macy shrugged. "I'm just telling you what she said."

"I agree with Macy. We should do what Phoebe would have wanted." Sawyer placed his hands palm-down on the table.

"No!" Susan yelled. Tears filled her wide eyes.

Sawyer sighed. "What difference does it make, Mom?"

"The difference," Susan spoke through gritted teeth, "is being able to bring flowers to my daughter's grave where I know she will rest forever versus scattered remnants of her floating among oil slicks from waterski boats, feces-covered goose feathers, and a million years' worth of fossilized fish poop!"

Dale put his arm around his wife and squeezed her shoulder. "We'll get her a nice spot facing west toward the Olympics. It'll have a built-in vase for flowers."

"Lilacs were her favorite, but they're only available in May." She sniffed. "We'll have to wait six months."

The door opened behind me, and I turned to see Andy burst into the room with Clyde trailing close behind him. Andy had a wide-eyed look of grief and anger, even more than when I'd seen him earlier. He scanned the room, his desperation to locate an ally etched across his face. His gaze landed on me, and his knees nearly buckled. I rushed over and wrapped my arms around him. His whole body shook with sobs and incoherent words.

As his tears dampened my neck, I was reminded of holding him when he was a little boy of five years old mourning the loss of his father.

I felt as helpless now as I had then.

Andy pulled away and wiped his face with his forearm.

"Susan. Dale. I—" His voice was ragged.

Dale held up his hand. "Stop. Just stop." He glared at Andy. "Did you do this? Did you kill our baby girl?" His voice broke.

Andy cupped his hands in front of him like a pauper begging for bread. "Dale, you've got to believe me. I loved her. I could never—"

"Why do they think it's you then?" Ivy crossed her arms.

Clyde stepped in front of Andy before he could respond. "I've advised Andy to refrain from commenting in public."

Ivy gasped. "It's not in public, Clyde! And how can you take his side?"

"I'm not taking his side. I'm ensuring the situation is handled in the most ethical way possible for all concerned." He turned to Jane and me. "Ladies, I think it's best you take Andy back to your room for now."

I looped my arm through Andy's. "Come on. Let's get you something to eat."

Jane grabbed his other arm, and we began to lead him toward the door. Just as I reached out for the knob, it opened, and Frank and Elaine walked into the room.

"Just where do you think you're going?" Frank snarled. "You're not leaving my sight, murderer."

"I'm not a murderer!"

"Oh yeah? Well, I've got six witnesses that say otherwise."

"What are you talking about, Frank?" Andy jerked his arms free from Jane and me. He whirled to face his accuser.

"I'm talking about your friends, Andy. The ones you are so close with, they've taken a week off work to be here for your wedding." He jerked his thumb over his shoulder. "I just found 'em in the bar. They all say they saw you fighting with Phoebe last night. One of 'em said you grabbed her arm real aggressive-like when she tried to leave."

"I didn't mean to hurt her. I was just trying to get her to stop and listen to me."

"Oh, Andy," Jane murmured.

"I didn't do this! As a matter of fact, the reason Phoebe and I were fighting was 'cause of you, Frank!" He poked Frank in the chest.

Elaine let out a whimper.

"Me?" Frank snorted. "That's ridiculous. Why would you be fighting because of me?"

Andy drew closer to him until they were practically nose-to-nose. Well, more like Andy's nose to Frank's receding hairline. "You're a crook, and Phoebe was just starting to figure out how crooked you are."

Frank's left eye twitched as he played the staring game with Andy. Andy raised his eyebrows but didn't blink.

Dale stood. "Frank, what's he talking about?"

Frank pushed Andy away. "Nothin'." He pointed at Andy. "I'm not gonna let you drag me under with you. You know what you did."

Clyde stepped between them. "Andy, go with Charlotte

and Jane."

Andy heaved an angry sigh and stormed out the door. Jane followed him.

Neal had moved back to the porthole. He had a grim expression as he leaned against the wall with his arms and ankles crossed.

Ivy scowled, and next to her, Lily shredded a piece of tissue.

Macy stood behind Susan, massaging her visibly tense shoulders. I couldn't tell if Susan was angry at Macy for positing the idea of cremation or if she was simply upset about the whole situation. Either way Macy seemed to be giving her best efforts to get back into Susan's good graces.

Dale slumped into his seat, looking bereft. Sawyer dropped his head into his folded arms like he was playing the head down, seven up game in elementary school. Clyde had both fists on his hips, while Frank's were balled at his side. Elaine stood trembling next to Frank. She reached out to touch his shirtsleeve, and he jerked his arm away from her. She looked up at me and then quickly averted her gaze.

It was too late, though. I'd already seen her fear.

Chapter Seven

"THIS IS A nightmare." Andy walked into the elevator with his shoulders slumped. "I knew this cruise ship was a bad idea."

I pressed the button to go down one level to the seventh floor. "It was my understanding you and Phoebe were in a bit of a pickle. Jane and I were only trying to help."

"I know. I'm sorry if it sounds like I'm blaming you. I had Aunt Jane on speaker with Phoebe in the room when she suggested it. Phoebe thought it was the perfect solution. I tried to get her to wait until we'd had a chance to talk it through, but she insisted we do it. I think she thought it would simplify things. I knew in my gut it wouldn't. If you've got family problems, you're not going to escape them by going on a cruise…especially if you bring the whole family with you."

"What happened in the security office?" I asked.

"He questioned me, took my fingerprints, he even had the ship's doctor examine me to see if I had any scratches from Phoebe defending herself."

Jane gripped his arm. "That must have felt so undignified."

"Undignified doesn't even begin to describe it. Oh, and he gave me this." He pulled a small envelope from his pocket and handed it to me. "No point in me keeping it."

I peeked into the envelope and found the sapphire ring. "Oh, Andy. Are you sure you—"

The elevator doors opened, and I gasped. Xavier Mesnier stood on the other side.

"Just the person I was coming to find." He held the door open.

"I've already told you everything I know." Andy's tone was defensive.

"I am not speaking to you, Monsieur Cobb. I am speaking to Madame McLaughlin."

I touched my fingertips to the base of my throat. "Me? Why me?"

"I will explain once we get back to my office."

Jane stepped between us. "If my sister's a suspect, then she needs to call our lawyer."

"She is not a suspect."

I tucked the envelope with the ring into my purse. "Jane, it's okay. Take Andy to our room. I've got our list of questions, so this will give me the opportunity to get some answers. I'm sure this will only take a few minutes."

Jane knit her brows together. "That's what Andy said. Now he's the prime suspect."

OFFICER TAYLOR WAS back at his desk, as was his cohort,

Lonnie Irving. Irving looked to be about ten years older than Taylor, but where Taylor's complexion was deep brown, Irving's was nearly transparent except for the freckles that dotted his nose and cheeks. Taylor's irises were almost as dark as his pupils, but Irving's were a shade of iridescent blue-green that could most accurately be described as the color of Baja Blast soda. Rarely was that color seen in nature. Finally, Taylor's dark curly hair was the yin to the tang–I mean yang–of Irving's flaming orange crewcut that stood straight up, a half inch from his scalp.

Both men rose from their chairs when we entered the office, but upon seeing us, they sat down again.

Taylor gave me a smirk. The man enjoyed seeing me dragged back into their lair.

"Follow me." Mesnier raised his right hand.

As we entered his office, I was surprised to see it wasn't the sparse utilitarian style of the outer room. Instead, it was an old-world style, with overstuffed brown leather chairs, a freestanding globe, a green banker's lamp, antique brass nautical instruments in mahogany shadow boxes, and fully stocked floor-to-ceiling bookshelves.

"Have you actually read any of these books, or are they for show?"

He placed his hand across his chest. "I am wounded that you believe I could possibly be such a charlatan."

"No offense intended. I've found in my life as a librarian that avid readers tend to make less of a fuss about it. Their books are worn from being so well-loved they make for terrible displays."

"I must be the exception, then. I have read nearly every book on these shelves." He took his seat and tented his fingers. "I should have known you were an educated woman. You have that...*je ne sais quoi* quality that speaks to a broad and enlightened mind."

"You should know, then, that my enlightened mind might register flattery when it hears it. Also, do French people actually say *je ne sais quoi*? I thought that was only for the benefit of the American movie audience, like *sacre bleu*." I exaggerated the stereotypical guttural sound of the phrase.

He laughed and wagged his finger at me. "Aha. *Oui*, you *are* a bright one. The saying may be a bit old-fashioned. However, I am a bit old-fashioned myself." He gave a dismissive wave at our surroundings. "As you may have noticed."

"Xavier. May I call you Xavier?"

"*Bien sûr*."

"Xavier, since we've established that we're both intelligent, educated people, let's cut to the chase. I'm sure you're a great investigator, otherwise you wouldn't have this job. However, if you believe my nephew could possibly have committed this horrible crime, you're not as good as you think you are. Incompetent and impolitic are two words that come to mind."

He raised his left eyebrow and allowed his mouth a slight twitch of amusement. "For someone who does not intend to offend, you certainly have the gift for slicing through a person."

"I'd apologize, but you must know, Andy is the world to

me. His father—my brother Bernie—died when he was small. My sister Jane and I never had children of our own, but we had Andy. He's a good man, and he loved Phoebe very much, even though..."

He leaned forward and rested his forearms on the desk. "Even though?"

"Even though she could be difficult."

"Difficult in what way?"

"Stubborn."

He raised his brow again.

I tilted my head. "Are you implying I'm stubborn?"

"I said nothing of the sort. I do not know you. It would be disingenuous, however, to say I have not observed a strong-headed tendency."

"Trust me, I've earned it."

He watched me, no doubt waiting for me to elaborate. When I didn't, he said, "I suppose you are wondering why I wanted to speak with you."

"I assume it's because you'd like some insight into the situation from someone other than Andy. Or perhaps you want to compare his answers to mine."

"That, and, like I said, I have been observing you and you seem to be quite perceptive. I was hoping you might assist me by sharing your insights."

I emitted a humorless chuckle.

"Did I say something funny?"

"Unintentionally, I'm sure. Although, considering the fact I know you must be aware—perhaps not at the time, but certainly now—that my husband's traveling companion was not his wife, it's difficult to imagine you thinking of me as anything but obtuse."

He stared into my eyes with an intensity I felt down to my toes. This time I saw a smidge less pity than when I'd introduced myself on the gangplank and a dash more intrigue mixed with amusement. I even thought I caught a twinkle in there somewhere.

"I do not find you obtuse, I find you completely...acute." He cleared his throat and sat back in his chair. "I mean, astute."

I felt my cheeks warm at the inadvertent compliment, and it had the desired effect. I felt compelled to cooperate with him. "How can I assist you in finding Phoebe's real killer?"

"Being adjacent to both Andy and Phoebe, you have a unique insight into their relationship and their families' dynamics."

"Yes and no. Andy and Phoebe haven't been together for even a year. I know some, but my knowledge of her family is limited."

"Tell me about last night. There was an argument."

"Earlier at dinner, something upset Phoebe and she left the dining room, but it didn't have anything to do with Andy."

"What was happening at that time?"

"Her uncle Frank was bickering with her father."

"About?"

"Frank and Dale are very different, despite having both grown up in the same privileged household. Frank embraced the benefits his family wealth has afforded, while Dale has shunned it. Well, sort of. Frank was heckling his brother about the fact the family business Dale has loudly criticized has also bankrolled his so-called vagabond lifestyle. Frank was claiming he keeps the business afloat and Dale just cashes the paychecks while simultaneously badmouthing the excesses of affluence."

"After Phoebe and Andy left, did everyone continue with their dinner, or did anyone else leave?"

"Pretty much. Sawyer and Macy–Phoebe's brother and his girlfriend–came over from their table to see what the hubbub was about and ended up staying to eat with us in the vacated spots."

"What is your perception of her brother?"

"I enjoyed our conversation. Where Phoebe was high-strung and high-maintenance, Sawyer is more laid-back like his father, very *go-with-the-flow*. Phoebe always said he's not very ambitious. She tried to get him involved with Braithwaite Industrial, but he wanted nothing to do with it. From what I've seen and heard, he seems content to spend his winters skiing and his summers hiking for the rest of his life."

"What about after dinner?"

"Jane and I went back to our stateroom for a glass of wine and some peaceful reading."

"I see." He glanced at his notes. "What can you tell me about Andy's mother, Rhonda? She is staying in the room next to you, correct?"

"She is."

"What was her relationship with her future daughter-in-law?"

"Pretty nonexistent. Andy hasn't had a great relationship with his mom for quite some time, so I don't think he brought Phoebe around her much, if at all. In fact, I think he said they only met once."

"And what has been the reason for this estrangement?"

I sighed. "Rhonda hasn't been the most reliable of mothers since my brother Bernie died from cancer. Andy was only five. Her grief led to long-term depression, which meant there were days she couldn't even take care of herself, much less her kid. Jane and I did what we could to help raise him. Even after she moved out of state when he was eighteen, Jane has always done her best to be there for him for all the milestones. I've been more involved than Jane over the past dozen years or so because I live closer."

"So, you are more than simply his aunt."

"I didn't have kids of my own. My husband said he didn't want them." I swallowed my bitterness. "He traveled a lot, and I only worked part-time at the library so for Andy's sake I did what I could to fill in the gap of his dead father and emotionally absent mother. By his teen years, Rhonda had basically abdicated her role altogether, physically and mentally MIA. She's struggled with...well...staying present in her own life, much less his, if that makes sense. I don't know how else to put it."

"Drugs?"

"Probably of some sort. Definitely alcohol. Look, Andy has forgiven her—mostly—and he knows she's been through a lot, but that doesn't mean he wants to have much of a relationship with her. He's been through a lot, too, but without a mother he could count on."

Xavier blinked at me a few times. "Would Rhonda have any animosity toward Phoebe?"

"I think the reverse. Phoebe had resentment toward Rhonda for letting Andy down all those years." My stomach dropped. That noise I'd heard. I glanced up at the ceiling and then let my gaze settle on his face. He was scrutinizing me, but I couldn't read his conclusion. "Does this mean Rhonda's a suspect?"

"She is not at the top of my list, but everyone is—"

"Everyone is a suspect. Got it. But you should be able to see who killed Phoebe on the security cameras, right?"

"Unfortunately, that is not the case. For some reason, several cameras on the Perseus, Capri, and Aegean levels have an anomaly in their recorded feed, including the stairwells between them."

"An anomaly?"

"Forty minutes of blank footage on all cameras."

"Whoa."

"Indeed."

"I'm still not clear on something. Phoebe was discovered on which floor?"

"Capri. On the VIP sundeck."

"So, the fifth floor. Andy is staying on the seventh floor, same as Jane and me. I don't recall anyone in our group staying on the fifth floor."

"They are not."

"So why was she there?"

I meant it as a rhetorical question, but he shrugged and said, "Perhaps to meet someone, perhaps to relax in the Jacuzzi."

"Jacuzzi? Is that where she was killed?"

"She was found submerged in the water." He tented his hands once more. "It's my understanding Andy went to school to be a computer specialist of some sort?"

His insinuation crept up on me like bony fingers sliding onto my neck, gripping my throat so I could barely breathe or swallow. "That's not…I don't…he didn't…" I struggled to get out an entire sentence. "He went for a year, but it wasn't a good fit. He transferred to the teaching program."

"I assume he gained a working knowledge during that year."

"A working knowledge of the basics, maybe, but not hacking into a private security system and deleting video."

"I am not necessarily suggesting he hacked in to delete video."

"What are you suggesting, then?"

"He could have disabled the cameras."

"Isn't it possible they just didn't work?"

His mouth twitched. "All the other cameras were working, and those cameras worked before the murder. Come now, Madame McLaughlin. You do not expect me to suspend my disbelief to that extent."

I inhaled and shrugged. "He didn't do it."

He stared at me for a bit and then slapped his palms on the desk. "We play a game."

"Excuse me?"

"You like games, no?"

"I like Yahtzee and Scrabble. I don't like mind games."

"These games are strategy games, are they not? They use your mind?"

"That's not what...you know what? Never mind. Let's play."

I was surprised to realize that despite my growing irritation with Xavier Mesnier, his attractiveness not only didn't diminish, but it somehow increased. I'd never experienced that before, and it unnerved me. I willed myself to tamp it down, but I was losing the battle.

He cleared his throat. "Let us set aside for the moment the means, motive, and opportunity your nephew may have had for committing this crime. Statistics say nearly sixty percent of murders are committed by a known acquaintance, often by a husband or boyfriend, but we will also set that aside for now and focus on the remaining friends and family."

"That discounts the forty percent committed by strangers."

"The preponderance of those living on this boat who are unknown to you are very much known to me. Longtime residents and staff make up the vast majority, and I promise you, I have done stringent background checks on all employees. Let us start with those closest to the younger Madame Braithwaite. What was her relationship like with her parents?"

"I've explained to you, my knowledge is limited, since

Andy and Phoebe only started dating about eight months ago or so. What I've seen of their relationship, though, is Phoebe and her parents were very close. By all accounts, Phoebe was the golden child."

"Could that have bred resentment in her brother, uh"—he peeked at his notes—"Sawyer?"

"Maybe, but I never heard that. Andy said Sawyer was very protective of her, especially after the stalking incidents."

"Yes, Monsieur Cobb mentioned that to me as well."

"There you go. That blows your *it can't possibly be a stranger* theory right out of the water. Have you even checked the manifests or the newly hired staff? Maybe one of them was her stalker and made their way onto the boat."

"First, I did not say it cannot possibly be a stranger. I merely recited the statistics. However, since we are going there, were you aware that in three out of four stalking cases, the perpetrator has some connection or prior relationship with the victim?"

"I did not. You can't possibly be implying Andy was her stalker. They didn't even know each other back then!"

"That is exactly my point. Perhaps Monsieur Cobb was an obsessed fan of her video channel and insinuated himself into her life."

I stood from my chair and glared at him. "Why do I get the feeling you're trying to pin this on Andy, and nothing I say will change your mind?"

"HOW DID THAT go?" Jane jumped up from the sofa when I entered the suite. "What did he want?"

Andy's blue eyes had always held an element of sadness, but they were even more forlorn than usual.

I had to decide: Put a positive spin on things or give it to him straight?

"He wanted my insight into Phoebe's family dynamic. He kept talking about statistics and how the majority of the time the victim has a relationship with their killer." I held up his business card. "He said I should call him if I think of anything else."

Andy let his head fall back against the sofa. "I can't believe this is happening. What am I going to do? I've lost the love of my life, and now her murder is being pinned on me."

Jane sat next to him and placed her hand on his arm. "We'll figure it out. I promise." She jerked her chin toward me. "Aunt Char and I have been training for this for practically our whole lives."

"What do you mean?" he asked.

"All those mystery shows we've watched."

"Aunt Jane, I've seen every episode of *Grey's Anatomy*. That doesn't mean I'm capable of performing surgery."

I sat on the chair next to the sofa. "Andy, we saw Phoebe on the Mykonos deck when we went to check in at the muster station before the ship left port. She was talking to someone and appeared upset. We couldn't see them, and when we asked her about it, she claimed she'd been alone the whole time. Any idea who that could have been?"

His eyes widened briefly. "I guess it could have been anyone, but she never mentioned having an argument. What did you see?"

"Nothing. Whoever it was, they were behind a big plant. She claimed she was talking to herself."

There was a knock on the door. Jane and Andy both appeared as alarmed as I felt. Just as had happened that morning, I opened it to find a grim-faced Xavier Mesnier, along with his sidekicks, officers Irving and Taylor.

"What now?"

Xavier pointed two of his fingers at Andy. Irving and Taylor squeezed past me and headed over to my nephew.

"Monsieur Cobb, rise, *s'il vous plaît.*"

The fear and confusion in Andy's eyes would haunt me for the rest of my life.

"Auntie Char, what's happening?"

Taylor grabbed his arm and pulled him to standing.

"Monsieur Cobb," Xavier said. "I am detaining you for the murder of Phoebe Braithwaite."

"Why are you doing this?" I got close to his face. "You have no evidence. Statistics don't always tell the whole story!"

He stepped back and held up a clear plastic bag. In it was a steak knife, covered in blood. "Statistics may not, but fingerprints certainly do."

Chapter Eight

JANE AND I took turns pacing the suite, which had begun to feel quite small. Claustrophobic, even. Currently, she was circling the kitchen while I chewed my cuticles on the sofa.

"What are we going to do?" Jane started opening cabinets. "I need wine."

"It's just after three o'clock," I snapped.

"Time is irrelevant at sea. We've probably crossed a dozen time zones in the past twenty-four hours. Where's the corkscrew? Where's the wine, for that matter?"

"I don't know. I just got here twenty-four hours ago."

She opened a drawer and pulled out a pacifier. She held it up with a distasteful sneer. I felt like I'd been punched in the gut. She winced and threw the pacifier back into the drawer, bumping it closed with her hip.

It had never occurred to me Gabe and Kyrie Dawn not only came here as a couple, but they'd also come as a family. I glanced at the table and imagined them laughing as their baby attempted to eat spaghetti for the first time. I pictured them snuggling together on the sofa to watch Gabe's favorite movie, *The Maltese Falcon.*

"Maybe you should call Kyrie Dawn. She probably knows where the corkscrew is." My tone was sharp.

Jane slammed a cupboard shut. "Look, I know you're stressed and this whole situation is terrible, but no need to take it out on me. We're in this together, remember?"

"Sorry. It's just all too much."

Jane picked up the phone. "Windsor?" She paused. "Yes, this is her sister, Jane. We were looking for the wine bottle opener." She listened to his response. "Well, if it's not too much trouble." Pause. "Okay, thank you." She put the receiver back on the hook. "He's coming to take care of it."

"Jane, forget about the wine. Concentrate. We've got to figure out how the murder weapon had Andy's fingerprints on it."

She leaned against the counter. "Until Mesnier held up that knife, I didn't even know how she'd been killed."

"That was intentional, I'm sure of it. One of those techniques they use to catch a slip of the tongue. Xavier said she'd been *found* on the fifth floor submerged in the hot tub, but he didn't say how she'd been killed, or even where. I'd assumed that's where she'd been killed and that she'd been drowned."

"Oh, we're on a first name basis with *Xavier* now, are we?" The doorbell rang. Jane waved me off. "I'll get it. I'm closer."

Windsor walked into the suite, holding a bottle of red wine in one hand and a bottle of white in the other.

"Afternoon, ladies. In the mood for some wine?" He held up the bottles for our inspection. "I have a pinot noir and a chardonnay."

"Yes, please," Jane said.

He furrowed his brows. "Pardon, madame, but which did you mean?"

"Both." She sat next to me on the sofa.

"I see." He set the bottles on the counter and opened a drawer. "For next time, if you'd rather not have to call on me, all your gadgets and tools are in here."

"I thought I looked in there," Jane muttered.

A thought occurred to me. "Windsor?"

"Yes, Mrs. McLaughlin?"

"You can call me Charlotte."

"I'd rather not, ma'am."

"Okay, well, um, you keep an eye on things around here, right?"

He removed the foil from the pinot bottle. "I do not spy, if that's what you're implying."

"Not at all. I was wondering if you might have an awareness of the comings and goings on this floor."

"Sounds a bit like spying." He twisted the opener into the cork. "I value the privacy of our residents, like yourself. Discretion is an important service I provide."

"He's got a point," Jane said.

Discretion, as in looking the other way when men like my husband brought their mistresses on the ship…and their love child. I cleared my throat. It sounded like a garbage disposal. Jane gave an involuntary giggle.

"I'm just going to lay my cards on the table," I said. "I assume you know our nephew Andy has been detained by

Xavier Mesnier for the murder of his fiancée, Phoebe Braithwaite."

"I do." He deftly removed the cork with a pop and poured the wine into a glass swan-necked decanter. "I was sorry to hear it."

"Did you happen to see or hear anything...unusual last night?"

He rested his hand on the decanter. "Unusual?"

"Yes, like, for instance, I thought I heard some racket during the night. It sounded like it came from next door."

"From Ms. Cobb's room?" He opened a glass-front cabinet and pulled down two wide-mouthed goblets. "Red first?"

"Yes, please. I don't suppose you know anything about a loud noise coming from Rhonda Cobb's room next door? It would have been just after midnight."

He pursed his lips. "Like I said, discretion is priority here. I try to make it my business to *not* be in others' business unless they involve me directly." He poured the pinot from the decanter into the glasses.

"I'm involving you directly. Rhonda was our sister-in-law, and Andy is her only son."

He set the glasses of pinot on the table in front of us.

Jane picked up her glass and took a sip. "Good choice. Now let's try the white."

Windsor gave only the slightest look of surprise before he headed back to the kitchen and began opening the chardonnay. "I don't want to get anyone in trouble."

The hair on my arms rose, along with goose bumps. "No one's getting into trouble unless they did something wrong."

"Come on, Winnie, spill yer guts."

I gave Jane a pointed look. She shrugged.

"The wine is delicious." She held up her glass. "Salut!"

I sighed. "Windsor, Andy's future is on the line."

He kept his back to us, grunting as he wrangled the cork out of the bottle. When it finally released, he yelped.

"You okay?" I asked.

He nodded, still with his back to us. He inhaled deeply, his shoulders rising and falling in dramatic fashion. When he spoke, his Queen's English accent was gone, and in its place, an estuary English accent. "You didn't hear this from me."

JANE POUNDED ON Rhonda's door. "Open up, Rhonda. We know you're in there."

After a few moments, the door opened a crack. Rhonda's bloodshot eyes peeked through the slit.

"What?" she croaked.

"We need to talk." I gave her my best *disappointed-librarian* look.

We followed her into the cabin, which was a studio with one king bed, a single recliner chair, a tiny dining table for two, and a kitchenette. Her wavy brown hair was mussed in the back, like she'd been taking a nap. She slumped onto the bed.

"You're already in pajamas? It's not even four o'clock."

She had the dazed gaze of someone under sedation.

"Rhonda." Jane snapped her fingers.

She turned to look at Jane and then back at me. "What?"

"Two whats, no answers. What did you take?"

I pulled a chair away from the table and sat. Jane did the same, crossing her arms.

"Just a little something to help me sleep." She rubbed her eyes.

"Why are you trying to sleep in the middle of the day while your son is being detained on a murder charge?" I asked.

"I didn't know what to do." She threw her hands in the air. "I don't know how to fix this."

"You can start by telling the truth about the noise I heard last night. I know Phoebe came to see you."

She puckered her lips, then pulled them back into her mouth until they disappeared. She repeated this motion three more times, her mouth moving faster with each repetition.

"Rhonda!" Jane slapped the table.

Rhonda stopped mid-pucker. "Okay, okay, but don't be mad."

I closed my eyes and took in a slow, deep breath. The woman was family, but she had hit my very last nerve. Through gritted teeth, I said, "What. Happened."

Rhonda wrung her bony hands. Although her hands had a few sunspots, her skin was supple for a woman in her late fifties. She must practice a diligent nightly routine of hand lotion. When everything settled down, I'd have to ask her about that.

"I texted Phoebe last night. I asked her to meet me to

talk."

"Why?"

"I wanted to explain to her about Andy's and my relationship. I'm sure he's told her all sorts of awful things about me. I tried to friend her on Facebook, but she never accepted my invitation to connect. I didn't want to go to the wedding feeling like my son's new wife hated me without even hearing my side. That's why I didn't go to dinner last night. I couldn't face everyone and all their judgment. I know I haven't always done right by him, but I've done my best."

Jane guffawed.

"Whatever, Jane. You're one to talk. You act like you've always been there for him, but you've lived hundreds of miles away for the past several years. The truth is, the only one who's truly always been there for him is you, Charlotte. I know there's not much I can say that would ever make up for how I've let him down, but I do love him, and I'm trying. I really am." She buried her face in her hands and began to cry.

"Oh, come on."

I glared at Jane. "Hey, show some compassion." I got up, walked over to the bed, and sat next to Rhonda with my hand on her heaving shoulder.

In between gulping sobs, she said, "I thought if I could talk to her, she'd talk to Andy and convince him to give me another chance."

"So, she came here?"

"It was late, and she wasn't in a good mood from the start. I tried to plead my case, but she was really mean to me."

"What did she say?" I rubbed her shoulder.

"She said"—Rhonda emitted a half-hiccup, half-gulp—"she said she had more important things to deal with than my pathetic attempts to worm my way back into Andy's life." She began to wail.

"Rhonda, pull it together," Jane said. "We're trying to keep Andy from going to prison for a murder he didn't commit. Stop making everything about you."

Rhonda scowled at Jane. "You sound just like her. Nobody cares about my feelings. My husband died!" She poked her own chest with a firm finger. "I took care of him for two years while also trying to take care of a toddler. I alternated between changing diapers and cleaning up puke. I watched the love of my life wither away while trying to make life as normal as possible for our son." She turned the finger toward Jane and poked the air. "You were in California. Don't talk to me about things you know nothing about."

Jane pulled her mouth taut. Once again, she crossed her arms. Now she was clearly pouting.

I stroked Rhonda's hair. "It sounds like there's a lot we need to talk through after all of this is dealt with. I know you love Andy and you want to help him. Anything you can remember about the conversation might help. Anything at all."

Rhonda bobbed her head and inhaled twice. "She came in already agitated. I asked her what was wrong, if she and Andy had a fight, she said yes, but that wasn't why she was upset."

Jane straightened in her chair. "She said that?"

Rhonda gulped. "She basically was like, *what do you need, Rhonda? I don't have time for this.* I started to talk to her about losing Bernie, how hard that was for me, but she held up her hand." Rhonda raised her hand. "Like this. She said, *I will not have you use my wedding to try to make up for thirty years of neglectful parenting.* As if it's always been this way."

"I don't blame her." Jane lifted her chin.

I shot Jane a look I hoped was full of daggers. I was trying to get Rhonda to open up to me, and Jane wasn't helping by antagonizing her. "What happened next?"

"She went to leave, and I tried to stop her."

"Did Phoebe say what else had upset her other than her fight with Andy?"

"All I know is, it had something to do with family and something to do with work."

I raised my eyebrows at Jane. "Andy said there was shady stuff happening at Braithwaite Industrial."

"We should talk to Frank," she said.

"Do we have to?"

She looked down her nose at me, and I sighed.

"Fine, but I need you watching my back. Literally."

Chapter Nine

WE FOUND FRANK sitting alone at Azure Lounge's bar near the observation deck, nursing some sort of amber-colored liquid on the rocks. I edged up next to him on one side while Jane hopped onto the stool, flanking him on the other side.

"Am I dreaming? I must be dreaming because I've had this exact fantasy."

"Come on now, Frank, doesn't the misogynistic pervert routine ever get old?" Jane asked.

"Jane!" I barked.

I despised Frank's attitude as much as anyone, if not more, but we needed to keep our eye on the prize, and that was solving this murder so that Andy didn't spend the rest of his life in prison for a crime he didn't commit.

"Sorry about my sister, Frank. We're just really upset about Andy."

"And Phoebe?" He gave me a pointed look, and I immediately felt awful.

"Yes, of course, I'm sorry. I meant both what happened to Phoebe and also what's happening with Andy."

Frank swigged his drink. "From what I'm hearing, all the

evidence is pointing in Andy's direction."

"That's convenient, isn't it, Frank?" Jane said.

"What's that supposed to mean?" he grunted.

I leaned back and peered around his broad body to catch my sister's attention. She craned her neck just enough to make eye contact with me, and that's when I realized what she was doing. She wanted to play good cop/bad cop, with me being the good cop, since Frank had often expressed his *admiration* for me. It would have been helpful if she'd alerted me before we got into the bar.

"Where's Elaine?" I asked.

He lifted the glass to his lips. "Getting ready."

"For what?"

"Seventies night." He took another sip.

"You can't be serious!" Jane said. "Your niece was just"—she lowered her voice to a whisper—"*murdered.* Now we're all gonna disco dance?"

"Show must go on." He slammed his glass on the bar. "Bartender! 'Nother one!" He stood, slightly wobbly. "I gotta take a leak. Make sure he isn't stingy with my pour."

With that, Frank weaved his way out of the bar and into the hall.

"Hey, Egan?" I called to the bartender, a handsome man in his mid-to late-twenties.

He glanced up from pouring Glenlivet into Frank's glass. "Yes, ma'am, what can I do you for?"

"Were you working last night?"

He gave me a confused look. "I was. Did you accidentally leave something at your table? We've got a lost and found down on Capri. I'd start there."

"No, I was wondering if you witnessed an argument last night."

"Oh, that little scuffle between the bride and groom? Yeah, anyone within a hundred feet heard that. I try to mind my own business, but they were making it pretty hard. Well…I should say she was. I couldn't hear what he was saying, but she was screeching like a barn owl."

Jane leaned forward. "So, you wouldn't describe them as being equally upset?"

He wrinkled his forehead. "That's tough to say. My mum got scarier the calmer she got. Some people are like that. If you're asking, were they both loud, nah. She was definitely winning that category."

"Can you remember what she was saying?" I asked.

He tilted his head. "Mostly just a lot of, *you don't know what it's like*, and *you have no idea what I'm dealing with*. Stuff like that." He mimicked Phoebe by raising his voice several octaves.

"That doesn't give a lot to go on." Jane said.

"One more question." I tapped the bar. "I know much of the bridal party was here and saw the fight. Anything stand out to you?"

"A lot of 'em thought it was funny."

"Nice group of friends," Jane muttered.

"No cap," he said.

"I'm sorry?" I must have heard him wrong.

Jane scoffed. "Ignore her. She's too old and out of touch." She turned to me. "I learned from the TikTok *no cap* means *I'm not lying or exaggerating.*"

I tightened my mouth. "First, you're older than me. Second, I'm pretty sure you lose all credibility for being hip when you call it *the* TikTok."

Egan nodded slowly, his lips puckering into a knowing smirk. "No cap."

I turned back to him. "Anything else?"

"Nah, she stomped off, the boyfriend tried to stop her, and that really didn't go over well. He was about to go after her, but one of the guys blocked him from leaving."

"Which guy?" I asked.

"Dunno. Tall, skinny. Kinda beige. You know the type?"

I tilted my head. "You mean he was tan?"

"Nah, I'm not talking about skin color. I'm talking about personality. The way he dressed. The overall vibe. Beige. Basic. Bland. Boring."

Hmm, Duncan was a sales executive who traveled a lot for work. He liked to say he knew the best steakhouses in each city of America, and the last time I'd seen him, his waistline supported the claim. He wouldn't be considered thin by any stretch.

Andy's best man, Vance, was tan-complected. Half Black and half Japanese, Vance liked to refer to himself as *Blasian.* He and Andy had known each other since elementary school. A car mechanic with multiple tattoos and piercings, Vance was far from bland.

"You're sure it was someone he knew?" I asked.

"Sure seemed like it. Now that I think about it, though, that guy actually wasn't with the others. He came into the bar after the fight had already started."

"But Andy knew him. You're pretty certain of that."

"Yeah, he calmed him down, and then he went after the girl."

"Wait. You mean Andy went after the girl, right?"

"Is Andy the tall skinny bloke?"

"No."

"Then, no. That guy went after the girl."

Jane had been quietly observing our conversation. "We've got to figure out who that was."

"I agree."

Frank meandered back into the bar and attempted to launch himself onto the stool. He didn't quite make it and ended up on his ample rump. "Oof!"

"Geez, Frank." Jane tried to pull him up, but he proved too heavy for her.

I got off my stool and helped her heave him upright. "Let's get you back to the room."

A smarmy smile washed across his face.

I narrowed my gaze. "Don't even think about it."

JANE AND I did our best to keep Frank upright as we made our way to his and Elaine's stateroom on the sixth floor, also known as the Aegean deck. They were in 615, halfway down the hallway from the elevators on the right side.

We propped Frank against the wall, and Jane held him in place with her shoulder while I knocked.

Elaine opened the door in dramatic fashion...*literally* in dramatic fashion.

Her strawberry blonde hair was once again teased into a round helmet style, this time with a silky purple and pink paisley hairband that matched her mini dress—designed to show off her new breasts—and knee-high go-go boots. Her chandelier earrings swung above her shoulders.

Her eyeshadow was lime green, with heavy black eyeliner to accompany her frosted faux lashes. She'd given herself an amoeba-shaped black mole above her upper lip. If it were real, it would be the type of thing a dermatologist would be quite concerned about.

She eyed me, perplexed, and then at Jane and Frank. "It's about time. I've been texting you for an hour."

"Elaine," Frank slurred, "those weren't texts. It was just a bunch of tiny pictures."

"You know I like to text only using emoji." She lowered her voice and addressed Jane and me. "Frank really likes it when I send the eggplant and the peach. It's fun, like a puzzle to solve, and it doesn't require me to spell good. Spelling's never been my thing. Or math. I was good at art, though. I once posed nude for an art class, in fact."

I'd have preferred not to have that visual.

"He had a few too many pre-funk drinks," Jane said. "I don't think he could decipher his own name through the lens of all that scotch."

Jane pushed him toward the door, but Elaine scooted out of the way. He had too much momentum, so he ended up face-down on the plush entryway rug.

"Elaine." This time, her name came out in a moan, muffled by the rug's fluffy strands of gray (I suspected) polyester/silk blend.

Elaine rolled her eyes. "Frank, I can't believe you did this. We're supposed to leave for dinner in a few minutes." She nudged him with her boot. "You gotta get up. Your leisure suit is on the bed."

"We're gonna leave you to it." Jane waved a terse goodbye.

"Wait! Are you going to the seventies' night dinner?"

"Oh, uh..." *Come on, Jane, rescue me.*

Jane shrugged. "I don't know, Elaine. Last night was a lot."

"Oh, come on! This is supposed to be a fun trip. It's only fun if everyone participates."

I dipped my chin. "This was supposed to be a wedding cruise, and the bride is dead. She's been murdered. The groom is in custody. Doesn't it seem...inappropriate to be partying at a time like this?"

"Nonsense! If there's anything to take away from this situation, it's that life is short. Phoebe would have wanted us to dress up and have fun."

I wasn't so sure about that. Last night, a sullen Phoebe had pouted about having to wear a costume to pacify Andy. "We'll think about it." I glanced at Frank, who was still facedown on the ground. "Good luck."

As we turned toward the elevators, someone called our names from behind us. At the end of the hall, Macy stood in the open doorway of her cabin.

"Charlotte, Jane," Macy repeated. "Could I speak with you for a moment?"

Jane shrugged.

"We've got a few minutes to spare," I said.

Macy led us into the suite she shared with Sawyer. The sound of running water in the bathroom indicated he was taking a shower.

Macy sat at the dining table, so Jane and I followed suit.

"Is everything okay?" Jane asked.

Macy let out an anxious sigh. "I'm not sure. I saw something, and it may not be a big deal at all, but I needed to tell someone just in case it's important."

"What did you see?" I asked.

Macy chewed her lower lip. "Today, in the captain's lounge, I noticed that Neal was acting strange."

So, I wasn't the only one who thought that was odd.

"He kept looking at his phone," she said. "Staring at it. At first, I figured he was trying to sneak in some work. I thought that was tacky, considering the circumstances. I decided to sneak a peek before I accused him, and I couldn't believe what I saw."

Jane leaned forward. "What was it? Porn?"

Macy pursed her lips. "Practically."

I knit my brows together. "That's unfortunate for Lily and embarrassing for Neal, but I don't see how that could possibly relate to what happened to Phoebe."

Macy gave a knowing look. "It *was* Phoebe."

"Wait, what?" Jane's voice rose two octaves and three decibels.

"I know. Crazy, right? I couldn't believe it."

"What..." I tried to phrase my next question as delicately as possible. "What was Phoebe, uh, what did the photo, uh, what kind..."

"The kind you're thinking. She was dressed, sort of, but in something skimpy and sexy. I didn't get a good look, because first, *eeww*, and second, Neal noticed me hovering and shoved his phone in his pocket."

Jane looked like she'd gotten a whiff of bad fish. "What a pervert. I wonder how he got the photo." She gasped. "You don't think she was cheating on Andy with her own brother-in-law, do you?"

I groaned. "I hope not. That would make this whole thing even worse. Maybe he stole it from her private stash of pictures."

Jane slapped the table. "What if he were her stalker?"

"That makes no sense," I said.

Macy's eyebrows raised. "Doesn't it? I mean, think about it. Her brother-in-law becomes obsessed with her, but he can't let his wife find out, so he finds a sexy picture of her and, well, you know."

"Gross," I said. "I don't know, and I don't want to know."

Macy continued, "Soon, it's not enough just to have her picture. He needs her to know how he feels, but he can't tell her directly, so he sends anonymous messages and gifts."

Jane fervently nodded. "That would explain how he knew to send stuff to her house! That was always a question, how the stalker got her home address."

"Macy, do you think the picture might have been a screenshot of one of her YouTube videos?" I asked.

"No, I don't think so. I mean, I haven't seen many of them, but I've seen enough to say she didn't post that kind of stuff. That's more of an Only Fans kind of thing. Although, I don't even know if Only Fans existed before she shut down her accounts."

I raised one brow. "Do I want to know what Only Fans is?"

Jane laughed. "You do not."

BACK IN OUR suite, I flung my phone on the counter.

Jane yawned as she walked past me and dropped into a chair. "It's always the ones you least suspect."

"Are you saying you didn't suspect Gabe was a cheater?"

"I never liked the guy, and I could definitely see him having some weird fetish like watching videos of a girl sucking peanut butter off her toes, but no, I didn't think he was capable of constructing an entire double life. Frankly, I didn't think he was that interesting."

"Me neither. Obviously." I slumped onto the sofa and put my feet on the coffee table. "I can't believe Elaine still thinks we should dress up and go to dinner."

Jane yawned again. "We do have to eat."

"Okay, and?"

She shrugged. "I'm just saying, if we have to eat dinner anyway, it's not the craziest idea to get dressed up in our costumes. We paid good money for them, and it's not like we'll have many chances to wear them."

"Speak for yourself. I got mine at Goodwill."

"Char, you're the only millionaire I know who shops at the thrift shop."

"Hey, if it's good enough for Macklemore, it's good enough for me. I've found some high-end stuff there, especially the U District location. Besides, I still don't feel like a millionaire. I keep thinking I'm going to wake up and discover it was all just a crazy dream. Or nightmare. What do they call that? Lucid dreaming?"

"I don't know, but I can tell you that Gabe is dead, the money is real, and Andy needs us to do everything we can to figure out what happened to Phoebe. I say we put on the costumes. Let's do this thing. Get us some fondue, and while we're there, do a little snooping, ask a few questions. We aren't doing Phoebe or Andy any favors by starving ourselves or staying in for room service."

I narrowed my eyes. "What costume did you get?"

She gave me an impish smile. "You'll see!"

Chapter Ten

"I FEEL RIDICULOUS."

Jane arched her left brow as she eyed me up and down. "It's not the worst thing I've ever seen."

"It is. Don't lie to me. It's atrocious."

I'd already stared at my reflection for ten minutes trying to decide what adjustments could possibly be made so I could be seen in public. My costume—a denim pantsuit with paisley blouse built into the seams, which I'd purchased from a thrift store but never tried on—was ill-fitting, particularly in the bust area, and generally unflattering.

"Stop fidgeting."

"I can't. The shirt is that scratchy kind of polyester that makes your skin crawl." I shimmied my shoulders, then I yanked the collar to one side in hopes of relieving the claustrophobic feeling it gave me.

"You're being dramatic."

"Easy for you to say. That *Solid Gold* dancer outfit you've got on looks like it was custom made for you."

Jane was taller and slimmer than me to begin with, but in her four-inch heels, she was like a golden flagpole to my disco scarecrow. Her lamé jumpsuit, instead of giving the appearance of an overstuffed sofa from 1973 like my costume, made her look like an Oscar statuette. Her wavy dark hair had been hidden beneath a long, blonde wig and she'd added thick, white-tipped eyelashes and white lipstick to complete the retro look.

Her vibe was Donna Summer at Studio 54. Mine was Roy Clark from *Hee Haw*.

"You look cute, Char. I don't know what the problem is."

"The problem is that this thing is too baggy everywhere but my boobs."

She pulled and yanked the outfit, frowning, until it met some level of approval. "It will have to do."

"Not a glowing compliment."

"You should've gone to a costume rental place. They have everything." She scrunched her nose. "And their stuff doesn't smell like it's been stored in a damp attic for thirty years."

I tipped my nose to my chest and attempted to inhale. "I don't smell anything."

She reached into her rhinestone clutch, pulled out a bottle of perfume, and spritzed me.

"Hey!"

"You'll thank me later. Ready?"

I sighed. "This feels like a bad idea."

THE DINING ROOM had been transformed from Roaring

Twenties to groovy seventies since the last time we were here. Each table had disco ball vases filled with multicolored daisies. Strobe lights darted from wall to wall, and the waitstaff wore ruffled shirts under their normal tuxedo uniforms.

Jane pointed at our assigned table. "Looks like Elaine managed to get Frank off the floor."

"Barely."

Frank was leaning against an annoyed Elaine with his eyes only partly open and his mouth hanging mostly open. If his tongue suddenly lolled out of the corner, I wouldn't have been surprised. Understandably, Dale and Susan weren't there, and neither, obviously, was Andy. Rhonda was also MIA for the second night in a row.

Lily and Ivy sat next to each other at their table, with their husbands on each side of them. The twins wore coordinating A-line halter dresses—Ivy in fuchsia, Lily in lavender—with matching silk headscarves. The color choices spoke to the difference in their personalities. It was difficult to tell if their dark under-eye makeup was intentionally smudged or the result of intermittent crying bouts.

Clyde had gone full *Superfly* with his white suit, white loafers, and white fedora.

My gaze rested on Neal, and a whimper escaped me.

"What's wrong?" Jane said, looking around. "Is someone hurt?"

I closed my eyes, inhaled deeply, and opened them again. Unfortunately, I hadn't mistaken what I'd thought I'd seen. "Neal is wearing the same outfit as me."

"You're kidding." Jane grabbed my arm as she scanned the room. When she finally spotted him, she squealed. "That. Is. Hilarious." She wheezed with laughter. "You guys must shop at the same thrift store."

I raised my chin in an attempt to project more nonchalance about the embarrassing faux pas than I felt. "Let's sit down before anyone sees me."

We scurried over to our table and launched into our chairs. Frank's eyes flew open, and for a moment he appeared to not know where he was. He blinked at me, and then at Jane.

"Have I traveled back in time?" He pulled back from Elaine and his eyes widened. He glanced down at his own outfit, which he'd apparently forgotten putting on his body, and then back at Jane and me. "I knew those 'shrooms were a bad idea."

Elaine gasped. "When did you do 'shrooms?"

He shrugged. "Nineteen seventy-one. No, maybe seventy-two."

"Evening, ladies and gentlemen." Ulfric, the maître d, arrived at our table. "How is everyone tonight? Will the others be joining us?"

We all glanced at each other. No one knew what to say.

Finally, Jane took a crack at it. "Uh, not sure if you heard, but the bride is…deceased."

He placed his open hand over his heart. "I did hear something terrible had happened, but I did not know it was her. You have my condolences. And to the groom."

"He's in jail for her murder," Frank slurred.

"Oh my."

"He didn't do it," I said with as much emphasis as possible.

Ulfric swallowed. "Oh." After a moment of awkward silence, he backed slowly away from our table.

"Charlotte?" Elaine tapped her chin with her long red coffin nails. "I know it's kinda dark in here, but is it my imagination, or are you and Neal Alcorn wearing the same getup?"

I let my head hang.

"It just means Char has good taste," Jane said.

"Does it?" Elaine asked. "I hate to say it, but it looks better on him. Which, I guess makes sense, since it's obviously a man's costume."

"Since when are polyester coveralls made to look like denim only for men?" Jane pounded the table. "Even in the seventies they believed in equal rights for women. The ERA and all that."

"Jane, you're not helping," I mumbled. "Also, only thirty states ratified the ERA by the end of the decade."

"I'm all for equal rights." Elaine sniffed. "That doesn't extend to costumes clearly not designed to hold your boobs."

"I need a drink." I pushed away from the table.

As I walked to the bar, I could hear Jane protest that our server Haimi would be taking our drink orders shortly.

It wasn't about the drink. I needed a moment to pull myself back together before I lost my temper and made a scene.

I attempted to nonchalantly lean against the bar like I'd

seen so many times in the movies. I clenched my fists together and bounced them off the bar top.

The bartender, Egan, glanced at me. "Be right with you." He poured liquor into a silver cocktail shaker.

"No problem."

He poured the cocktail out of the shaker into a martini glass and set it on the counter in front of another patron. He slid over to me, taking in a fuller view of my outfit as he did so.

"You decided to go with the whole shebang, I see." His broad smile was accompanied by an Irish accent.

"I know it's ridiculous. I'm not sure what I was thinking. Can I get a double vodka martini, extra dirty, extra olives, please?"

"Whoa, sounds like somebody's either trying to drown their sorrows or getting ready to dance." He began pouring from various bottles.

"Oh. Oh, no. No, no. I don't dance." I wagged my finger.

He held the shaker next to his ear and sloshed it back and forth. "You will by the end of the night if you keep drinking these." He poured the contents into a glass and placed it on the bar. "Anything else I can do for you?"

"Uh, no, I'm good, thanks." I began chugging my martini.

"Let me know if you change your mind."

Oh my. Did he just wink at me? I'm old enough to be his mother. Maybe not his mother but definitely his aunt.

As he moved down the bar to help another customer, I

observed the table where the remainder of the bridal party were seated. While they'd all been in the captain's lounge earlier, I'd not been introduced to most of them. I'd known Vance for several years, but the others I only recognized from photos Andy had posted and tagged on social media. He'd always been careful not to include Phoebe in any of the pictures since her stalker had never been caught.

First in my line of vision was Duncan. I hadn't noticed earlier, but he'd lost about twenty pounds since the last photo I'd seen of him at Andy and Phoebe's Labor Day barbeque a couple months prior. Had his motivation come from knowing he'd be on this trip with Nikki, the Eastside real estate agent he was currently chatting up? He couldn't have been the man Egan the bartender described earlier, the one who'd followed Phoebe after her fight with Andy, because he was well under six feet tall.

Nikki appeared to be tolerating Duncan's story, but she didn't look enthusiastic. Nikki, who was supposed to have been Phoebe's maid of honor, was the kind of girl I'd always found intimidating when I was younger, despite the fact if we were standing next to each other, I'd loom over her. Barely five feet tall, with tiny features and a tiny waist, she'd been a cheerleader at Washington State University. According to Phoebe, she was the one who got vaulted to the pinnacle of the pyramids like a Kurt Adler star atop a Christmas tree.

Nikki's costume was a florescent orange Lycra minidress that contrasted brilliantly with her deep-brown skin and thousand-watt smile.

On the opposite side of Duncan, the other bridesmaid, Serena, plucked the elastic string of her beaded bracelet as she observed his conversation with Nikki. I'd have suspected she was an elementary school teacher even if I hadn't known she was a coworker of Andy's. She wore her light brown hair in a slick ponytail, little if any makeup, and she had kind brown eyes that gave her the aura of being a safe person. Although I knew she was in costume for the event—purple flared pants and a tie-dyed blouse with a giant yellow happy face in the middle—in Andy's social media posts she wore a collection of cardigans with kitschy themes such as school supplies, various holidays, all the seasons, and an occasional fictional reference. Her favorite seemed to be one with a *Lord of the Rings* motif including lines of elvish script all down the back.

Andy had often described Serena as bookish and introverted. I imagined this scenario, a whole week at sea socializing with the likes of Nikki and Duncan, was especially torturous for her.

Duncan must have made a joke, because Nikki emitted a boisterous inauthentic laugh. He leaned back to catch Serena's reaction as well. She mustered a slight smile but not more than that. When Duncan once again turned his back to her, Serena rolled her eyes and swigged her red wine.

"Have you discovered anything of interest?" a deep gravelly voice with a French accent spoke into my ear.

I whirled to face Xavier, expecting him to be wearing a flirtatious grin to match the effect the timbre of his voice had on my now-tingling spine, but instead he was stone-faced.

The only hint of emotion was bemusement as he took in my costume. Thankfully, he refrained from commenting. I'd be of no help to Andy if I got thrown in the same cell…or brig or wherever they were detaining him…for whacking my purse upside the head of the chief security officer.

He, of course, wore no costume, only his standard uniform.

"I, uh, what do you mean?"

"Come now, Madame McLaughlin. It is clear you are trying to spy on those young people in hopes of determining possible suspects and exonerating your nephew."

"Well, now that you mention it, have you looked into the bridal party? Since, as you said, these crimes are often committed by someone acquainted with the victim, I'd think they'd be on the top of your list."

"They are, of course, on the list. I have my men researching everything they can about each member of the Braithwaite-Cobb wedding party, including yourself. Perhaps you can shed some light on them as well?"

On the one hand, I didn't like Mesnier. Okay, so maybe I liked him a little, but not at that exact moment, while he held my nephew on suspicion of murder. On the other hand, the sooner the real killer was identified and caught, the sooner Andy's name would be cleared.

I turned back to the table where the non-family members of the wedding party were seated. I could sense Xavier move in closer to hear my analysis.

"I don't know a lot. Mostly just bits and pieces I've picked up over time and conversations."

"What was his relationships to the victim?" Xavier dipped his chin at Duncan.

"Duncan and Andy met at trivia night at a pub in Seattle a couple years ago, but they've become closer in the past few months. He went through a bad breakup recently, so Andy has been putting in extra time with him." I gave Xavier a pointed look. "That's the kind of guy Andy is. He's the friend who's always there for people when they need him."

Xavier raised his eyebrows. "This...*Duncan*, he is a recent friend of your nephew?"

"Recent compared to Vance. He's the man on the other side of Nikki. Vance and Andy have known each other since high school."

"The, uh, how do you say, stalker you mentioned to me earlier, what can you tell me about that situation?"

I turned around. Xavier was closer than I'd expected. I blinked rapidly, and he stepped back a few inches.

"Remember, this is all second- and thirdhand from Phoebe and Andy. It went down before Andy and Phoebe met."

"Remind me, *s'il vous plaît*, where did they meet?"

"I believe they met at the same pub where Andy met Duncan."

"Interesting."

"You're thinking Duncan could be her stalker."

He gave a wry smile and wagged his finger. "Uh, uh, uh. That is not how this works."

I blew out a sigh. "As I was saying, a few years ago, Phoebe started making her silly YouTube videos. I've never quite understood what causes someone to go viral or gain a massive following simply for recording their daily life, but there's an audience for it and she found it. It wasn't just about her, either. She recorded her family, their vacations, holidays. She opened their lives up to the public. Kind of like the Kardashians but a lot less glamorous."

"The Braithwaites, they are wealthy, are they not?"

"They're not Kardashian wealthy. They're well off. The business her father co-owns with her uncle is successful, but not to the point of funding the type of lavish lifestyle you might think. That's what's so crazy about this new era of social media and celebrity. Phoebe once told me the video with the most views was one where she and her brother tried to bake a cake for their mom's birthday. Three million people have watched it."

"Three million." He whistled. "That is a lot."

"At least one of those three million became obsessed with Phoebe. Started sending gifts, letters, all anonymous. Phoebe typically answered as much of her mail as possible, but something about these letters felt off to her, so she set them aside and didn't answer. Eventually, the frequency and intensity of the letters became overwhelming. Phoebe shut down the channel, deleted all her social media, and went dormant."

"Did the harassment cease?"

Jane popped up next to us. "Whatcha talkin' about?"

Xavier reared back.

My sister glowered at me. "Thanks for leaving me with Frank and Elaine. Now Sawyer and Macy are there. Frank's heckling Macy because she doesn't have any vices, and he sees that as a character flaw. He said, *No drinking? No gambling? No cigars? Might as well kill me now*, like *that* wasn't a totally insensitive thing to say. Meanwhile, Sawyer seems distracted by the other table and isn't even defending her. Talk about your barrel of monkeys."

Xavier blinked several times with a blank expression on his face.

I glanced back at our table. Macy wore a purple sequined jumpsuit with long bell-shaped sleeves that flared dramatically at the bottom. Her large silver hoop earrings matched her silver necklace and locket. Sawyer wore a white suit with a black open-collared shirt like John Travolta in *Grease*. His sandy-blond hair was slicked back. He watched Nikki and Duncan's interaction like it was a reality TV show.

Nikki saw him surveilling her and then forced a laugh as if Duncan had said something amusing. Duncan crinkled his forehead in confusion, but he eventually joined her laughter.

It reminded me of middle-school antics.

I said to Jane, "I'm in the middle of explaining to Officer Mesnier here about Phoebe's stalker and why he should be looking for that person instead of her loving fiancé Andy."

"You're definitely barking up the wrong tree with Andy." Jane slapped his bicep but immediately removed her hand as soon as she saw his scowl. "Sorry." She turned to me. "Did you tell him about Neal?"

"Not yet."

"By Neal, do you mean Monsieur Alcorn?"

"Yeah," I said. "We had to help Frank get back to his

room this afternoon. As we were leaving, Macy called us down to her suite."

"Macy Keeling, the girlfriend of Sawyer."

"Yes. That one over there." I indicated our table. "She's wearing the purple jumpsuit. She said she saw that Neal kept looking at his phone. She thought maybe he was working and tried to catch him. Instead, she saw he was looking at a picture of, get this—" I paused, expecting him to exhibit signs of anticipation. Instead, he remained stone-faced, maybe bored, even. It wasn't as fun to deliver this bombshell to someone who appeared as though I were reciting my grocery list. I waved away my disappointment with my hands. "Phoebe."

I spotted the slightest twitch of interest in his left brow.

"Only not just any picture," Jane said. "It was a naughty picture. A private, *naughty* picture."

"Hmm."

"That's it? *Hmm*?" I understood playing cards close to the vest, but this was ridiculous. "Come on, that's got to fall under the category of suspicious."

"Perhaps. Do you know how he acquired the photo?"

"No, we only found out about it an hour or so ago," I said.

Jane narrowed her gaze. "You should be thanking us."

"Pardon?"

She jutted her chin. "We seem to be making more progress on this case than you and your goons are."

"Those *goons* as you so disparagingly put it, are former Navy SEALS."

Jane scoffed. "Like I haven't heard that line before. Not every guy can be former Navy SEAL."

Xavier scrunched his face. "Pardon?"

"She's met a lot of liars and frauds on internet dating sites," I clarified.

He cleared his throat. "Before you arrived, Madame Cobb, Madame McLaughlin was just about to tell me if the activity ceased after Madame Braithwaite removed her content from the internet."

"This formality thing is getting old. It would be a lot easier if you would call us by our first names. Jane." She touched her chest. "Charlotte." She pointed at me. "And Phoebe, God rest her soul."

He gave no indication whether he intended to change the way he addressed us.

I said, "The answer to your question about whether the harassment ceased, is not completely. The Braithwaites had to change her phone number to unlisted, move across town, switch their mail delivery to a PO box, and had her assistant filter every letter and package. Anything that seemed suspicious got routed directly to the investigating officer."

Jane said, "She went to work for her uncle at Braithwaite Industrial. Even though it was public information that the company was partly owned by her father, the site is heavily guarded and monitored by a high-tech security system."

"They did that just to protect her?" he asked.

"Oh no," Jane said. "They already had that in place. Frank has it on lockdown. Which is another point we wanted to make. Andy said Phoebe was all worked up about some shady guys Frank's been doing business with lately. She'd been feeling less secure since those thugs had been coming around."

Serena appeared next to me, holding an empty glass. "Are you guys talking about Phoebe's creepy uncle?" Her words were a little slurred, and she smelled like wine.

Jane eyed Serena. "Maybe."

"She definitely had a beef with him." Serena waved her glass at Egan and then set it on the bar.

He gave her a brief but appreciative head bob.

This close to her, I could see that the beads on her bracelet were black except for one light turquoise crystal in the middle. Aquamarine. I'd seen one like it before, on Andy's wrist. His center bead was red. Ruby.

Their birthstones. Matching bracelets seemed oddly intimate, even for close friends. Whose idea was that, and how had Phoebe felt about it?

"A beef?" Xavier knitted his brows.

"Yeah, you know, I saw them arguing."

Xavier's mouth twitched. "Pardon?"

"When?" I asked.

"The first night," Serena said.

"Last night?" I blinked twice at her. "You mean the night she was murdered?"

She blinked back at me. "Well, yeah, I guess so."

"And you did not think this was pertinent information to report?" Xavier didn't blink at all. He just stared at her like another head was sprouting out of her shoulders.

"I forgot, I guess."

"What time was this?" Xavier gritted his teeth.

Serena gazed up at the ceiling. "Uh, had to have been like twelve fifteen, twelve thirty. I left the bar just after midnight. I'd accidentally gotten off on the fifth floor because the old lady I was riding the elevator with pushed the button and I was kind of tipsy, so I forgot to push six until it was too late. I knew I could take the ramp up to six, so I went that way, and I saw Phoebe yelling at her uncle."

"What did you hear?" I was stunned that she hadn't thought to report the argument.

"She said something about getting a call from one of their clients about strange noises coming from one of the crates. She told him she knew what he was doing, and she was going to blow the lid off the whole operation. He tried to calm her down, but she wasn't having it."

"Then what happened?" Jane asked.

"Frank stormed off, and I ducked back around the corner."

"Why?"

She looked at me like I was stupid. "Because I didn't want to talk to her." She picked up her now-full glass from the bar. "I'm not sure if you know this, but Phoebe doesn't–didn't–like me all that much." She wobbled back to her table and plopped down.

Xavier observed Frank, who was resting his head on the table in front of him, and then back at me. "Tell me exactly what happens at Braithwaite Industrial."

"I have a better idea. Why don't the three of us go talk to Andy? He can tell you exactly what Phoebe told him."

"Alright."

I put my hand on his forearm and immediately removed it. "Please, don't tell him about Neal and the photo just yet. I don't know what he knows about it, but if he doesn't know, the last thing Andy needs right now is to find out his fiancée may have been unfaithful."

As soon as the words were out of my mouth, I knew I'd made a terrible mistake.

I'd just given Xavier one more reason why Andy might have wanted to kill Phoebe.

Chapter Eleven

ANDY JUMPED TO his feet and opened his arms for a hug from Jane and me.

"No touching," Xavier said.

The room where he'd been held for the past several hours was basically four white walls and the cot on which he'd been laying. A water bottle and an empty paper plate sat on the floor next to the cot.

"Did they feed you?" I asked.

He slumped back onto the cot and rested his forearms on his legs. "Yeah. Officer Taylor brought me a turkey sandwich."

Xavier crossed his arms and widened his stance. I was certain it was an intimidation tactic that had served him well in his previous life as an international man of mystery or whatever he was.

"Monsieur Cobb, I have been speaking with your aunts regarding the happenings at Madame Braithwaite's place of employment. They seem convinced it is related to what happened to her. Could you enlighten me on any details of which they may not be aware, *s'il vous plaît*?"

Andy scrunched his face. "You think someone related to

Frank's business might have done this?"

"I merely am attempting to place all the puzzle pieces together. Did you not express concern to your aunts about her work?"

"I can tell you this. She was concerned. She told me multiple times, including last night, that something wasn't right there. I guess it's an open secret in the family that Frank's always been the type of guy who likes to ride the line between illegal and unethical. According to Phoebe, he never batted an eye regarding the unethical. Lately, she's been starting to worry he'd begun crossing the line into the illegal."

"What evidence did she have to support this theory?"

"I'm not sure she had any. That's what she was trying to do in the weeks and days leading up to the wedding. She was trying to accumulate the proof. Frank had some new clients, and they made her very uncomfortable."

"Being uncomfortable is not evidence of criminal activity."

"Let me break this down for you in a way that you might understand why she was alarmed by what she was seeing." Andy ran his fingers through his hair. "So, her family is in the storage business, specializing in shipping container storage. Her grandfather started the company and then passed it on to his two sons, Frank and Dale. Dale was never too keen on participating. He's always claimed it was a matter of principle. Calls himself a conscientious objector to his own inheritance. Frank says his brother is flaky and just doesn't want to work. Says Dale doesn't like to get dirt under his fingernails. Dale says Frank has dirty hands, but he means it metaphorically."

Xavier grabbed a notepad and a pen from his inside pocket. "Where is the business located?"

"Their property sits right on Salmon Bay, between Lake Union and the Ballard Locks."

"Ballard's the cultural hub of Seattle's Scandinavian community," I explained to Xavier. "A large portion of the residents are involved in deep-sea fishing and other nautical endeavors."

"Right." Andy agreed. "Even though the Braithwaites aren't Scandinavian by name, the grandmother or great-grandmother emigrated from Norway as a young girl and settled with her family in Ballard. Dale and Frank's dad was raised there and like everyone else he knew became a deep-sea fisherman. After his sons were born, though, he decided he needed to stick close to home, so he bought a large chunk of land and started Braithwaite Industrial. Phoebe said initially the business had been broader, but Frank found focusing on the storage aspect was more lucrative with less liability than industrial supply."

"So, Frank worked their father's business, but Dale did not. How did Phoebe get involved?" Xavier scribbled something on the notepad.

"When Phoebe still had her YouTube channel, she was bringing in a decent amount of money, and creating that content was her full-time job. After she shut everything down, she needed to support herself. Frank offered to hire her as the office manager." Andy gave a sad smile. "I don't think he anticipated she would interfere in the stuff he had going on."

"If I may ask, do you know approximately how much income Madame Braithwaite received as a result of her videos?"

Andy shrugged. "I never asked. The last thing I wanted was for her to think I was a gold digger. At one point she mentioned she was making a couple thousand dollars per video. She posted one to two videos per day, pretty much every day for several years. If I had to guess, two hundred and fifty thousand a year for the last couple years she was active would be a conservative estimate."

Xavier whistled. "Half a million dollars is not a small amount of money for such a young woman." He paused and focused his gaze onto Andy. "Or a young man."

I cocked my head. "That in and of itself should prove to you Andy didn't do this."

Xavier raised both brows. "How do you surmise this?"

"She was killed before they got married. Why would he kill the golden goose, so to speak, before the wedding? As her husband, he stood to inherit a lot of money. As her fiancé, he gets nothing."

"Perhaps. Or perhaps she wanted him to sign a prenuptial agreement and he got angry."

"That's ridiculous," I said.

Xavier ignored my reply. "Continue with your explanation, *s'il vous plait*," he invited Andy.

"A couple months ago, we were on our way to a surprise thirtieth birthday party for a friend when Phoebe remembered she'd left their gift on her file cabinet at work. She'd gotten delayed by a client yelling at her about a billing issue and was worried we'd be late for the party, so she'd run out of her office without the thirty-year-old scotch she'd bought especially for the occasion. Our friend was born in Scotland, and...well, anyway, she insisted we stop by her work to grab it. I waited in the car. When she came back a few minutes later, she was upset. I tried to press her on it, but she didn't want to talk about it. It was only after we'd gotten home that night, she said Frank had been meeting two guys in his office. It gave her a bad feeling."

"Did she explain what struck her as unusual about the meeting?" Xavier asked.

"Well, first, Frank was never there that late. He likes to breeze into the office around ten, leave for lunch around eleven thirty, come back at one, and then leave for the day by two thirty to avoid traffic. He'd already left for the day as far as she was concerned, there was no meeting in the online calendar, and he'd never mentioned it. Beyond that, it was the guys he was meeting and how they acted when they saw her."

"What do you mean?"

"She heard voices she didn't recognize and was worried there was a break-in. They sounded Russian or Eastern European. But then she heard Frank's booming voice. She tried to sneak in without him spotting her, mostly because she didn't want to get roped into a conversation when we were already in danger of being late for the arrival of the birthday boy at the surprise party. She never told me anything about what they were saying, but Frank caught a glimpse of her as she reached for the bottle. I guess the two guys whipped their heads around and gave her a death glare."

Xavier wrinkled his forehead. "Death glare?"

"Yeah, like, they wished bad things against her."

"Did she describe the men?"

"Not in too much detail, only that they looked like henchmen."

Xavier frowned. "I am afraid none of that information is very helpful. Her gut feeling that two business associates of her uncle are bad men is not evidence of anything."

"You'd have to have seen her when she got back in the car. She was shaking. I told her if her gut instincts were that it was unsafe there, she should quit. She got mad at me. And then on Sunday, she told me she doesn't want to ride together. She'd meet me at the docks because she needs to deal with something. She almost missed the boat."

"Ship." Xavier waved his hands. "No matter. So, you were angry she nearly missed the ship for your wedding? That was the subject of the argument on the observation deck?"

Andy rolled his head back and held up his palm. "What? No. I was worried, but not angry. When she stormed off at dinner, I followed her and once again, I told her she should quit her job. Her uncle's a real jerk and she doesn't need to be dealing with him anyway, but if he's into something illegal or dangerous, she needed to get out of there. She accused me of being overbearing and controlling, which is crazy. I let her do whatever she wanted—"

"Oh, Andy." Jane sighed. "*Let* her?"

"You know what I mean. I supported her, encouraged her. I just didn't understand why she'd keep working for her uncle. She said she was trying to save her family business and I couldn't know what that was like because my dad is dead and I don't really talk to my mom."

"Ouch," I said.

"Did I try to convince her it would be better if she quit? Sure. But why would I kill her just because we had a disagreement?"

"People have killed over less," Xavier said.

"Well, I didn't."

"Did she tell you what she was doing when she nearly missed the ship's departure?" Xavier's left eyebrow arched.

"Only that she'd gotten a call from a customer who'd seen something they felt needed further inspection. I asked her about it later that night, if that was why she had gotten upset at the dinner table. I think she was really scared, and that's why she was acting so erratic."

"Scared of whom?" Xavier asked.

"Her uncle. I believe Frank Braithwaite may be involved in smuggling."

"But you say you have no proof of this."

Andy gave Xavier wide, crazy eyes. "You're just determined to pin this on me, aren't you? I'm trying to explain to you: she didn't want to talk to me about it because she knew I'd be more convinced she should quit if I knew it was dangerous, not because she was afraid of me."

"I will reach out to the authorities in Seattle to see if

there is anything to back your story. I will also speak with Mr. Braithwaite and his brother."

"Dale has no idea what's going on with that business," Andy said.

Xavier uncrossed his arms and put his hands on his hips. "He may not. However, we may need his authorization to investigate these claims of smuggling at the location. That is a very serious charge."

"Andy," I said, "do you think Frank is smuggling drugs?"

"I don't know. That would be my first guess. I don't know what else it could be."

"Over the years in my field I have seen people smuggle all variety of items, from shark fins to counterfeit electronics to weapons and even human beings," Xavier said.

Jane made a gurgling sound. "Oh, I hope he's not into human trafficking. That would be horrific."

"Monsieur Mesnier—"

"Xavier, please."

"I don't think you believe Andy did this any more than we do. So, why don't you let him go?"

"I cannot. If he is not the perpetrator, someone else on the ship is, and I would like them to believe I am focused on Andy as a subject. I believe that was an intended byproduct of this crime."

"It's not fair to hold him. Can you at least allow him to go back to his room and be on house arrest? You can post a guard."

Xavier gave a rare smile. "I have a better idea. You can babysit him."

Chapter Twelve

"YOU GUYS DON'T have to share a bed. I can sleep on the fold-out couch." Andy held his suitcase in one hand and a duffle bag in the other.

"Aunt Jane and I used to share a room as kids. There's no reason why we can't share one for a few days."

"I appreciate you getting me out of that room. I thought I was going to be stuck on that cot forever."

Jane came out of the bedroom where she'd slept the past couple days with her suitcase. "I still think it's pretty crappy Xavier's trying to use you as a red herring so he can lure out the real killer."

"I get it," I said. "We all want to know what really happened, and if the killer thinks they got away with it, they may get overly confident and unintentionally reveal themselves. I'm relieved to know Xavier doesn't really believe Andy did it. Or at least he mostly thinks that."

Andy dropped his bags and took a seat on the sofa. He put his face in his hands. I moved to sit next to him, rubbing his shoulder like I had when he woke up crying from a dream about his dad as a little boy.

He removed his hands from his face. His were the saddest eyes I'd ever seen.

"I haven't even had a chance to process the fact she's gone." His voice was ragged. "We had so many pl-plans."

My heart felt like it was physically being squeezed by some unseen force. Despite every challenge he'd faced, he pressed forward. When he was eight and his new basketball coach had pulled me aside after the first practice to gently suggest perhaps it wasn't his sport, I told him he'd never meet any kid more willing to keep trying than Andy. By the end of the season, he'd received the *most improved* award. Persistence and resilience were his core values, and yet time and again he'd been rewarded with more loss and setbacks.

No matter what I thought of Phoebe or their relationship, I desperately wanted things to work out for him. Even the most tenacious optimists reached their limits and lost hope if they never tasted the fruits of their efforts.

"I'm so sorry. I'm so, so sorry." They were the only words that would come out of my mouth.

Jane took the chair adjacent to us. "Andy, you've had more loss in your young life than anyone should have to experience. It's not fair. But you've gained a tremendous amount of resilience, and I know that will carry you through this. The pain will never go away, but just like when your dad died, you will learn to live with this loss as well."

He broke. His sobs were childlike, with snot and spit scattering everywhere. The wailing came from the deepest parts of his soul, a lifetime of accumulated grief rising to the surface: watching his dad suffer and then losing him when Andy was just learning to tie his shoes and ride a bike without training wheels. His mother forgot most of his birthdays and all of his school events. Now the tragic death of his fiancée, lying in a makeshift morgue less than seventy-two hours before they were supposed to be married.

The injustice of it all was more than I could bear.

"Andy."

His shoulders continued heaving.

"Andy," I repeated.

He wiped his slobbery face with his sleeve and gave me a baleful gaze. His eyes were bloodshot and red-rimmed.

A knowing passed between us, something only those who'd lost a significant other could understand. It was the bond that formed within two grieving people in a momentary glance of *I see you. I've been there. I get it.* It was something I allowed myself to feel only in private, when I didn't have to worry about the pitying gazes of friends or the shameful embarrassment I felt whenever my sister declared my husband unworthy of grief, but Andy needed to connect with that tender part of me, no matter how painful.

I gave him a resolute nod. "We're going to find who did this and hold them accountable. You have my word."

THE NEXT MORNING, I peeked out my window and saw nothing but icy waters and snow-covered hills. According to the schedule, we were in the vicinity of Tracy Arm Fjord, about forty-five miles south of Juneau. The itinerary for this sailing had only one stop—Victoria, British Columbia on the second-to-last day—with the rest of the trip at sea. The residents had voted not to have any other ports of call on this voyage because they thought it would be more relaxing to float around off the Alaskan coast rather than dock in various places to get on and off the ship. Plus, it was just plain freezing outside.

Did any of them regret that decision since they were stuck onboard for at least four more days with a killer running loose on the ship?

Jane was still asleep in the bed next to me, so I quietly tiptoed out of the room with the intent of making coffee. After a few moments of staring at the glass carafe, I once again called Windsor to bring a pot.

As I'd requested, he lightly tapped on the door as opposed to ringing the bell. But he still marched the tray over to the kitchen counter.

"Would you like me to pour for you?" His voice was barely above a whisper.

"Only if you pour one for yourself."

He startled. "That would be highly unusual."

"Humor me."

He poured each of us a cup, and I motioned for him to sit.

He perched at the edge of one of the high-backed chairs like he was waiting for a starting pistol to alert him when to take off for the hallway.

His eyes darted anxiously. "I can only stay for a few minutes. I have other guests to attend."

"I understand. I was hoping to pick your brain a little

bit."

"Pardon?"

"I understand about discretion. Technically, I rented all the rooms housing the wedding party, so you're not breaking any residents' confidentiality by speaking to me about what's happening in those rooms."

He stared at me over the brim of the teacup. "I'd say that's a stretch. You're in luck, though, because my loyalty is first and foremost to the residents and owners of this ship."

"Great. What have you seen in Frank and Elaine Braithwaite's room?"

"What is the number?"

"I think 615."

"That's not my area of responsibility."

"Which of the rooms are in your area?"

"Not every stateroom has a full-time butler. That is reserved for the larger suites. The other residences can request service, but we have limited staff who attend to the entire floor. I may be in the vicinity at times, but I don't go into those other rooms. I am strictly limited to servicing the eight penthouses up on Santorini, suites 600 and 601 down on the Aegean level, and then your suite along with 700 here on the Odyssey level."

"Phoebe's room was 601, wasn't it?"

"Yes, ma'am."

"Did you see anything, anything at all, that might be connected to her murder?"

Windsor knit his brows together. "She arrived shortly before the ship departed. She never requested service of any kind. She had the DO NOT DISTURB sign on her door when I went to do turndown service Sunday night, so I never entered her room."

I exhaled and my shoulders sagged. "I was hoping maybe you saw something that might help Andy."

He cocked his head to one side.

"What does that look mean?" I asked.

"Something just occurred to me."

"Okay..."

"Around eleven thirty that night, I had gone down to Aegean to collect any room service dishes or trash that might have been left outside suites 600 and 601. Typically, I do that around ten, but there was a party in penthouse 800 that required my attention."

"Those are some long hours."

"It can be, yes. Some voyages are quieter than others. Anyway, there wasn't anything to collect. As I was making my way toward the elevators, I passed younger Mr. Braithwaite on the way to his room."

"Sawyer?"

"Yes, I believe so. He was clearly intoxicated, stumbling down the hall. I was concerned he wouldn't make it, so I turned to watch and make certain he got into his room safely. Only he didn't go to his room."

"Where did he go?"

"To his sister's room next door. He pounded until she let him inside. Once she'd closed her door, I left the vicinity."

"You're saying Sawyer was with Phoebe late Sunday night in her room?"

"He was."

I KNOCKED ON the door to room 600. No answer. Had Sawyer and Macy gone to breakfast? I rang the bell to be sure. I heard some noise coming from within the room, so I rang again.

The door opened a sliver to reveal Sawyer's eyes, barely open and squinting back at me from under his shaggy bangs.

"Charlotte? What are you doing here so early?" His voice was a hoarse whisper.

"It's after ten."

"Like I said…"

"I need to talk to you. Can I come inside?"

Sawyer jerked his thumb over his shoulder. "Macy's still sleeping."

"Okay, well, can you meet me for coffee at Azure Court up on Mykonos?"

"I don't get all these names. What floor is that?"

"Nine. It's next to the Azure Lounge by the observation deck."

"Give me fifteen minutes to get dressed and brush my teeth."

Sawyer didn't look significantly more alert when he walked into Azure Court. He wore black board shorts and an ice-blue T-shirt with some sort of surfing logo on the front. His hair was mussed, unbrushed, and still hanging in his puffy eyes.

He flopped into the seat across from me. "I think I drank too much last night."

"I'm more curious about how much you drank on Sunday night."

He wrinkled his forehead. "The night of the twenties party?"

"Yes."

"I didn't drink that much at dinner, but then I met up with the group that had gone to the bar. We were over there." He indicated the bar adjacent to the café.

"Who was there with you?"

"Uh." He held up his fingers and began ticking off names. "Duncan, Vance, Serena, and Nikki."

"Not Macy?"

"No, after dinner she had a migraine, so she went back to our room and fell asleep. She slept until Andy woke us up pounding on our door the next morning."

"How long were you at the bar?"

He blinked a couple times. "Not sure. Why does this feel like an interrogation?"

"It's not, I'm just trying to put together a timeline of where everyone was and when. After you left the bar, where did you go?"

"Back to my room."

"That's not true."

"What do you mean? Of course, it is."

"Someone saw you go to Phoebe's room just before midnight."

He tilted his head, with a faraway look. His gaze widened. "That's right! I did. I tried to get in, thinking it was my room, but my key wouldn't work. Probably because it was the wrong room." He hit the palm of his hand against his forehead. "Duh. Anyway, I knocked on the door, trying to get Macy to answer, but when it opened, it was Phoebe. All this time I thought it was a dream."

"Do you remember what happened when you went into her room? Did she say anything?"

His face showed deep concentration. "She was rambling and venting. I can't remember about what. I know she was mad at Andy. I'd heard from the guys at the bar they'd had a big fight in front of everyone, super embarrassing. But she was upset about some other stuff, too. Phoebe had a tendency to be high-strung, lots of drama, so I usually tuned her out when she went off like that." He sighed. "I wish I would have listened."

"Were you awake when she left?"

"I think…" He squinted. "I think she got a text. Whoever sent it, she was irritated. She was like, *now I gotta deal with this bitch.*"

I bobbed my head. "Rhonda."

"Yeah. Makes sense. Pheebs wasn't a fan."

"Something doesn't make sense to me, though. Andy went to Phoebe's room the next morning, but no one was there. He had a key, and when he went inside, her bed hadn't been slept in."

Sawyer twisted his mouth to one side. "It's pretty hazy, but I think after she left, I passed out on the couch. I'm not sure what time I woke up, but I know it was still dark. Of course, up here we're only getting like six hours of daylight, so that doesn't mean much. Who goes to Alaska in November anyway? You couldn't even book a regular cruise this time of year, did you know that? I had a buddy who wanted to celebrate his twenty-fifth birthday by going to see the northern lights. We thought we'd take a cruise up here, but we ended up having to take a ferry out of Bellingham. It took almost two full days, and it wasn't exactly luxurious."

"Yeah, so anyway, when you woke up, was Phoebe there?"

"I dunno. I didn't look. I think I just stumbled back to my room and crawled into bed with Macy. I tried to get frisky, but she wasn't having it."

"If you smelled anything like when you opened your door this morning, I don't blame her. It was like you'd slept for three years in a vat of beer and whiskey."

Sawyer covered his mouth and checked his breath. "Sorry. Things got out of hand after the disco party. Everybody mourns in their own way, right?"

"Can you think of anything else that happened that night that was unusual or stands out in hindsight?"

He puckered his mouth until his upper lip was touching the bottom of his nose. "Man, I really wish I could. I don't wanna believe Andy coulda done this."

"He couldn't. He didn't."

"You have to say that 'cause you're his aunt."

"I say that because I know him, and I know what he's capable of doing or not doing. He's devastated."

Sawyer scratched the blond scruff on his right cheek. His

knuckles were scratched and scuffed.

"What happened to your hand?"

He pulled his hand away from his face to examine it. "Would ya look at that."

Chapter Thirteen

NO AMOUNT OF coaxing Sawyer's memory brought the information I sought to the surface. He hadn't noticed it, so he wasn't sure when it had happened. He thought it was unlikely to have happened Sunday night, but he couldn't rule out the possibility.

After I finished my coffee, I decided to head down to the Capri level where Phoebe's body had been located. I wanted to visit the scene in hopes something might stand out to me. I was definitely a visual rather than auditory processor.

As I rode the elevator alone down the four floors, I tried to sort out everything in my mind. I tended to have more luck solving problems when the information was arranged in a linear fashion. The timeline for Phoebe's night was beginning to take shape.

After storming out of the dining room, she'd ended up on the observation deck just outside the Azure Lounge, where the groomsmen and bridesmaids had been drinking for at least an hour at that point. Andy followed her there, they argued, and then she stormed away to parts unknown.

The next time anyone saw her was around eleven thirty when Sawyer accidentally mistook Phoebe's room for his own, as Windsor witnessed. Sawyer spent only about thirty minutes with Phoebe before Rhonda summoned her up to her room on the seventh floor, Odyssey. Rhonda and Phoebe had a minor tiff, and Phoebe left a few minutes later. The security footage verified this part of Rhonda's account.

Sometime between midnight and six in the morning, Phoebe was killed. Unfortunately, Sawyer was little to no help in determining what time it was when he woke up on her couch and stumbled next door or whether Phoebe was there at the time.

Had Phoebe returned to her room after her conversation with Rhonda and then left again? Or, considering her bed hadn't been slept in, had she never made it back to room 601 at all?

The elevator doors opened onto the Capri deck, level five. This was the level where I'd entered the ship and checked in at the registration desk. Along with the beauty salon, marketplace and boutiques, ice cream parlor, and fitness center, it was also where the security office was located.

The VIP deck and the hot tub where Phoebe's body had been found were on the bow area. The tub was on an elevated platform with steps leading up the side. Even standing on my tiptoes I couldn't see into the tub, which made more sense of the fact no one had noticed something was awry until maintenance climbed up to test the chemicals early Monday morning.

I assumed the area would still be cordoned off while the investigation was ongoing. To my surprise, two couples were sitting in the hot tub. On the lounge chairs next to the tub were several white fluffy robes and striped towels.

I couldn't understand why, even if it were allowed, anyone would want to be soaking in the spot where a dead body was found floating a day prior.

A young man was posted at the entrance. He asked my name and room number, verified my status on some VIP list, and allowed me to go through the double glass doors that exited to the deck.

Although it was sunny, the temperature was anything but balmy. I clutched my sweater to my chest, wishing I'd grabbed a coat. I couldn't even imagine how cold it had been out there Sunday night, but perhaps since we'd only left Seattle a few hours before it hadn't been as frigid as I thought.

The people in the hot tub stopped their chatter and observed me. I could only see them from the shoulders up.

One of the men, with dark gray thinning hair and a gold chain wrapped around his overly tanned neck, raised his eyebrows up and down. "Would you like to join us?"

"No thanks. I'm just looking around." I contemplated how to phrase my next question, but couth wouldn't do me any favors. "Are you aware a woman was found dead in this hot tub yesterday morning?"

"Yeah, but they got it cleaned up pretty quick," the man said.

"It doesn't creep you out to be in there?"

One of the two women made a sour face. "They drained the water. It's fresh."

I didn't know how to respond to that. "Yeah, okay. Well, enjoy."

I walked away from the foursome and scanned the deck. I wasn't sure if the crew had already cleaned all traces of Phoebe's murder or if I was looking in the wrong place. Xavier had never clearly specified where she was killed, only where she'd been found.

I made my way toward the two stairwells. The ship had been designed to connect each level with covered ramps. If I were to go into the alcove to my right, it would take me up to the sixth floor. The alcove to the left headed down to the fourth floor, Perseus.

Just inside the shadows, I saw a small brown smudge on the wall of the corridor. It had the look of dried blood, and perhaps the imprint of a portion of someone's hand. It was only about an inch long and half an inch high. I took a few more steps into the corridor but saw no other markings. Maybe it wasn't recent. Maybe it wasn't even blood.

But maybe it was.

I wasn't huge into Greek mythology, but I remembered the story about how Perseus killed Medusa and rescued Andromeda from a sea monster. Hopefully, the spirit of Perseus would be helpful in locating Phoebe's phone and something on it would reveal the monster who'd killed her.

The ramp was not well lit, and it got darker the farther I went down the corridor. I had a flutter in my stomach, my breathing was quick, and my hands buzzed with adrenaline. Despite the cold temps, it was still broad daylight and four people frolicked in the hot tub just feet from me, so I wasn't sure why I felt so tense.

I rounded the corner for the rest of the downward trek but stopped when metal scraped behind me. I turned around but saw no one. Still, I sensed I wasn't alone. Toward the bottom of the ramp, I swore I heard a footstep. I walked faster until I stepped onto the flat ground.

I quickly ducked around the side of the walkway and held my breath. After a few moments with no sound, I had nearly convinced myself I was being paranoid.

I pulled my cell phone out of my pocket and turned on the flashlight. I shined it around the darkened corridor that led to a set of metal double doors. Beyond those doors there was some sort of noise, but I couldn't make out what specifically I was hearing. Perhaps a boiler room or something.

I continued to scan the metal walls and cement floor. I saw nothing unusual, and certainly not a phone. I got over to the far wall and ran the light along the side. Lots of scrapes, as though items had been stored in this area.

Then something caught my eye.

In the dimness, it appeared like black paint had splattered against the wall. I held my phone closer.

It wasn't black. It was dark red. It wasn't paint. It was blood.

My hands shook, causing the light to jump up and down.

I turned to go back up the ramp and shrieked.

A tall, dark figure stood in the shadows staring right at me.

Chapter Fourteen

"SHHH!" THE MAN'S voice urged from the shadows. "I'm not going to hurt you."

"Neal? Is that you?" I shined my phone flashlight in his direction, and he immediately blocked the glare with his forearm.

"Hey!"

"What are you doing here, Neal? Why are you following me?"

"Will you put that thing down?"

I lowered the light until it no longer shone directly in his eyes but kept it focused on him. I wanted to know exactly where he was.

"Thank you."

"You scared the heck out of me, Neal."

"Sorry." He ran his hand through his hair. "I wanted to see what you were doing. You looked like you were onto something."

I made a buzzing sound. "*Ehhh.* Try again." I returned the light to his eyes.

"It's true!" he squawked, but his own grimacing face called him a liar.

"Neal, you should never play poker."

He sighed and slumped his shoulders. "You're not the first person to tell me that." He stepped slightly to the left and out of the light.

"You were acting squirrelly all day yesterday. You're keeping a secret, and it has something to do with Phoebe's death."

He held up his hand. "No, I swear I'm not. Not about her death."

"Then what?"

He shifted his weight between his feet. I was certain he was about to confess to their affair but instead he said, "Last night I texted her, asking her where she went."

I expected him to elaborate, but he didn't. It took me a moment to connect the dots. "You're looking for her phone!"

He sheepishly rubbed his neck. "When you said they didn't find her phone, I realized I was probably one of the last people to text her. I knew that wouldn't look good."

"You're right. Not to mention the half-naked photo of her you were staring at all day."

He didn't bother hiding his shock. "How did you—" He inhaled deeply. "It's not what you think."

"You don't know what I think, but I can tell you that having a sexy photo of your sister-in-law doesn't bode well for your character defense."

Even in the dim light I saw the color drain from his face. "Please don't tell anyone."

"I won't have to tell anyone. It's going to come out regardless. When they find her phone and see you two have been texting each other things your significant others wouldn't be happy about, the first place they're going to look is your phone."

"Maybe the killer threw her phone overboard."

"Did you?"

"I didn't kill her, Charlotte! I loved her!"

His confession echoed off the metal walls.

"Oh, Neal." I made a disgusted groan.

He hung his head. "It was over a long time ago. Well, for her. Not for me."

"Were you Phoebe's stalker?"

He jerked his gaze to mine. "No! I swear! It was one of her fans."

Typical martyred cry of a guilty man. Cheating 101: always play victim and deflect when accused.

"I don't know, Neal, it's not looking good for you. You were one of the last people to text her, you'd had an affair, and were still in love with the woman even though she was marrying someone else. How is anyone supposed to believe you weren't her stalker and her killer?"

His shoulders slumped.

"Tell me the truth. Why did you follow me down here?"

"I am desperate to find her phone before anyone else. I searched the area near the hot tub. When I saw you coming down the hall through the glass doors, I tucked behind a pole and hoped you wouldn't see me. I figured Andy must have told you where to look, so I was hoping you'd lead me to it and then I could get it from you."

"Andy didn't tell me where to look because he doesn't know where her phone is either. He didn't kill her."

I took a step closer, trying to see his expression in the ambient light, then another. The closer I got, I realized how tall he was. At five foot eight inches, I was used to looking eye-to-eye with many men without having to crane my neck too much. With Neal, my head was tilted at a forty-five-degree angle. He had to have been at least six-three, if not taller, but he hadn't struck me as large because he was so slender.

"It was you."

"I told you; I didn't hurt her. I promise you."

"No, I mean it was you who stopped Andy from following her after their fight."

He furrowed his brow. "Did Andy tell you that?"

"No. The bartender said somebody kept Andy from going after Phoebe, but it wasn't one of the groomsmen, and it wasn't Sawyer. He said the man was tall and thin."

"Andy never knew when to give her space. Phoebe needed time to process her feelings, but he always pushed. I came into the bar and saw them arguing. He wasn't backing down, and I saw the panic in her face when she ran away."

"What did the text say? The one you sent to her."

"I just said I needed to see her, to talk. After I got Andy to calm down and gave her enough time to escape, I told him I'd try to talk to her on his behalf."

"And did you?"

"No. I never found her, and she didn't text me back. She probably thought I was trying to talk to her about being together, but I wasn't. I only wanted her to be happy." A whimper escaped him.

"Hmm. I'm curious about something."

"What?"

"Why did you say you gave her time to escape? That sounds so ominous. You know Andy would never hurt her."

"I don't know that. The police are saying he's their number one suspect, and, like I said, when she took off, she was freaked out."

"Okay, first, they aren't the police. They're onboard security. Second, they're being completely myopic hyper-focusing on Andy simply because he was her fiancé and they had a fight. Lots of people fight—that doesn't mean they murder their significant other. There's no other evidence to tie him to this crime. No bloody clothes, no defensive wounds."

"Perhaps you forgot about his fingerprints on the murder weapon?" a familiar French-accented voice boomed from the dark corridor behind Neal.

I yelped. "Dang it, Xavier, my heart can't take this many jump scares!"

He moved out of the pitch darkness and into the darkness augmented by my phone's flashlight.

"Are you saying you are in need of medical attention?" What was visible of his face showed concern.

"No, I mean, you can't be appearing like that out of nowhere when there's a killer on the loose. You frightened me."

"Our primary suspect should not be on the loose. He should be in your cabin, monitored by you or your sister."

"Andy's not your killer and you know it. However, he's in our room, and Jane is there with him." I hoped it wasn't a lie. They'd both been asleep when I'd left to confront Sawyer, and I'd been gone for quite a while.

"What are the two of you doing in this area?"

Neal held his hands in the air. "I was just following her to see what she was doing." His voice raised several octaves with his lie.

I clicked my tongue. "Oh, Neal."

Xavier cocked his left eyebrow. "Are you saying I should not believe him?"

"If you believe him, you're probably a terrible detective."

Xavier made a sound that at first, I thought was him choking, but then I realized he was attempting to suppress a laugh. "Perhaps we shall finish this conversation in my office."

"Wait. Xavier, I think this is where Phoebe was killed." I shined my flashlight against the wall, illuminating the blood spatter. "Come look."

He didn't move.

"I'm telling you. I think this is blood." I jiggled the phone, causing the light to bounce up and down on the wall.

"I'm aware."

"You knew she was killed down here? You made it sound like you believed it happened near or in the hot tub."

"You may have gotten that impression, but it is not because I said it. I told you what I wanted you to know, and you made assumptions."

Neal remained silent. He wasn't a complete dummy.

"If you knew this was the spot, why didn't you cordon it off? There's still evidence on the walls that should be protected."

I folded my arms, which caused the flashlight to aim at my feet and thrust Neal and Xavier into the shadows. When Xavier spoke, it sounded even more ominous.

"Outside of my team, only one person knew this was the location of the crime. The killer. And, apparently, his aunt."

Chapter Fifteen

IT HADN'T OCCURRED to me that my snooping to solve the case and exonerate Andy might backfire and create more problems for him…and me.

Xavier escorted us away from the crime scene and up to his office. Officer Irving was seated at his desk, but Taylor's was unoccupied.

"Lonnie, will you go to suite 701 and verify Andy Cobb is where he is supposed to be?"

Irving gave me a suspicious once-over, and left the office.

"You two, follow me, *s'il vous plait.*" Xavier jerked his finger toward his office door.

Neal waved me ahead of him, as if he were being chivalrous, not cowardly. I was pretty sure he was shaking in his beige Dockers and sensible shoes. How I hadn't realized he was the one Egan was talking about simply from the description of bland, boring, and beige, I had no idea. His banality served as a cloak.

I sat in one chair. Neal sat in the other. Xavier eased himself into his own chair and rotated it back and forth, looking between the two of us.

"Who would like to go first?"

Neal pulled at his starched white collar and stretched his neck.

I jerked my thumb at him and made an exasperated face at Xavier. "You're seeing this, right? It's like he took a class on how to appear guilty."

The corner of Xavier's mouth twitched. "In my experience, innocent nerves can sometimes appear as guilt."

I flicked my hand. Whatever.

"You do recall, Madame McLaughlin, you are the one in the hot seat. What did your nephew reveal to you about the crime?"

I hinged my jaw, inhaled, and growled through gritted teeth, "As I have said, and continue to say, Andy did not do this. He told me nothing because there is nothing to tell." I punctuated my statement by slapping my palm on his desk.

He didn't flinch.

"Why don't you ask Neal about his desperate need to find Phoebe's phone before anyone else." I sat back in the chair, feeling ready to fight the next person who implied, indicated, inferred, or flat-out stated Andy was a murderer, and I was an accessory after the fact.

A hint of amusement played on Xavier's face before he redirected his attention to Neal. "Monsieur Alcorn, you are husband to one of the sisters of Phoebe, correct?"

Neal nodded but didn't speak.

"Which of the sisters? Forgive me, they are so much alike. Twins, yes?"

This got a reaction out of him. Neal leaned forward, almost looking angry. "They are nothing alike. My wife, Lily, is a saint. Ivy is rude, crass, and obnoxious."

"How long have you been married?"

"Nine years this past April. We met in college, dated three years or so, got married at twenty-four."

"That would make Phoebe approximately fourteen when you met her sister." Xavier tented his fingers, a gesture I'd seen him make more than once in previous interactions.

Was this a tell, and if so, what did it signify?

Pink began to creep up Neal's neck. "Sounds about right."

"Gross," I said. "You've known her since she was a child."

Neal's face grew pale as he stared straight ahead.

Xavier observed him for a moment. "Would you like some water, Monsieur Alcorn?" He pointed at the fully stocked bar in the corner.

Strange that the head of security had alcohol in his office, but this was a private residential ship, and many of the ways the staff operated had struck me as unusual.

Neal cleared his throat twice. "Yes, thank you."

Xavier handed Neal a glass and leaned against the front edge of his desk. He folded his arms and watched Neal suck down the water like a man who'd been stranded in the Sahara. After Neal finished the last sip, he handed the glass back to Xavier.

"Thanks."

"*De rien.* Of course. Do you need a refill?"

"No, I'm good."

Xavier observed him again for a moment. "We are on

this ship, out to sea, and sometimes it feels as though we are in a state of suspended reality here. Does it not?"

I had no idea where he was going with this line of questioning, but I was intrigued. Beads of sweat had begun to form at Neal's temples. Xavier had him nervous, and I was here for it.

"I s-suppose."

Xavier tilted his head. He ran his tongue across perfect white teeth and made a clucking sound. "We are, in fact, an extension of the real world. You Americans, you have a saying, what happens in Las Vegas, stays in Las Vegas."

I stifled a giggle. "Something like that."

"It is a myth. You may mistakenly believe that what happens on this ship stays on this ship. That is not true. Choices always have consequences, no matter where the actions take place."

Neal was fully squirming now. I suppressed a squeal of glee. I was feeling chockfull of all the petty emotions I'd swallowed.

"Regardless of the gilded adornments, the luxurious accommodations, the water and glaciers surrounding us at this moment, reality remains. Phoebe Braithwaite is still very much dead."

His statement landed with a thud.

There was a difference between knowing something in your head and hearing the words out loud and then allowing the truth to pierce your heart. I'd always known denial was a powerful coping mechanism, but it took living through loss to understand it could only shield a person from grief for so long before cracks began to form and pain seeped through.

As Xavier's pronouncement hung in the air, my chest felt squeezed like it was in a vise. I'd been so focused on exonerating Andy; I hadn't completely faced the reality. Phoebe was gone, killed in a brutal way. She was never coming back. She and Andy were never getting married or having the children they'd talked about. Her young life was over.

From the agony on Neal's face, he was also only just beginning to come to terms with the truth of what had happened. He appeared heartbroken—more heartbroken than normal for a brother-in-law.

A sob escaped him. Xavier registered alarm and surprise.

I put my hand on Neal's shoulder. "He's going to find out eventually. If you lie or hide things, he won't believe you when you tell him you didn't hurt Phoebe."

Neal buried his face in his hands. Between sniffles, he began to tell his story.

"For years I'd seen Phoebe as Lily's little sister. A kid. When she started her YouTube channel, I thought it was cute. We watched all her videos because we were trying to support her. I figured it would boost her confidence."

"Did her confidence need boosting?" I asked. "I've always known her to be quite strong-minded."

Neal dragged his hands down his face, resting his fingertips on his mouth. "She started the channel because she was lonely. Phoebe was an oops baby, and no one let her forget it. Dale and Susan didn't have the twins until they were in their early to mid-thirties, and then Sawyer came along about four years later. They were done having kids. Or so they thought. Phoebe was conceived backstage at a Grateful Dead concert in the nineties. Susan was forty, Dale was even older. They hadn't been super attentive to their kids prior to that, but the added *burden*"—he made air quotes—"of another baby made them resentful. All they ever wanted to do was party and follow their favorite bands around the world. They hired a nanny, who basically raised the kids. You can imagine the impact it might have on a kid to be told your very existence interfered with your parents living their best lives."

"I had no idea," I said. "I feel awful. I always judged her harshly for being so inflexible and difficult. I thought she was a spoiled prima donna. Turns out she just needed to feel in control of some aspect of her life."

"When did the relationship become romantic between the two of you?"

I glanced at Xavier. I couldn't get a read on whether he'd been touched by Neal's story.

Neal swallowed. "It was in the middle of the stalking incidents. She'd called me one night around two A.M., saying she thought she'd heard a noise outside the house. Dale and Susan were off in some yurt worshipping Jimmy Buffet, and Phoebe was all alone. Sawyer spends winters up at Snoqualmie skiing and instructing, so he wasn't around either. Lily and I live about ten minutes from the Braithwaites' former home. At Lily's request, I got in my car and drove over there. Phoebe was a mess. She was in hysterics. She'd found a package on the front porch with no return address and no postage. It was clear it had been dropped off, not mailed."

"What was inside?" My fingers gripped the arms of the chair, my nails digging into the leather.

"All her favorite candy. She liked the sour stuff. You know, the kind of things that the mere thought of them makes the hinges of your jaw tingle and your mouth fill with saliva?"

I felt the sensation as he described it.

Xavier sucked in his cheeks and swallowed.

"Anyway, it was confusing to Phoebe because, on the one hand, it was clear the person was trying to do something nice for her, and there wasn't a threatening note or anything, but the intrusiveness of having someone know your home address and invade your personal space that way—well, it freaked her out. It took me quite a while to get her to calm down. I made her some tea, turned on the fireplace, and put on a romantic comedy to take the edge off. I guess I hadn't thought that through very well. I was trying to be the big brother, but what I'd done was create a very intimate setting, right after coming to her rescue. It would have been totally inappropriate even if I weren't married. I took advantage of her vulnerable state and the fact she looked up to me. But when she looked up *at* me with those big blue eyes I..."

He couldn't finish his statement.

"Was this an *affaire du coeur* or merely a physical relationship?"

I shot Xavier a look. It was clear that, for Neal at least, this was an affair of the heart as much as a sexual one. Xavier responded with a double eyebrow raise.

Neal sniffled. "I fell in love. I know it was wrong, but

you must understand, Phoebe was extraordinary. She was the kind of person who brightened every room she entered. Charlotte, you know."

"I'm sorry. That wasn't my experience, Neal. The night Andy introduced her to me, I had a difficult time understanding what he saw in her, other than her beauty. She was sullen and irritable and impossible to please. I worried he was setting himself up for a lifetime of falling short of her expectations."

Xavier turned to me. "That statement does not do your nephew any favors. It could be construed as a motive."

"I'm saying that was *my* impression. Andy was head over heels."

"I get it. Lily, she's my wife, and I love her. She is a wonderful woman, wife, mother to our two boys. But Phoebe, she was..." Once again, he struggled to find the words. "She was lightning in a bottle."

"How long did the romantic relationship endure?" Xavier asked.

"About a year or so." Neal's ability to speak buckled under the weight of his shame.

"Does your wife know about the affair?" Xavier narrowed his gaze.

A look of horror washed across Neal's face. "She wouldn't kill her own sister!"

"I merely asked a question." Xavier said.

A reasonable one, in my mind. If Lily had discovered the affair, she had a motive. No one ever suspects the meek, timid ones, but they were just as capable of exacting revenge as anyone, maybe even more so. People like Lily fly under the radar, and they sometimes harness their invisibility for ill intentions.

Neal banged his fist on the arm of his chair. "She wouldn't hurt Phoebe. I can't imagine anyone would hurt Phoebe intentionally."

Xavier clasped his hands and rested them on the desk in front of him. "But they did." He seemed to heavily weigh his next words. "She was stabbed repeatedly. Our onboard physician has estimated between one and two dozen wounds."

A wounded yelp escaped Neal. I felt my chest constrict at the thought.

"That's a lot of anger. Hatred, even," I said.

"I agree. You did not answer my question regarding your wife, Monsieur Alcorn."

Neal took several deep breaths to regain his composure. "As far as I'm aware, my wife doesn't know about…what happened between Phoebe and me." He gave Xavier a pleading gaze. "I beg of you, don't tell her. We have kids. A life together. Nine years of marriage." His voice cracked at the end.

"Perhaps you should have thought of that prior to bedding your wife's sister."

I winced. Not that it wasn't true, it was just brutal. Clearly, Neal was hurting. I knew Lily must be grieving as well. Dropping this bomb on her would only magnify her grief.

On the other hand, it did create a motive, and the only

way to discover what Lily knew about the relationship was to ask.

"Am I in the clear?" Neal fumbled with his fingers in his lap.

A guffaw escaped Xavier, but then he recomposed himself. "No, you are not exonerated. This investigation is ongoing. You have given me no proof you were not involved in the stalking incidents. For all I know, you delivered that box of candy and then returned to the scene a second time to offer your protection from the crisis you created."

"I didn't! I was at home when she discovered the box! You can ask my wife."

"Oh, I will." Xavier leaned back and crossed his arms.

Realization dawned across Neal's face. The only way to explain to Lily the need to know the timeline of his whereabouts at the time of the stalking incident would mean Xavier suspected him of being the stalker. That would lead to more questions and inevitably reveal the affair. There wasn't really a way around it. If she hadn't known before, it was going to break her heart.

Even worse, if she had discovered the affair, Lily Alcorn had a strong motive for murdering her sister.

Chapter Sixteen

"WHERE HAVE YOU been?" Jane greeted me with a frenzied expression as I walked into the suite.

"Trying to exonerate Andy."

"Why didn't you wait for me?"

I laughed. "You were sawing logs like you were about to build a three-bedroom cabin in the woods. There was no way I was about to wake you from whatever dream you were having. Has Andy made an appearance yet this morning?"

"Yes, he's binge-watching a show in the bedroom. Come, sit down, and tell me what you've been doing."

When I'd finished my recap, her eyes were wide as saucers.

"Do you think Lily did this? More than a dozen wounds." She shivered. "I can't imagine the type of animosity that could have fueled that kind of attack, but finding out your husband was having an affair—with your sister, no less—would definitely cause most people to feel murderous." She paused. "Not that you did."

"I didn't get the opportunity to find out. Hard to say what I'd have felt if I learned of the affair before Gabe's death, even if I only had a moment to contemplate it before I knew he was gone. I must say, it's hard to comprehend anyone getting so angry as to ruin their own future because their partner was unfaithful, but I guess it happens."

Jane guffawed. "It's not hard for me to imagine at all. If I coulda killed Gabe a second time, I might have."

"Jane!"

"Sorry, maybe you can forgive him posthumously, but I can't."

"I haven't…forgiven him, so to speak. I'm just dealing with the feelings. It's not like I can change anything he did or make him feel better—if he even felt guilty about it at all—but I've gotta live with myself the rest of my life, and holding bitterness against someone unworthy of that much energy isn't how I wish to expend it."

"Phoebe's murder had to have been a crime of passion, don't you think?"

"It looks that way, but I don't know that I'm ready to make that leap yet. Yes, that many stab wounds feels personal, but it doesn't necessarily mean it was not premeditated. I've known people to hold rage for long periods of time, meticulously plotting their revenge."

"What kind of people are you spending time with?"

"You mean besides you?" I laughed. "I should clarify. I know *of* people who do that, from reading true-crime novels and listening to podcasts."

"Aren't those people usually psychopaths?"

"I'm not a psychiatrist or psychologist, so I can't say. Maybe. I've just watched too many shows and read too many books where people went down the wrong path of thinking because they got set on an idea."

"You mean like Xavier Mesnier believing Andy killed Phoeb—"

The door creaked. Andy shuffled into the living room. His wavy hair was disheveled, his shoulders were slumped forward like an old man, and his face had somehow lengthened about three inches. Andy was never what you'd call a perky child—he'd taken after his mother in that way—but this was exceedingly mopey, even for him.

"Hey, Aunt Char. Any news?"

"I was just telling Aunt Jane about my morning." I patted the sofa between Jane and me. "Sit, and I'll tell you all about it."

Andy sat between us the way he had when he was five and we were helping him grieve the loss of his father. I'd felt equally helpless then as I did now. And it was about to get even worse.

"I keep coming back to the idea that Phoebe's phone is the key to knowing where she went that night and who she talked to. I went snooping around near the hot tub and then down to the lower level. I ended up in this storage area. Guess who showed up?"

"Who?"

"Neal appeared out of the shadows and nearly gave me a heart attack."

Even in his stupor Andy reacted with surprise. "Neal?"

Jane nodded vigorously. "Neal. He was looking for Phoebe's phone, too."

Andy squinted and scrunched his nose. "Why would

Neal be looking for her phone?"

He always got pouty when he concentrated, but I could tell he was trying to process what she'd said.

"You know, he told me not to go after her. The other night when we had our fight."

"I know." I put my hand on his forearm. "Did Phoebe ever mention…" I tried to carefully form my question. "Did she ever say anything about Neal and what role he played in her life?"

Andy tilted his head. "Well, yeah, I mean, she said he was protective of her, and he really showed up for her during the whole stalker thing. Why?"

Jane cocked a brow and pursed her lips into an *I'm-not-telling-him-you-tell-him* face.

I sighed. "Neal was really there for her. I mean, like *really* there for her."

I waited for recognition to pass across Andy's face. When it finally did, the sight was heartbreaking.

"No," he whispered.

I waited for him to say more, but he didn't. He sat, shell-shocked, his forehead wrinkled and his mouth pulled taut.

"He swore it was over before you and Phoebe began dating."

He jerked his head to look at me. "How is that supposed to make me feel better? She kept this practically incestuous relationship from me. He met her as a child. Who harbors a crush on a child? It's disgusting."

"He says it was only later, during the stalking, that things shifted between them."

"Oh, so noble. He waited until he couldn't be prosecuted legally."

Jane pointed her index finger. "I have a feeling it's this reaction that she was trying to avoid by not telling you."

Andy jumped to his feet and began to pace the living room. "Nobody gets to judge me for how I'm feeling right now. She could have told me, but she didn't. If she would have explained, I could try and wrap my head around this. But she didn't. She let me chum it up with him at family dinners. We played golf together. We'd grab a beer every once in a while. The whole time he knew what my fiancée was like in bed. I feel like a fool." He stopped pacing and leaned against the dining room table. "She made a fool out of me, and I almost committed to spend my life with her."

Jane joined him and rested her hand on his back. "Andy, she was young. Neal acknowledged he took advantage of her, her youth, and her vulnerability. She was scared, and he acted like he was rescuing her, but he was a predator, too. He's to blame here, not Phoebe."

His shoulders heaved. "She should have told me."

"You're right," I said. "She should have. It's not easy, though, to tell someone you love, someone whose admiration and respect means so much, that you did something that makes you feel ashamed. You never know how the other person will respond, and even if they say it doesn't matter, you worry about it changing their view of you forever."

"So does Mesnier think Neal had something to do with...what happened to Phoebe?"

"He's still keeping all his theories close to the vest. He

seemed to have an inkling something might have happened between Neal and Phoebe before I even brought up the photo."

Andy stood upright. "What photo?"

My stomach churned. Yet another thing I didn't want to have to tell him. Maybe Jane would play the heavy on this one.

Jane cringed. "Yikes. Don't look at me."

Andy inhaled deeply and let out a long, exasperated breath. "Just tell me. I'm numb at this point."

His pained expression said that wasn't true, but he was probably too worn out to get any angrier or more upset than he already was.

"Neal had a sexy photo of Phoebe on his phone. Macy caught him staring at it."

Andy closed his eyes, his mouth pulled downward. He took several cleansing breaths and then opened his eyes.

It was as if he'd transformed from the mild-mannered Andy we knew to the Incredible Hulk. Anger oozed out every pore, like lava from a volcano. His face reddened, and his chest rose and fell quickly.

He stomped to the glass slider, slid it open, and walked onto the balcony. Frigid air blew into the cabin. He placed his hands on the railing and screamed at the top of his lungs, a wounded animal roar, wail, and a howl all in one. In fact, I might have heard something echo back to his call from beyond the steep glacial cliffs of the Tracy Arm Fjord.

He bowed his head and stood motionless for a moment. Eventually, the wind must have gotten to him because he returned inside and slid the door shut. He rubbed his arms.

"I won't ask you if you're okay, because I know you're not," I said. "Is there anything I can do?"

Between gritted teeth, Andy said, "Bring Neal here. Now."

Chapter Seventeen

LILY ANSWERED THE door. It wasn't that I was surprised to see her, but I realized in that moment that I hadn't prepared what I would say to her.

"Charlotte? What are you doing here?"

I gulped. "I, uh, I was wondering if Neal was here."

Her brows drew together. "Why, no. I was actually starting to worry. He said he was going to explore the ship, but that was a few hours ago, and he's not answering my calls or texts."

I held up a finger. "You know, now that you mention it, I thought I saw him down near the shops. He's probably looking for a gift for you. I'll try to catch him there."

I turned to walk away, but Lily called out to me.

"Char, wait! Would you like some coffee? I made a whole pot, thinking he'd be back by now. I've already had three cups waiting for him. Join me?"

On one hand, I didn't want to join her. She had the personality of an overripe banana.

On the other hand, a chat over coffee presented an unexpected opportunity to sniff around and see what she may or may not have known about her husband's affair with her sister.

"I'd love to," I lied.

I was certain my smile was as forced as my enthusiastic tone sounded to my own ears, but Lily didn't seem to notice.

Lily and Neal's stateroom was a one-bedroom. The living space was smaller than my unit, but at least no one had to sit on the bed like in the studio apartments.

Lily poured coffee into two mugs. "How do you like it? Cream? Sugar?"

"Yes, please." I took a sip after she was done. "That's pretty good. I still haven't figured out how to use this kind of system."

"That's because you're a boomer. It's a millennial thing."

I spit out the coffee I'd just sipped. "I beg your pardon! I'm not a boomer. I'm Gen X!"

Lily shrugged. "Sorry. I'm not good with ages."

I swallowed all the insults I wanted to hurl at her, along with another sip of coffee. Instead, I chose to go the compassionate route. "How are you holding up? I can't imagine how difficult it is to lose your sister, especially in such a…tragic and horrific way."

Lily appeared stoic. She bobbed her head a bit as, I assumed, she formulated her jumbled thoughts into a cohesive sentence.

"Yes."

Okay, maybe her thoughts were simpler than I gave her credit for. "Were you and Phoebe close?"

Lily's mouth formed a straight line. "I thought we were. It turns out she wasn't the person I believed her to be."

Here we go. I had to sit on my left hand to keep from rubbing my palms together like the schemer I was.

"How do you mean?" *Does that sound innocent enough? Am I pushing too hard?*

Lily's mouth pulled into a frown. "Nothing. Never mind. Forget I said anything. None of that matters now."

Rats. Not what I'd hoped for. "You know, I recently lost someone under...complicated circumstances as well."

She eyed me from just above the rim of her mug. "Did you?"

"My husband. He died in a car accident with his mistress and their baby."

Lily's eyes widened. "Oh wow. That must have been quite traumatic."

"It was. Quite. Not only was I grieving the loss of someone I loved, but I also had to grieve his betrayal, with no chance of reconciliation. No opportunity to hear his explanation. No way to scream at him and say all the things I needed to say. And no apology. He may be resting in peace, but I haven't been living in peace."

Lily pursed her lips and stared out the window. "Would you have wanted reconciliation?" She turned back to me. "If you had the chance today? If he were still alive, I mean."

I shrugged. "Hard to say. I'm not someone who likes to leave things unsaid. I can't stand loose ends. It would have been nice to get to decide, one way or the other, but that choice wasn't available to me." I sipped the coffee. "What about you?"

Once again Lily stared out the window. The ship was

stationary, anchored in the fjord. The snowy peaks and floating chunks of ice seemed to have mesmerized her.

"I think I'd like to know. I'd like to have an explanation and an apology." She turned to me, her blue eyes even brighter in contrast to the red blood vessels that had appeared from all the crying she'd been doing. "You said it best. It felt like a betrayal, and now there's nothing that can make it right."

I tried to use a gentle tone as I delivered a harsh message. "It didn't just *feel* like a betrayal, Lily. It *was* a betrayal."

Her eyes welled with tears, and she gave me a sad but grateful smile. "Thank you for saying that, Charlotte. It's nice to talk to someone who understands and validates how I'm feeling. My mother and Ivy don't get it. They told me I was overreacting."

It took a moment for her statement to penetrate. "Wait. Your mom and Ivy know about...what happened? And they're okay with it?"

She pinched her face. "Well, of course they know. How could they not?"

I held up my hands in mock surrender. "I didn't even know what you knew."

Lily tilted her head and gave me a strange look. "I mean, isn't it obvious?"

I stared at her, dumbfounded. "No. When did you find out?"

She gave an exasperated sigh. "When I called her up and asked her point blank. She admitted it. She didn't even sound the least bit sorry."

"That must have been a difficult conversation."

"After I hung up, I was crying, and I called my mom. She was in Denver having her chakras recentered or whatever. She told me I sounded selfish, and had I not even considered how Phoebe felt? I just hung up the phone." She wiped a tear from her cheek. "I've never felt so misunderstood."

"If you don't mind my asking, what made you suspect something was going on?"

"I saw them together and I just knew. I felt like I'd had a knife thrust into my back." As soon as the words escaped her lips, her eyes flew open in horror. "Oh gawd!" She covered her face with her hands. "I can't believe I just said that." Tears flowed heavy now. "I didn't mean that, it just hurt so badly."

I put my hand on her shuddering shoulder.

"Lily, I'm so sorry. I can't even imagine how hard it was to see two people you love so deeply in the act of betrayal."

Her hands slipped partway down her face so only her mouth was covered by her fingertips. "Huh?"

"I mean, it was tough enough for me to hear it secondhand. I don't know how you were able to deal with seeing in the flesh. Your sister...with your *husband*."

"I'm sorry?" Her hands slipped the rest of the way. "What?" She squinted at me like I was a bug she wanted to squish. "What do you mean?" Her mouth gaped open, and she shrieked, "What do you mean?" She jumped to her feet and looked at me accusingly, as if simply by delivering the news, I was culpable. "Phoebe? And *Neal*?" She nearly roared his name.

I'd made a grave error. I opened my mouth and then closed it again when no sound escaped me. Just as I opened it again, hoping something might come out of it to undo what I'd just done, Neal entered the suite.

He glanced at Lily.

His normally timid wife stared at him with a frenzied, deranged expression. He immediately turned to me, then his bewilderment turned to terror visibly washing over his entire being as he finally registered what was happening.

His focus dropped to his feet. "Charlotte, what did you do?" he whispered in a low growl.

"What did she do?" Lily screamed. "What did *she* do? How about, what did *you* do, Neal?" She spat his name out of her mouth like a piece of rotten fish. "Did you screw my baby sister? Did you?"

She rushed over to him. He winced, bracing himself.

She pushed his shoulder. "What did you do?" she screamed into his face. She pushed him several more times, and he took it because he deserved it. She was petite, so she kind of had to jump a little to reach his shoulder. Every time she pushed him her cries became more agonized until her final push had hardly any energy behind it. He grabbed her wrist and pulled her close.

Lily began to sob like a toddler who'd been separated from their mother. Neal held her tight, allowing her to slobber against his chest.

"I'm so sorry. I'm so, *so* sorry." He repeated this phrase over and over again while he stroked her hair.

I stared longingly at the door while they played out the scene, but Neal caught my gaze with a warning glance. I eased back against the sofa. Nothing quite so fun as being held captive while a couple fought.

Lily pushed off from him and slumped onto the cushion next to me. Neal stood in the center of the room, looking uncertain.

"Neal," I began, "I didn't mean to—"

He held up his hand to stop me from finishing my sentence. "I find that hard to believe."

Lily stomped her foot. "You don't get to act self-righteous and offended right now." She sternly pointed at one of the chairs, and he obeyed.

"It was a misunderstanding," I said. "Lily said Phoebe had betrayed her. I thought she meant with you."

"I meant because she chose two girls, she barely knew to be in her bridal party instead of her own sisters."

I bared my teeth. "Oops."

Neal glared at me.

"In my defense, it was about to come out anyway."

"Yeah, when I told her. In my own way." He crossed his legs.

Lily jerked her head to look at me. "Why was it going to come out?"

I pursed my lips and pointed at Neal. "You wanna take this one?"

"Not particularly."

To Lily I said, "Neal was caught snooping around, looking for Phoebe's phone this morning."

"What was on her phone that you didn't want anyone to find?"

I had to hand it to Lily. She'd gone from church mouse to lioness in the blink of an eye. I hadn't thought she had it in her.

On second thought, that wasn't a point in her favor in terms of exonerating her from Phoebe's murder.

Neal continued to keep his mouth shut, so I jumped in to explain once more.

"He texted Phoebe Sunday night, asking to meet with her to have a conversation. He arrived at the bar around the time Andy and Phoebe were fighting on the observation deck. When Phoebe stormed off, he prevented Andy from chasing after her."

Lily lifted her chin. "She always needed her space when she was upset."

"Right. That's what he told Andy."

Lily leveled a steely gaze at Neal. "Such a knight in shining armor. Always coming to her rescue. But we all know you did it so you could have her all to yourself."

Neal leaned forward with an earnest expression. "No. It's been over for a while. I was just trying to help."

"I don't believe you."

He shrugged. "I don't know what to tell you. It's the truth."

Lily gave a mirthless chuckle. "Forgive me if I don't trust a single word out of your filthy, lying mouth."

Neal sunk back into the chair, looking defeated.

"He told Xavier Mesnier, the head of security, the same

story," I added. "He got nervous because he figured he was one of the last people to text Phoebe. Also, I'm guessing, he suspected there might be something on her phone that would indicate their relationship wasn't strictly platonic. Macy noticed him looking at a photo of Phoebe that seemed to be the type shared privately not publicly."

Lily shot him a look of pure revulsion. "You have nudes on your phone of other women? The phone you let our kids watch videos and play games on? What if Cassidy had found a naked picture of her aunt? How would you have explained that?"

Neal stared forlornly at the carpet in front of him, chewing on his bottom lip.

Lily emitted a disgusted sigh. "So, what, the security guy thinks you killed her because you were trying to cover up your affair? Is that it?"

He continued to gnaw his lip in silence.

"I left before Xavier was finished talking with him," I said. "But I got the impression Xavier hasn't ruled anyone out as a suspect in this case."

"Except me and the rest of our family, obviously."

I gave her a pointed look. "Everyone's a suspect."

Lily's gaze darted around the room. "Oh my gawd, that includes me!" Her gaze landed with an angry thud on Neal. "You jerk! Because you couldn't keep it in your pants, now I'm a murder suspect. I hope it was worth it."

I gave him a look of warning and willed him to not respond. I had a feeling if he opened his mouth to defend himself in any way, she'd launch herself across the room and choke him until he became unconscious.

I wouldn't stop her.

I hadn't had a particularly high opinion of Lily previously, but this new iteration—the woman scorned—I kinda liked her. She had spunk and a spine I didn't know she possessed. Plus, there was a feeling of solidarity among people who've experienced similar trauma. As with Andy's and my shared grief, Lily and I were now involuntarily bonded by the betrayal of our loved ones.

The one thing she had that I didn't was the ability to look her husband in the eye and let him know exactly how he'd hurt her. I wanted to believe I'd also have corked my tears and let Gabe have it with both barrels, but I'd been robbed of that opportunity by his penchant for extra cheese on every burger he'd ever ordered.

"Lily, I can tell you didn't know about Neal's inappropriate relationship with your sister," I said. "I'll be sure to convey my thoughts about that to Xavier Mesnier. As for being upset with Phoebe about not having you as a bridesmaid in her wedding, well, I don't think anyone will believe that's a motive for murder."

"I didn't kill her. The truth is, I wish she were standing in front of me, right now, alive and breathing."

I gave her a sympathetic nod. "I know. I get it."

Lily folded her arms. "I don't think you do. I wish she were here so I could murder her myself."

Chapter Eighteen

I SHUT THE door to room 668, relieved to be out of there. I could still hear Lily giving Neal an earful, with little to no response from him.

He was penitent enough I thought their marriage had a chance to recover once Lily was done making him suffer for his infidelity. Some couples therapy would help, too. But only time would reveal if the affair was a death blow to their relationship or a chance to start fresh.

I would have bet money neither of them was responsible for Phoebe's death. Since I knew Andy didn't do it either, my pool of suspects had started to narrow.

I still felt like Frank needed to be at the top of the list. Whatever was going on at Braithwaite Industrial Storage had concerned Phoebe enough she'd almost missed her own wedding cruise. Not to mention that Frank was just sleazy. He was guilty of something. I could feel it in my bones.

Rhonda was still a possibility, although unlikely. Video footage showed Phoebe had left their late-night meeting on her own two feet. Unless they'd met up again, during the security camera blackout, Rhonda was probably in the clear.

Although it wasn't impossible Dale and Susan had killed

their own daughter–I'd seen enough *Dateline* to know it did happen–I'd seen nothing to indicate a motive. In fact, after talking with Neal, Phoebe had a stronger motive to kill her parents than the other way around.

Sawyer had opportunity but not motive, and if he'd had something to hide, he wouldn't have admitted to being one of the last people to see her in her room. Of course, I wouldn't have even known to ask about it if Windsor the butler hadn't told me. Still, Sawyer had no reason to want his baby sister dead.

The only sibling I had yet to interview, was Ivy. The truth was, Ivy intimidated me. She had a brash personality, and unless a reasonable opportunity presented itself, I had no plans of questioning her. Her husband was a lawyer. Corporate or not, Clyde still had the ability to threaten a lawsuit, and now that I had become aware of my sizable assets, I kind of wanted to hold on to them.

That didn't mean I wasn't planning on poking around and trying to determine where Ivy had been the night Phoebe was killed.

I believed, deep in my gut, that this attack was not done by a stranger. Someone had lured Phoebe to the storage area on the fourth floor, and I couldn't imagine a scenario in which she'd have left her room in the middle of the night to meet someone she didn't know.

Tonight's dinner would give me an opportunity to observe the bridal party and the family to see if anyone acted suspicious.

The dress code for the evening was as your favorite fictional character. Perhaps the killer's choice of who to represent—and whether hero or villain—would be their tell.

I also hoped I wouldn't be in a matching outfit with Neal again.

THE STRANGE THING about having a murder occur in the middle of a cruise while out to sea was that after the initial shock had morphed into a numb, sorrowful form of acceptance, this new reality where grieving family and friends still dressed in costume for dinner parties no longer struck me as odd.

What Xavier had said regarding suspended reality while at sea rang truer than I could have imagined.

Not wanting to haul a ridiculous amount of clothing for seven events in my suitcase and garment bag, I'd picked a simple re-creation that could be made with my own clothing and a few small accessories.

Miss Marple, the sleuth in several Agatha Christie novels, was an older woman with sparkling blue eyes. Beyond that, most descriptions were about her personality rather than her appearance. I'd brought a gray pencil skirt, a white blouse, gray cardigan, silk scarf, and a gray wool bucket hat. I had a nice strand of silver pearls that were my grandmother's, which I was expecting to bring a level of sophistication and class to my wedding attire. Now that the wedding wasn't to be, I wore the strand with my costume. I didn't know if Miss Marple wore pearls, but I felt confident neither did anyone in the Braithwaite-Cobb bridal party.

Jane came out of the bedroom wearing a brown and white faux fur one-shoulder dress with jagged edges. Her hair was swept into a chignon.

I blinked twice. “Wilma Flintstone?”

She sputtered. “No! Jane. Like Tarzan and Jane.”

“You’re looking pretty hot for a woman who’s almost sixty.”

Another offended huff. “In three years!”

I shrugged. “It was a compliment.”

“Keep it.” She eyed me up and down. “Decided not to participate?”

I grunted. “Rude. I’m Miss Marple.”

Jane gave me a look of incredulity.

“What?”

“Charlotte, we’re both Jane.”

I still didn’t get it. Then it hit me. “Ohhhh.” Miss Marple’s first name was Jane.

“Right.”

I squared my shoulders. “No one will notice.”

“LET ME GET this straight.” Frank was chuckling, pointing back and forth between Jane and me. “You’re Jane, playing Jane, and you’re *not* Jane, but you’re playing Jane too?” He slapped the table as he burst out in laughter.

“We’re not the same Jane,” I mumbled.

This only made Frank laugh harder. He was wearing the

same pinstriped gangster suit from the first night on the cruise.

"Who are you supposed to be?" I asked, dropping into my seat.

"Bugsy Siegel." He straightened his lapels.

"Bugsy Siegel isn't a fictional character, Frank," I said.

"Sure, he is. From that movie with Warren Beatty."

Jane leaned over and whispered into my ear, "It's not worth it."

Elaine swatted at Frank. "No, silly. Bugs Bunny wasn't in *Who Framed Roger Rabbit*?"

She was adjusting her cleavage stuffed into a red-and-white polka-dotted dress, so it took her a moment to notice we were all staring at her.

She stopped smacking her gum. "What?"

"Where'd you find a sexy version of a Minnie Mouse dress?" Jane asked.

Elaine gave a knowing smile that revealed the color of her gum was purple. "I got a friend. She has all the cute costumes. Sexy princess, sexy pirate wench, and...oh look! That girl must know my friend. I swear she rents out that sexy teacher costume, too."

We all turned to the dining room entrance.

Standing in the doorway, a woman pulled down her very short plaid skirt. She wore a white midriff-baring blouse, the ends of which were tied between her breasts into a bow. A loose striped tie hung around her neck, her long legs were covered in sheer black thigh-high stockings with lace cuffs and her stiletto heels were at least three inches, if not higher.

She had black horn-rimmed glasses on her heavily made-up face, complete with a fake mole above her scarlet red lips. She still wore her beaded bracelet.

I could have sworn Frank said *hubba* under his breath.

"Serena?" I said, awe and surprise in my voice.

"No! It can't be." Jane swatted at me.

"Oh, it is. It doesn't look like her, but it is," I said.

Serena had transformed from frumpy schoolmarm into a racy stereotype befitting of a Van Halen music video muse. All eyes were on her as she entered the room, as intended.

Jane leaned toward me. "Looks like someone got tired of being invisible."

Serena made her way past Ivy, Clyde, Lily, and Neal, their faces agape, to a nearby table where Vance and Duncan sat with their tongues practically hanging out of their mouths. Nikki watched the scene with pinched expressions and crossed arms, observing the men make fools of themselves over Serena's revamped image.

"Who are you supposed to be?" Nikki said.

"Cameron Diaz's character in *Bad Teacher*." Serena had altered her voice to sound more coquette than normal.

"I saw that movie. I don't remember her wearing an outfit like that. I don't even think she had glasses." Nikki sniffed.

Serena tipped her nose in the air. "I was going for a general vibe, not exact." She went to pull out her chair, but both Vance and Duncan jumped out of theirs to try to get to it first. Duncan won the race, much to Vance's dismay. "Thank you." Serena batted her eyelashes at Duncan, the same man she'd barely tolerated the night before.

The whole situation struck me as odd. Odd was becoming an ever-present vibe with this group.

Serena caught me watching her. She gave a broad smile, but it didn't reach her eyes. "Ms. Charlotte, is Andy coming soon?"

I furrowed my brow. "Oh, no, he's not coming. He's confined to our cabin for now."

"He texted me this afternoon saying he'd been told he could come to dinner."

"Did you hear that?" I asked Jane.

"I never saw him this afternoon, other than peeking in on him briefly, but he was taking a nap."

I turned back to Serena. "I think you must be mistaken."

I'd barely gotten the words out of my mouth when Andy walked into the dining room. An audible gasp went up from all three tables. He was dressed like Indiana Jones.

He pulled out the empty chair next to me.

"What are you doing here?" I asked.

He shrugged. "Mesnier said I was free to come to dinner."

Frank glared at Andy. "So, they're just letting suspected murderers run around the ship unsupervised?"

I tilted my chin toward Frank. "You're not in the clear either, you know."

He glowered at me. "I've done nothing wrong."

Andy snorted. "Sell that to someone willing to buy it."

Serena rose from her chair and made her way to our table. She touched the back of the vacant seat next to Andy.

"Do you mind if I join you? I'm not enjoying the company at my assigned table."

"Of course." Andy appraised her. "You look nice."

She gave him a thousand-watt smile in response. "Thank you."

Frank's enthusiastic nod was even more vigorous than Andy's. "Never hurts to have a lot of eye candy around."

Everyone at our table turned a stink-eye on Frank.

"I'm only saying out loud what every man in this restaurant is thinking."

"You don't speak for me, Frank." Andy turned to Serena. "I'm sorry. He never learned that having money doesn't excuse a lack of class."

Serena touched Andy's hand. "I appreciate you sticking up for me."

Pink crawled up Andy's neck and into his cheeks.

Before I could comment, Haimi arrived to take our drink orders. As she went around the table, I found myself feeling unsettled. Serena's transformation and her clear interest in Andy had my wheels turning. She had an obvious effect on him as well. Could this mild-mannered teacher be a killer in disguise? Could she have murdered Phoebe to stop her from marrying Andy, a man for whom Serena appeared to have developed romantic feelings?

"Aunt Char." Andy nudged me.

"Oh, I apologize. Do you have any cowslip wine?"

Haimi's brows arched. "I do not even know what that is. Is it a red or white varietal?"

Jane laughed. "No need to be so obscure, Charlotte. Just

because Miss Marple drank cowslip wine doesn't mean you need to do so to play the part."

"It didn't hurt to ask. I'll have a claret or a burgundy."

Jane rolled her eyes. "Now you're ordering like Poirot. No one is holding you to the beverages of an Agatha Christie novel simply because you're dressed like Miss Marple."

Haimi said, "I believe I have a Francis Coppola Diamond Claret Cabernet Sauvignon."

Frank banged the table with his palm. "I changed my mind. I'm not Bugsy. I'm Don Corleone from *The Godfather*. Change my old-fashioned to the Coppola claret."

Haimi appeared startled at Frank's outburst but quickly recovered. "Ms. McLaughlin?"

"Yes, the claret works, thank you. Let's get a couple of bottles for the table in case anyone else wants some."

Haimi scuttled off toward the bar, and I turned to Andy. "I'm surprised Xavier let you out of the room. Did he say why?"

"He came by earlier, while I was trying to take a nap. You and Aunt Jane must have been gone, because the doorbell rang several times before I realized, once again, it wasn't in my dream."

Jane leaned forward. "I never left you alone. I was taking a nap, too. I have really great noise-canceling headphones."

"Ah, that explains why you kept ignoring the doorbell. I was about to pull it out of the wall so no one else would disturb my nap. Anyway, I opened the door, and Mesnier was there. He asked if you were around, Aunt Char, and I told him I didn't know where you were. He poked his head inside the cabin, and then told me I was allowed to go to dinner tonight."

"That's so strange. Just out of the blue?"

"Yeah. Maybe he's realizing he's got the wrong man."

"Or not." Frank pointed toward the entryway where Xavier Mesnier stood scanning the dining room, flanked on one side by Lonnie Irving and on the other by Pike Taylor. He spotted me, and regret crossed his face. It made my stomach sink. He lasered in on Andy, sitting next to me, and that sinking feeling became heavier, like I'd swallowed an anchor.

The three security officers marched to our table.

"Monsieur Cobb, *s'il vous plaît*, I need you to stand," Xavier said.

Andy closed his eyes, took a deep discouraged breath, and got to his feet. "What is it now?"

Irving grabbed Andy by the arm.

"Monsieur Cobb, I am officially placing you under arrest for the murder of Phoebe Braithwaite."

Serena emitted a yelp.

Irving pulled both of Andy's arms behind his back and zip-tied them.

I jumped to my feet. "Why are you doing this?"

"I am sorry, Madame McLaughlin. You must face the truth of your nephew's guilt."

"I will do no such thing. He's innocent."

Irving and Taylor escorted Andy out of the dining room, past the stunned faces of Sawyer and Macy, who'd just arrived.

Xavier turned to look directly at me. "We have found

more evidence linking him to the crime."

Jane pushed out from the table. "Evidence? What evidence?"

"We have located Phoebe's cell phone. I showed it to her parents, and they identified it by the case."

"Well, that's good, then," I said. "It should exonerate Andy, because it will show the last person who texted or called her to meet with them, and it wasn't him."

"Unfortunately, that is not possible. The phone has been wiped clean. It has been returned to factory settings. All information, all text messages are gone."

"I don't get it." Jane said. "How does that implicate Andy?"

"Because, Madame Cobb, the phone was found hidden in between the cushions of the sofa in your cabin."

Chapter Nineteen

SAWYER AND MACY approached our table, their expressions mirroring my own shock.

"What's going on?" he said.

Serena whimpered, and she blew her nose in her white cloth dinner napkin. When she pulled it away, her red lipstick had smeared, and her fake mole resembled a blob of melted dark chocolate on her upper lip.

My thoughts were rattled, and I felt unsure of my ability to speak.

Frank lacked no such confidence. "Looks like they've finally found the evidence to nail that piece of garbage for your sister's murder once and for all."

Sawyer's face paled.

"I can't believe it," Macy said. "I never would have thought Andy was capable…"

"He's not." I finally found my voice. "Andy didn't do this. I don't care what Mesnier says."

"Well, then how did Phoebe's phone get in your cabin?" Elaine said.

Sawyer jerked his head to look at me. "Her phone was in *your* cabin? Not in Phoebe's?"

"I don't know how, but that's where Mesnier said he found it. Jane, that's why he said Andy could come to dinner. He wanted to search our room."

"Is that even legal?" she asked.

"Maybe one of you ladies tried to help your nephew by hiding the incriminating evidence." Frank smirked.

"Is that true? Are you covering up for Andy?" Sawyer thundered.

"We're not." Jane's back arched in a defensive posture. "We're just as horrified by what's happened as anyone. We love Andy, but we would never abet him in covering up a crime."

"Andy. Didn't. Do this." I said the words through gritted teeth. "I'd stake my life on it."

"When you defend a killer, you're risking everyone's life." Frank's face was nearly purple. "Misplaced loyalty isn't a virtue."

"Let's go, Char." Jane tugged at my arm. "We can go talk to Xavier away from prying eyes and figure out what's going on."

I followed her out of the dining room, sputtering expletives under my breath.

"I know," Jane said. "I know."

We busted through the doorway of the security office; Taylor reached for his holster, and Irving jumped to his feet in a karate pose. When they saw it was only us, they returned to their tasks without acknowledgment.

"Xavier," I called in the direction of the closed office door.

"He's not here." Taylor spoke but didn't make eye contact.

"Where is he?"

Irving cocked his head to the side, so one of his eyes was pointing in my direction. "I'm afraid I can't give you that information. I will let him know you came to speak with him."

Jane and I stood in silence; the only noise was the tapping of their fingers on their keyboards. I waited for them to say something, anything, but they continued with their work.

"Come on, Jane, let's go find the real killer."

Before I turned away, I noticed Taylor's gaze flicked upward and his mouth tugged into a slight smile.

"What now?" Jane asked as I dragged her down the hallway away from the security office.

"I have an idea."

We got into the elevator, and I pressed the button to take us to level nine, Mykonos.

"Are we going back to the dining room?"

"No. I noticed a library and business center when we visited the bar."

"You want to read at a time like this?"

"No."

"You want to send a fax?" Jane smirked. "How 1995 of you."

"I want to use the computer."

"For what?"

"You'll see."

We entered the library—if one could even call it that, as it contained mostly outdated encyclopedias and worn paperback smut novels—and headed for the computer desk. I pulled out the chair and sat down. Jane hovered behind me.

"What are you looking for?"

I typed in a familiar website address and logged in.

"Char, is this really the time to be checking your notifications and friend requests?"

I ignored her and typed "Serena Price" into the search bar.

"Why Serena? She's just a regular girl. A teacher. She doesn't look like a killer. Although she showed up dressed to kill tonight."

"Exactly. Serena has been flying under the radar until now." I scrolled through the profiles—there were a surprising number of Serena Prices in the directory.

"You're not slut-shaming her, are you? Just because she put on some sexy clothes and red lipstick doesn't mean she's a bad person."

"I'm not saying that at all. However, I think her efforts tonight were for an audience of one."

I clicked on the profile with a thumbnail photo most likely to be Serena. Most of the profile was locked down to everyone other than her hundred eighty-eight followers, but certain posts and photos were visible because of the mutual friend tagged in them.

"Bingo."

"Andy?"

"Andy."

I clicked on a photo of Andy and Serena at their school carnival. They were both dressed as scarecrows, holding cornstalks. The caption read "We're so corny." Andy had commented below, "Hay, hay, hay speak for yourself!" Serena had hearted his response.

"Cute," Jane said.

"Yeah, unless it's her motive for murder."

"You think Serena got rid of Phoebe so she could be with Andy?"

"It's a classic motive. Did you see how flirty she was with him tonight?"

"I did, and I noticed he enjoyed the attention also."

"When I tell Xavier about this, don't bring up that part of it. He'll think they conspired to kill Phoebe so they could be together."

Jane made a dismissive sound. "That's ridiculous. You don't have to kill someone just break up with them."

"Sure, but right now Xavier is looking for anything to bolster his flimsy case against Andy."

"I just thought of something!"

I crooked my chin. "What?"

"I think we've found Phoebe's *stalker*. Get it? Stalker? Because she's holding a corn stalk?" Jane laughed at her own bad pun.

I groaned. "Good grief." I turned back to look at the photo. "Come to think of it, though, you might be onto something."

WE FOUND SERENA drowning her sorrows in Azure Lounge. She was posted up at the bar, sucking down a giant strawberry margarita through a thick blue straw. A few feet away, Duncan, Nikki, and Vance watched her from a rounded booth.

Jane sidled up on Serena's right, and I slid up on her left.

"That looks good." Jane waved her arms. "Hey, Egan, I'll have what she's having."

The bartender glanced our way and held up a finger.

Serena glanced sullenly first at Jane and then at me. "Did you find Andy?"

"No, we went to the security office, but we weren't able to speak with him." I tried to phrase my next question in such a way as to not scare her from talking to us. "Andy has always said how much he admires you, what a great friend you've been to him. That's why he insisted you were in the wedding, right?"

Serena gave an "mm-hmm" without removing her mouth from the straw. "He said he would have made me best person, but Phoebe didn't like that." She released the straw. "She said it had to be *girls with girls and boys with boys*." Her tone was mocking. "What are we, six-year-olds on the playground at recess? We're nearly a quarter of the way through the twenty-first century. I think the world can handle a female friend standing up for the groom."

"Agreed," Jane said.

Egan moved toward us. "What can I get for you ladies? I

believe I heard another quad-shot strawberry marg, and what else?"

Both horrifying and impressive. "You had him put four shots of tequila in there?"

"And that's after the two straight shots she took while she waited for the marg," Egan added.

Serena shrugged and returned to sipping through the straw.

"I'll have a hot toddy." I folded my hands in my lap.

Jane grunted. "You're not actually in your eighties, Miss Marple. Drink your age."

"Drink your age," Egan repeated. His laugh was choppy like a machine gun *rat-a-tat-tat*. "Good one. I'll have to use that."

"Were you and Phoebe close?" I asked.

Serena's eyes were halfway closed, and her mouth formed a sneer. "Close? No, we were not close. She tolerated me for Andy's sake. She was couture. Chanel, Prada, those shoes with red bottoms. I'm Goodwill and Lakeshore Learning school supply center. She was a celebrity with millions of fans. I have a hundred eighty-nine followers on social media."

"A hundred eighty-eight," Jane said.

Serena's eyes fluttered open to look at Jane. "Were you stalking me?"

"Speaking of stalking," I said, bringing her attention back to me, "what do you know about Phoebe's stalker?"

Serena wobbled a bit on the stool. She was now more than halfway done with her cocktail. "I know she used it every time she felt like Andy was slipping out of her claws."

Jane's wide-eyed gaze and raised eyebrows mirrored my thoughts.

"What do you mean *she used it*?" Jane asked.

"You know," Serena waved her hands in the air, "like, whenever he'd get mad at her. Suddenly her stalker would be back." Her words had begun to slur. "Cellaphane."

"Cellophane? Cellophane what?"

No, not cell-oh-phane, like it's s'posed to be spelled. Cell-uhhhh-phane, with an *a*. It was the stalker's username." She made air quotes. "Supposably."

I ignored her mispronunciation and my concerns about a fourth-grade teacher with poor grammar, instead choosing to focus on the implication of what she'd said. "You're telling us the stalking incidents continued after Andy and Phoebe met?"

Serena squinted at me. "You kinda look like Andy when I do this with my eyes."

"Well, he is my nephew," I said dryly. "Tell us about the stalking incidents that happened after Andy started dating Phoebe. It was my understanding they'd stopped a long time ago."

Serena puckered her lips and lolled her head back and forth. "Oh, they did. I'm pretty sure, at least. That's what I'm trying to tell you. She'd be mean to Andy, treat him like crap, and then blame it on stress because she had PTSD from her stalker or whatever."

"So, there weren't any incidents?" Jane said. "Just the aftereffects? The trauma of what she'd been through?"

"I mean, that's what I think, but sometimes she'd say she thought someone followed her to her car or was watching her from outside her house, just to get him to come over. Stuff like that."

"But you didn't believe it," I said.

"Nah. I mean, maybe, but I think she was just trying to give excuses for why she talked to him like he was a kid. He was always in trouble for one thing or another. He could never make her happy. She was so rude."

My heart sank. This had been my gut feeling about the situation as well. From what I'd observed, Phoebe had made Andy miserable way more often than she made him happy.

I didn't like these thoughts because I knew if I voiced them aloud, it would sound like he hadn't wanted to marry Phoebe, and someone might take that as a motive. The truth was, he loved Phoebe despite how she treated him, and he was determined to make things work between them.

"But you were there for him," I said. "Always there for him."

"Always." Serena slurped the remainder of her margarita through the straw and then she hiccupped. It was the saddest, most heartbroken hiccup I'd ever heard.

Egan set our drinks in front of us. "Another marg, Serena?"

Just as she opened her mouth to say yes, Jane interrupted. "I think she's good for now. We should probably get her back to her room."

"But you haven't even started your drinks," Serena whined.

"Hey, Egan, can you put these in to-go cups?" Jane asked.

"Sure thing."

"Serena," I said.

"Yes, Charlotte?"

"Can I borrow your phone? I forgot mine in the room."

Serena's eyes were barely open at this point. She slid it to me before resting her arms on the bar and her head on her arms. It was an older model iPhone with the fingerprint touchpad security feature.

"Give me your finger."

She held out her left index finger without question, and I used it to unlock her phone. She didn't even look to see what I was doing.

I quickly opened her texts and scrolled through, looking for anything to or from Phoebe.

I finally located their conversation, but I was disappointed. Nothing since we'd boarded the cruise ship. There were a few terse messages about dress fittings and a couple asking if Serena had seen Andy because Phoebe was trying to track him down, but nothing that overtly indicated bad blood or that Serena had lured Phoebe out on that fateful night.

"Anything?" Jane asked.

Serena began to lightly wheeze.

"Not that I can see," I said. "I think it's just a case of unrequited love but nothing that shows she'd kill over it."

"I can't say I'm not disappointed, but also I'm kind of hoping it works out for Serena and Andy."

I glanced around to see if anyone had heard her. "We

gotta watch what we say. If anyone suspects we weren't thrilled Andy was marrying Phoebe, that might make *us* suspects."

Jane pretended to zip her mouth shut and lock it with a key.

Serena let out a deep snore.

Chapter Twenty

FIRST FRANK, NOW Serena. This was becoming a regular occurrence for us, dragging drunken people to their rooms. Who might be next?

The bridesmaid suite, 612, was almost directly across from Frank and Elaine's room. We didn't bother to knock because we'd seen her cabinmate Nikki still pounding the drinks with the groomsmen when we'd hoisted Serena off the stool, out of Azure Lounge, and to the bay of elevators.

I propped her up against the wall. "Where's your key, Serena?"

She looked down at her outfit. "I didn't bring my purse."

"You had to show your ID at the bar, didn't you?" Jane asked.

Serena patted herself down, then started giggling. "I know where I put it."

She reached into her cleavage and pulled out two cards: her driver's license and her key. She handed the room key to me. I wiped off the under-boob sweat on my cardigan and unlocked the door.

"Honey, I'm home!" Serena sang. "Oh, wait, never mind. I don't have a honey." She pouted and flopped onto one of the beds. "The honey I want is in boat jail for killing the honey he wanted."

"He didn't do it," I repeated for what felt like the hundredth time in two days.

Had it only been two days? Two days since the world had turned upside-down.

Suspended reality indeed. In some ways it felt as though we'd just walked the gangplank onto the *Thalassophile of the Seas*, while on the other hand, with all that had happened, it felt like weeks had passed.

Serena was already asleep on the bed. I motioned to Jane that we should leave.

As I carefully shut the door behind us, I asked, "What's your impression of Serena regarding Phoebe's murder? Do you think she's capable of that?"

Jane leaned against the wall. "I think under the right circumstances, anyone is capable of anything. Do I believe Serena killed Phoebe? I don't, and I'll tell you why. I can see her being jealous and wanting Andy for herself. What I don't see is her setting him up to take the fall for it. Whoever did this wanted Andy out of the picture as much as they wanted Phoebe gone."

"Agreed. I feel like there's a piece of information rattling around in my brain that will make all of this make sense, but I'm so exhausted I can't quite grasp it to put it in place."

"Let's get some sleep." Jane yawned. "Maybe tomorrow things will become clear."

THAT DIDN'T HAPPEN, though. I tossed and turned all night while puzzle pieces floated through my semiconscious thoughts.

Even in my dreams, I had a sense there was something I knew, something important that could break the case wide open, but it was hidden among all the extraneous facts I'd gathered since Phoebe's body had been discovered submerged in the VIP hot tub.

One by one I'd crossed suspects off my list, and yet I still felt nautical miles away from figuring out who'd done it and why.

I finally resigned myself to the reality that I wasn't getting any more sleep, pulled on my robe, and wandered into the kitchen. I was surprised to find some basic staples in the fridge. Andy must have had them delivered while under house arrest.

Andy.

How had he slept now that he was officially under arrest? I wasn't even sure *where* he'd slept. Just because he'd been kept in the room without windows in the security office when they first detained him didn't mean he was there now.

I planned to visit the security office to give Xavier an earful later that morning, but any trouble I made might affect the way Andy was treated. I wanted to believe Xavier wouldn't retaliate against him for my behavior, but I couldn't be certain of it.

I found a glass bowl, and one by one I cracked eggs into it. Since it was only Jane and me for breakfast, I stopped at four. I added a bit of cream and some salt and pepper and then began absentmindedly whisking them.

Jane came into the kitchen. "I think if you beat those eggs anymore, you'll be reported to the authorities for abuse."

I'd created an orange frothy mixture with soft peaks. "I can't stop thinking about poor Andy."

"*Poor Andy*s won't do anyone any good. We need to solve this and exonerate him as soon as possible."

I pulled a frying pan out of the cupboard and turned on the stove. From the fridge I grabbed a stick of butter and cut off a pat, which I dropped into the now-sizzling hot pan. After allowing the butter to coat the bottom, I poured in the eggs. "I need a spatula."

"Don't look at me," Jane said.

I pulled out every drawer until I located one. I began to scrape the eggs from the bottom of the pan. "Shoot, I have the pan up too high. They're getting brown." I lowered the temp and frantically scraped the pan. "It's not helping. The pan's already too hot and they're getting ruined. Everything is ruined! And I can't do anything about it."

I buried my face in my hands. Gabe's death. His affair. His baby. Phoebe's death. Andy's arrest. In that moment of overcooked scrambled eggs, it all became too much.

I began to sob like I hadn't since I was a child. My parents had been the stoic kind, those of the generation who believed emotions were to be managed at all times.

The last time I'd allowed myself to give in to my sadness was when my grandmother had died unexpectedly of a stroke. My father had arrived to deliver the news while I was spending the night at a friend's house, and then he'd gone home to take care of my mother.

My poor friend had sat awkwardly patting my back as I'd cried and cried and cried, snot bubbles forming in my nostrils. I'd never lost anyone before, and my grandmother was the kind of person who knew how to make each of us kids feel like we were her favorite. She made me believe I was special in a world where I felt invisible.

My mother had locked herself in her room for four days and then came out like nothing had happened. She never talked about her mother again. Bernard, Jane, and I had known we weren't to talk of her again, either.

I'd learned that day that grief was meant to be private and short-lived and then put away like a memento box on a shelf in a dusty corner of the house.

From Jane's alarm when I removed my hands from my eyes, she'd absorbed the same lesson. I couldn't remember the last time she'd really cried, either.

"I'm sorry," I managed to say through shuddered breaths.

"Don't be. It was a long time coming."

"I ruined the eggs."

Jane grabbed the pan off the hot burner and placed it onto a cool one. She stirred the eggs with the spatula. "We'll melt some cheese on top, and they'll be great."

Jane went to the fridge and pulled out a block of cheddar. She located a cutting board and the cheese grater and began shredding. She plated some eggs and sprinkled cheese on top before handing it to me.

"*Voila.*"

"Thanks. Sorry again."

Jane made a sound like a buzzer. "*Ehh.* Nope. You shouldn't apologize for expressing emotion. We aren't doing this anymore. Stuffing our feelings hasn't served either of us well. Now. What's on the agenda for today?"

Jane scooped up some eggs for herself.

"There are two things I want to look into. First, I want to talk to Ivy. She's the only sibling I haven't been able to get a read on. Second, I want to do a little more digging into Braithwaite Industrial. Phoebe believed something shady was happening there, and I do, too."

"I have an idea." Jane picked up the phone. "Windsor, it's Jane Cobb. Is there any way you could book a spa day for me, Charlotte, and Ivy Evans?" She paused to listen. "Yes, and send the invitation to Ivy's cabin. I believe she's on the sixth floor." Pause. "Aegean. Whatever. Two P.M.?" Pause. "Great, thanks so much." She hung up.

"Spa day?"

"Who says we can't investigate a murder while getting pampered?" She shrugged.

"For someone who's always prided herself on living simply, you're adapting to the luxurious life pretty quickly."

"What can I say, dahling?" She affected the mid-Atlantic accent of 1940s movie stars and held her hand out like she was showing off diamond rings. "I love the finer things now."

⚓

AS SOON AS I opened the door to the spa, I felt transported. There were no windows, and the lighting was purposefully dim to create a calming effect. The scent being piped in through the vents was a combination of floral and cedar, and the speakers played soothing harp music.

"Hello, you must be Charlotte and Jane." The woman behind the desk spoke in dulcet tones. She had flaming red hair, green eyes, and skin that didn't appear to have ever experienced sunlight. "I'm Evangeline Irving, the spa manager here on the *Thalassophile of the Seas*. I hope you will find the experience we've created for you today to be very special. Mrs. Evans arrived a few minutes ago, and she's waiting in the quiet room."

Jane leaned toward me and whispered, "I forgot about the quiet room. I guess it's tough to question someone when you're not supposed to speak."

"How are your telepathy skills?"

"Follow me, ladies." Evangeline led us into a locker room. Except for one, all the mahogany cabinets were open and held a plush white robe. "Choose any locker you'd like, and when you're done changing into the robe, be sure to take the key from the lock. Your massage therapists will meet you in the quiet room, which is just around that corner." Evangeline pointed in the opposite direction from where we'd entered the locker room. "In there you'll find water and fruit."

"Great, thanks," I said.

Evangeline left Jane and me to change.

"Well, at least if we don't get any information, we'll be

able to decompress." Jane tied her robe.

"I'm not sure how I can relax at a time like this."

"Just go with it."

We found Ivy flipping through a magazine. She glanced at us and offered a smile as we sat in two recliners.

"Thanks so much for this. I really needed it." Ivy's whisper wasn't exactly quiet.

"You're welcome." The words stuck in my throat, along with the confession that we had ulterior motives.

Jane gave me a warning look. "We did too. Needed the pampering, I mean. Things have been so tense…for obvious reasons."

My sister stood and walked over to the refreshment table. Mint, cucumber, and lemon slices floated in a giant water jug. She grabbed a plastic cup and filled it to the brim.

Ivy leaned forward. "Look, I barely know Andy, but I knew my sister, and if she believed Andy was a good guy, I trust her. She had good instincts. Same with Clyde. He says he believes Andy is innocent. He may not be of much help to him as an attorney, but he's a good judge of character."

I put my hand to my chest. "I'm so glad to hear you say that. I understand things look bad."

Ivy's laugh was cynical. "Oh, it looks bad, all right. The fight. The murder weapon with Andy's fingerprints. The cell phone in your living room."

Jane retook her seat. "I still don't get how the phone ended up in our sofa."

"Clyde says that's as incriminating as the fingerprints on the knife."

"Andy's been in custody since Phoebe was found. When would he have had time to get the phone and hide it?"

Ivy held up her palms. "No idea. Somebody better figure it out, though, or Andy is in big trouble."

A petite dark-haired woman walked in through a side door. "Mrs. McLaughlin?"

"Yes?"

"My name is Sin Mee. I will be providing your massage today."

"Oh, okay, thank you." I rose from my chair. "I guess I'll see you two back here when we're done."

I followed Sin Mee into the hallway. She led me a couple doors down into a room that was nearly dark. In front of me was a massage table covered in crisp white sheets and pink rose petals. I could make out a small water fountain in the corner, which reminded me: I should have peed prior to the appointment. The smell of patchouli was strong, and I wasn't sure how relaxed I could be under the circumstances.

I was wrong. By the time she tapped me on the shoulder to let me know she was finished, I'd been asleep for at least ten minutes.

"You have much tightness in your deltoid and trapezius muscles. You have scar tissue in your knee, which indicates previous injury. Also, your hips…as tight as a porcupine in a teacup."

"Is that a saying?"

"You lack flexibility."

"I've been under a bit of stress lately."

"I recommend coming to see me once a week and doing

some stretching in between."

"Stretching is a great idea, but I'm only on the ship through Sunday morning."

"Oh, I was under the impression you are a resident and not a guest."

"It's complicated. My husband bought the condo. Now he's dead. I'll probably sell it."

"I am sorry. If you change your mind and decide to live on the ship permanently, I will create a treatment plan to help you."

"I appreciate that, but I doubt that'll be the case."

Sin Mee gave a quick bow. "I will leave you to get dressed."

I awkwardly slid off the massage table and reached for my robe, which hung from a hook next to the door. As I removed the robe, I saw my reflection in the mirror mounted on the back of the door. In this upright position, the Michelin rolls weren't as pronounced. My body looked round and soft. My hair was mussed, but my face appeared serene. My shoulders were no longer hunched. The person staring back at me looked refreshed.

Sin Mee's comment about living on the ship full-time was a crazy thought, and yet…

A knock on the door startled me.

"Mrs. McLaughlin? Do you need anything?"

"No thank you, Sin Mee. I'm coming out now."

BACK IN THE quiet room, I sat alone. The music had shifted from harp to sitar. I had a magazine in my lap, but my thoughts were elsewhere.

People really lived here, on a ship floating around the world. It was intriguing, even as common sense told me it was a ridiculous notion.

The door opened and Ivy was ushered in by her massage therapist.

"How was it?" I asked.

"Wonderful," she said. "Thanks again."

"My pleasure. I haven't had a massage in years. I needed it more than I knew."

"I heard from Phoebe about your husband, and all the unpleasantness. I'm sorry."

"I appreciate that. I'm coming to terms with the fact someone I trusted implicitly was capable of that level of betrayal."

"It must have really messed with your head."

"It did."

"When they figure out who hurt Phoebe, we'll probably feel the same way, huh?"

"How do you mean?"

"Unless it turns out to be a stranger—which I'm still hoping it was—someone in our family's inner circle did this. Someone who sat at my parents' table and shared a meal with us. Someone who looked us in the eye and then turned around and stabbed my sister in the heart. Literally."

A gasp escaped me. "Is that where she was stabbed? I hadn't heard."

"The head of security, the French dude, he said she was stabbed multiple times, but the fatal blow was likely the one to her heart. It feels personal, you know?"

"It absolutely does. What do you know about Phoebe's job and Frank's business? Anything suspicious going on there?"

Ivy reared her head back. "You think Braithwaite Industrial Storage had something to do with Phoebe's death?"

"I don't know. Andy said Phoebe had seen something that concerned her. That's why she was almost late for the ship's departure. She went to the storage facility to verify something."

Ivy's eyes grew wide. "Oh my gosh! She left me a message that afternoon. It didn't make any sense at the time because I thought she was talking about a wedding gift."

"What did the message say?"

"I can't remember exactly, but it was something about Russian dolls."

"Russian dolls?" Jane said as she walked into the room.

Ivy slapped her thigh. "I know! She said, *If I don't make it, ask Frank about the Russian dolls.*"

"RUSSIAN DOLLS. DO you think there are actual Russian dolls, or is it a secret code?" Jane shouted at me above the sound of the jets of the spa's whirlpool bath.

Ivy had elected not to share a skinny dip with her deceased sister's almost-aunts-in-law and instead chose to get a facial. I couldn't say I blamed her.

"I have no idea. Russian dolls are known for having many layers. It very well could be a metaphor. I was going to hit the sauna after this. Want to join me?"

"I think I'm about done. I'm having a hot flash on top of already simmering in boiling water. After I shower, I'll wait for you in the quiet room."

I grabbed a towel and wrapped it around myself as I climbed out of the pool. I pulled my robe over the towel.

"I'll see you in a bit. I'm sure I'll only be able to stand the sauna for about five minutes."

I walked down the hallway and located the door to the sauna. I poked my head inside. A blast of hot woodsy air assaulted me. It was empty.

I pulled the door shut, sat on the bench, and removed my robe so I was only in the towel. I took the wooden spoon and scooped water from the bucket to drizzle over the hot coals. I inhaled the cedar-scented steam, and it filled my lungs, scorching them from within. Sweat began to bead across my forehead and at my nape.

I ladled another scoopful of water and watched as the droplets danced across the sizzling coals. Another deep inhalation felt like the steam invaded every crevice of my bronchia.

I pulled my head to the left and then to the right. Between the massage and the warm, moist air, my muscles had loosened, allowing me to stretch farther than I had in a very long time.

I rolled my shoulders and pulled my right arm across my

chest. I repeated the movement with my left arm. A drop of sweat rolled down my back.

"Phew, it's getting toasty in here."

I regretted not bringing a cup of drinking water with me.

The red arrow on the thermometer pointed to 170 degrees.

I pulled on my robe and allowed my towel to drop to the floor. I picked it up and wiped the back of my neck and my forehead. I waved the towel to create a cooler breeze and reached for the handle. I pulled, but the door didn't open. I pushed. Still nothing. I yanked the handle back and forth several times, but it didn't give way.

"Hello? Anybody out there?"

Panic rose within me. Sweat was now pouring off my brow and into my eyes, the saltiness burning them.

Once more I jiggled the handle, but to no avail.

"Help!" I pounded on the door. "I'm stuck! Help!"

But no one came.

I watched as the thermometer's red arrow ticked ever closer to the danger zone.

Tick. Tick. Tick.

Chapter Twenty-One

"HELP!" I SCREAMED for what had to have been the twentieth time. "Help!" I pounded incessantly on the door to the sauna. "I can't get out!"

The more I panicked, the hotter it felt and the more trouble I had breathing.

"I'm stuck in here!" I yelled at the top of my lungs.

Muffled voices and scraping came from the other side of the door. It opened, knocking me backward, and fresh, cool air poured into the room.

"Oh, thank God." I rushed into the hallway.

"Mrs. McLaughlin, are you alright?" The spa manager's forehead was creased.

"I am now."

I grabbed a cup off the table and filled it with mint cucumber lemon water. I chugged the water and then refilled the cup. I repeated this three times until I felt as though my body temperature was nearly back to normal.

"I don't know what happened. I came through to check on the towels in the dryer and I heard you screaming. It wasn't loud, but I could tell you were upset. That's when I noticed this." Evangeline held up a shard of driftwood. "I think it's from the potpourri bowl." She indicated a teak bowl filled with chunks of wood and leaves on the table next to the water jug.

"What do you mean you noticed it?"

"It was jammed into the door handle. Like this."

Evangeline shoved the piece of wood under the handle and attempted to push the door. The wood blocked it from opening.

"I'm no expert on safety regulations, but I'd say having a sauna door that opens inward and can be blocked from opening from the outside might be a hazardous violation of some code."

Evangeline's face went from pale to nearly translucent.

"Did you say your name is Evangeline Irving?"

"Yes."

"Any relation to Lonnie Irving, the security guard?"

"He's my brother."

⚓

"I WOULD HAVE freaked out. Did you freak out? I would have totally freaked out."

We were on our way back to our suite, and I'd just given Jane the recap. She was not handling it well.

"You could have died, Char. It had to have been on purpose!"

"It was on purpose. No doubt. The question is…actually, I have a few questions." I held up my fingers and ticked them off one by one. "First, who knew we'd be at the spa? Second, how did they know I'd be in the sauna? Third, how did they get in and out without being seen?"

"Those are all great questions, but no matter what, it leads to one answer."

"What's that?"

"We're getting close to figuring this out, and someone is getting nervous. So nervous, they tried to stop you from investigating. Permanently."

We got off the elevator and headed down to our room. Xavier was leaning against the wall waiting for us.

"I'd ask to what do I owe this pleasure, but I find no pleasure in this visit." I was trying to be snarky, but it was disingenuous. Even after everything, I found a small amount of pleasure in seeing him. Hopefully, he couldn't tell.

"I assure you that I take no pleasure in hearing that you were in danger."

"Ah, so Evangeline called you?"

"She called my assistant and he let me know."

"Her brother."

"*Oui*. She told him the sauna was deliberately tampered with."

"Someone locked me in. Thankfully Evangeline heard me yelling for help."

Xavier shifted his weight between his feet. "I am relieved you were not hurt."

Jane arched her left brow at me.

"Now do you believe us that Phoebe's killer is still roaming around this ship? It's not Andy," I said.

"I feel I should perhaps keep a closer eye on you."

Jane coughed. I gave her a look of warning in return.

"I have the perfect place." Jane smirked at Xavier and then at me.

He gave her a questioning glance. "I am listening."

"Tonight is eighties night, and I'd really like to see you wearing a neon headband."

⚓

"THESE THEMED DINNERS become more humiliating with each one."

Jane stared at my hot pink taffeta dress. "It's not bad, although the pink is a bit much for your complexion."

She was once again dressed as Jane…this time Fonda. She had a one-piece metallic blue leotard, white tights, and coordinating blue leggings. Even at fifty-seven she could still pull it off. Much like the real Jane.

"You know what you need?"

"I hate to ask." I attempted to subdue my puffy sleeves, to no avail.

"Wait here. I've got just the thing."

She left me standing in front of my bathroom mirror trying to imagine what could possibly improve such a horrendous outfit. She came back clutching something in her hand.

"A zebra print belt!" She held it aloft like Rocky after winning the championship bout against Apollo Creed.

"You just happened to have a zebra striped belt in your suitcase?"

She shrugged nonchalantly. "You never know when it might come in handy." She reached around my waist and clipped the belt. "See? Told you. It's perfect."

I had to admit it was an improvement. Not a huge improvement, but an improvement, nonetheless.

She grabbed a comb and a bottle of hairspray from the bathroom counter. "Now, let's tease that hair of yours to high heaven."

⚓

"DID ANYONE GET off the ship today?" Haimi asked after taking our drink orders.

"I didn't know we could," I said.

"I was told a few passengers took skiffs over to the adventure center," she said.

Sawyer was wearing a T-shirt that read THIS IS MY '80S COSTUME in rainbow font. "I had a hard time sleeping last night so I downed a bunch of sleeping pills and took a much-needed nap."

Macy adjusted her neon yellow headband on her forehead. It matched her neon yellow tulle skirt and mesh fingerless gloves. "I tried to read my book on the observation deck, but the bar was blaring the Bee Gees' greatest hits. I saw some whales, though."

"I don't see the point," Frank bellowed. "It didn't seem very impressive to me." He wore the same pinstripe suit he'd worn the previous two evenings, this time with a teal crewneck instead of the white button-down. A piano tie loosely hung around his neck. Other than that, the only accessory he wore was his wedding ring.

"Yeah." Elaine's gum snapped over and over as she chewed. "It was mostly just nature stuff."

Haimi blinked three times. "Yes, the area is known for its unspoiled beauty." She held up her order pad. "I will be back with the drinks in a moment."

Frank grunted.

Elaine snapped her gum. She'd had the same general idea for a costume as Jane, only she'd topped her fuchsia bodysuit with a cropped geometric-patterned sweatshirt and purple eighties-era jogging shorts.

"We went to the spa," Jane said.

"Lucky." *Snap. Snap.*

"I don't know how lucky it was that she almost got murdered in the sauna," Jane said.

Everyone at the table turned to gape at us.

"What do you mean *murdered*?" Frank asked.

"Jane's exaggerating."

"I'm not, Char." She gave a wide-eyed look to everyone staring back at us. "Someone locked her in the sauna."

Frank sat back in his chair and waved a dismissive hand. "Pshh. I thought you were serious. The door probably got jammed."

"It did. By a piece of driftwood purposely wedged into the handle," Jane said.

Elaine grabbed at her throat. "I feel like I can't breathe just thinking about it. I've got claustrophobia."

"That's crazy," said Macy. "I'm so glad you were able to

escape. How did you get out?"

"The spa manager happened to pass by and heard me yelling."

"Why would someone lock you in the sauna?" Sawyer furrowed his brow. "Do you think it's because you've been snooping around?"

"What other reason could there be?" Jane asked.

I gasped. "I can think of one."

Everyone waited for me to continue.

"I can't believe I didn't think of this before. My"—I swallowed—"my husband used to bring his…girlfriend here. And their baby. What if this whole thing is retaliation on behalf of Kyrie Dawn?"

"No." Jane fervently shook her head. "No way. Nobody would kill an innocent woman, frame her fiancé, and then attempt to kill his aunt simply because of misplaced loyalty to a couple of cheaters. That makes zero sense."

"I don't know, Jane. You're trying to apply logic to a situation that by its nature is illogical," I said.

Sawyer crossed his arms. "I'd buy the idea of retaliation. Most of us believe Andy couldn't have done this. We know how much he loved her, and even though they'd only dated a few months, I spent enough time with him to see he was a good guy."

Frank snorted. "Sawyer, you literally lost five thousand dollars last year in a Ponzi scheme. Your judgment isn't exactly stellar."

"It wasn't a Ponzi scheme, Uncle Frank. It was a business opportunity, and there were several unforeseeable factors that led to its failure."

"Yeah, like the fact it was a scam. Although, I wouldn't exactly call it unforeseeable. One quick Google search showed that guy who took your money wasn't really a Turkish prince."

Pink crept up from Sawyer's chest to his cheeks. "He had several professional athletes on his board of directors."

"Yeah, and they all look like fools now, too."

Elaine swatted at Frank. "Lay off the kid. At least he's doing more than just being a ski bum."

"He's not a ski bum!" Macy hit the table with her fist. "He's a very talented instructor."

Frank held up his hands in mock surrender. "Look, all I'm saying is his endorsement of Andy's character doesn't hold a lot of weight with me. All the evidence still seems to point to him."

"Andy is a good kid," Jane said. "Also, Andy is locked in the brig. He obviously wasn't the one who tried to steam Char like a dumpling."

"That is a lovely visual." Xavier's voice boomed from behind me. "May I take one of these empty chairs?"

"Please." Frank indicated the open seat next to me. Suddenly, he was Mr. Congeniality.

Xavier pulled the chair away from the table and floated into it. Even the way he sat down was suave.

"I see you disregarded the theme once again," I said under my breath.

His mouth twitched at the corner. "I am not a guest."

In his defense, his gray suit was timeless. Ah, the French

and their innate fashion sense. It felt a little unfair.

"Mr. Mesnier, can you explain to my tablemates here that you're confident you've got the right man, so the supposed attempted murder of Charlotte at the spa today was nothing but an accident?" Frank asked.

Xavier tilted his head. "Monsieur Braithwaite, when we dock in Seattle, I will be handing over all the evidence I have gathered to the appropriate investigative body for them to pursue. In the meantime, it is my duty to keep the residents of this ship safe. Disregarding a possible crime because it does not fit a certain narrative would be a dereliction of that duty."

"So, you're saying you think it was on purpose?" Macy asked.

"I spoke with Evangeline Irving. She was adamant it could only have been intentional."

Frank scoffed. "But Charlotte wasn't really in any danger, was she? I mean she was in a luxury spa."

Xavier folded his hands and placed them on the table in front of him. "The sauna was set to one hundred ninety-five degrees, which is at the top end of the preferred zone. My understanding is Madame McLaughlin was in there for approximately ten to fifteen minutes before Evangeline opened the door. That is treading dangerously close to the longest recommended time at that temperature."

My breath grew shallow, as if I were back in the sauna fighting for fresh air.

"It's very scary," Elaine said.

"It is. Because Monsieur Cobb was detained, there is no

way he is responsible for both attacks."

"But it also doesn't mean he didn't commit the first one." Frank folded his arms across his chest.

"I concur. However, until I have a clear understanding of the motive for the attack against Madame McLaughlin, I must presume someone on this ship, other than Monsieur Cobb, has ill intentions toward the members of the Cobb-Braithwaite wedding party."

"You're saying we're all in danger?" came a voice from behind me.

Everyone turned to look at the late arrivals.

Dale and Susan looked like the aftermath of a night at the Palladium in 1983. Their costumes were an eighties hairband rocker (Dale) and a discount store version of Madonna (Susan).

Dale's black parachute pants had an absurd number of zippers. His shirt was intentionally ripped in multiple places as if he'd been locked in a cage with a tiger. Several of the holes had been hooked back together with giant safety pins. He wore a red bandanna across his forehead, which created distinct separation between the crown of his bald head and the long gray hair that hung down from below it.

Susan wore an all-black mélange of taffeta, tulle, lace, and fishnet. It occurred to me that she was a woman named Susan who'd attempted to dress up like Madonna in the era she played a character named Susan…in a movie about a woman trying to embody the style and dress of Madonna/Susan.

I wasn't sure if it fell under the category of irony or simply a coincidence, but it caused a giggle to bubble up, which I quickly suppressed. Unfortunately, the gurgling sound that came out of my mouth caught everyone's attention.

"Char, are you alright?" Jane asked.

I coughed. "I'm fine. I just got an unexpected tickle in my throat." I swigged my water.

Dale and Susan sat in the empty chairs opposite me. Macy rubbed Susan's back in greeting. Susan gave her a wan smile.

"What were you saying about danger?" Dale's question was once again directed at Xavier.

"It would be premature in this investigation to assume who is the perpetrator and their intentions beyond the crimes already committed," Xavier said.

"Crimes? What do you mean, crimes? Phoebe was killed. What other crimes?" Dale demanded.

"Someone tried to boil Charlotte in the sauna like that bunny in *Fatal Attraction*." Frank chuckled.

"Must you be so uncouth?" Elaine tsked and rolled her eyes at her husband.

"All I'm saying is that there's real danger." Frank shrugged.

"You don't have to be harsh about it." Elaine shook her head vigorously.

Dale squinted at his sister-in-law. "Elaine, I think you're missing one of those expensive earrings of yours."

Her eyes flew open, and her left hand flew to her left ear. She looked momentarily confused when she came into contact with an earring. Then she touched her bare right ear and cried, "Oh no!"

She patted her blouse and then pulled it away from her chest to peek down her cleavage. Apparently, she didn't find it because she jumped up, held out her hands, and screamed, "Nobody move!"

Frank's face turned purple. "How could you not notice it was missing?" he thundered.

"I don't know! Everybody, look under your chairs."

The group murmured but did as they were told. The earring was nowhere to be found.

Just as Elaine began to wail, Clyde ran into the dining room dressed like a member of Run DMC in a red track suit and a tan bucket hat. His eyes were wild, and he was out of breath.

"Clyde, what's wrong?" Susan sat up, alarmed.

"Have you seen Ivy?" Clyde asked.

"Not since this morning. Why?"

"She never came back from the spa. I woke up from my nap and realized she wasn't there. I went down there to see when she would be done. They said she left hours ago! I can't find her anywhere."

XAVIER GATHERED US all in the captain's lounge on the eighth floor and organized a search party for Ivy. Each group was given a walkie-talkie to report any updates. If it weren't for the circumstances, the sight of us all in our eighties gear would have been quite comical.

Vance would scour the Santorini level where we were currently congregated.

Duncan, Serena, and Nikki were assigned the Mykonos level where Azure Lounge, the dining room, and the observation deck were located.

Dale, Susan, Frank, and Elaine took the Aegean level. They would knock on all the doors since Ivy and Clyde's room was on that floor. The hope was perhaps she'd ended up in the wrong room somehow or had made an acquaintance and was unaware she'd been reported missing.

Neal, Lily, and Clyde would search Capri, the fifth floor. In addition to the registration desk, the boutiques and medical center, it was also the level of the VIP sundeck and the Jacuzzi where Phoebe had been found. No one mentioned that fact, but we were all quite aware.

Officers Irving and Taylor were sent to the Perseus level. Not everyone knew that was the level where Phoebe's death had actually occurred, and I wasn't about to bring it up, but I sensed that was why no members of the bridal party had been assigned that location. Hopefully, someone had cleaned up the blood since I was last down there.

Xavier, Jane, Sawyer, Macy, and I would look for Ivy on the seventh level, Odyssey, as well as the tenth (and top) floor, Kalispera.

We started on Odyssey. Sawyer and Macy took one side of the hallway while Jane, Xavier, and I took the other. One by one, we knocked on doors and rang doorbells, asking if anyone had seen a petite blonde woman with light-blue eyes and a fair complexion. It was still during dinner service, so many of our attempts went unanswered.

By the time Xavier, Jane, and I got to stateroom 703, I was feeling quite discouraged.

I pressed the doorbell.

"Rhonda's gotta be in there." Jane turned to Xavier. "She wasn't at dinner."

Xavier made a noncommittal hum.

"She hasn't been to dinner once. Rhonda has…issues." I rang the doorbell again. I pounded on the door. "Rhonda!"

After a few moments, someone fumbled with the lock. Rhonda opened the door a crack.

"Gawd, Charlotte. What is it now? I was trying to sleep."

"You're always trying to sleep," I said dryly. "We're looking for Ivy Evans. Have you seen her?"

Rhonda sneered. "Why would I have seen Ivy? That little snob wouldn't give me the time of day."

"She's missing."

This caught her attention. She allowed the door to open wider, revealing the dining table covered with dirty dishes and crumpled napkins. Her bedsheets were tangled and hanging off the side of the bed. The ship had daily maid service, but Rhonda clearly hadn't availed herself of it since boarding.

"What do you mean missing?" She caught sight of Xavier pacing behind me. "Oh, this is bad, isn't it?"

"I hope not," I said. "We're trying to find her. We invited her to the spa in hopes of getting information that might help Andy. The last time I saw her, she was in the quiet room waiting to be called by the hair stylist."

"Yeah, right before someone locked Charlotte in the sauna." Jane folded her arms.

Rhonda covered her mouth. "That sounds awful. Are you okay?"

"I'm fine. You swear you haven't seen Ivy?"

Sawyer and Macy joined us.

"No luck." Sawyer looked at Rhonda and then back at me. "I'm guessing she's no help. She's useless."

A flash of hurt crossed Rhonda's face. "Sawyer, I'm going to give you a pass because I know you're worried about your sister."

"I don't need your passes, Rhonda. You know, like the one you made at me when you got drunk at Andy's house the night we met?"

Rhonda's face lost all color. "I can't help you, I'm sorry," she mumbled as she shut the door, followed by the sound of a lock being engaged.

Macy placed her hand on Sawyer's forearm. "That wasn't very nice."

Sawyer yanked his arm away from Macy. "She doesn't deserve nice."

Xavier clapped his hands together loudly. "We have reached a dead end on this floor. Literally. Let us move up to Kalispera."

"Wait," Jane said.

We all waited, expectantly.

"Isn't Kalispera outside?"

"*Oui.*"

"Then, can we pop into our room really quick and grab

some jackets? Despite the name, these legwarmers aren't going to do a whole lot for me in the freezing Alaska night."

"Good idea," I said.

Sawyer and Macy followed us into our suite while Xavier waited in the hall. I noticed Macy was wearing just a V-neck T-shirt.

"Macy, would you like a sweater or coat?" I asked.

"Yes, please. Thanks so much." She rubbed her throat. "I'm not prepared to be out in the cold."

I grabbed a long wool coat, a black ski parka, and a cable knit cardigan from my closet. I handed the parka to Sawyer, the wool coat to Macy, and pulled the cardigan over my shoulders.

Jane came out wearing a thick lavender puffy jacket. "Doesn't match, but it'll have to do."

We exited our room, and I shut the door behind us. I could have sworn I caught Xavier trying to hide a smile.

I'd already had the feeling I looked utterly ridiculous, and his reaction cemented my belief.

As we walked toward the elevator, a squawk came across Xavier's radio.

"Irving for Mesnier. Over."

Xavier pressed a button and held the radio to his mouth. "Mesnier here."

"We've completed our search of Perseus. Nothing out of the ordinary here. Would you like us to head down to Marina?"

"Please. When you're done, meet me on Kalispera."

"Will do. Over."

Xavier clipped his radio back onto his belt.

"What's Marina?" I asked.

"That is the crew quarters. She is not likely there, but we must explore the entire ship."

After a quick elevator ride, we exited onto the Kalispera deck.

Either the pamphlet or the welcome video had mentioned *Kalispera* was Greek for *Good afternoon*, and they'd named it that because it was the best location on the ship to get unobstructed views of sunsets. I supposed it also had good views of sunrises, but they had to choose one or the other to promote.

There were no staterooms, only a bar, a smallish pool, and a sundeck with lounge chairs. There was also a two-and-a-half-foot-wide running track marked out with a pink stripe across the deck. Apparently, if you ran that track twenty or so times, you'd have run a mile or something. I didn't understand why someone would choose that over the treadmill, and it was probably quite annoying to any sunbathers to have some sweaty person jog past them every few minutes.

Not that it mattered on this sailing. For the duration of the trip to Alaska, the Kalispera level had been closed. It was too cold for anyone to be hanging around drinking or swimming, so the bar was battened down and the pool had been covered. Everything else was covered with canvas and tacked into place to protect from the harsh arctic elements.

I pulled my cardigan tight, wishing my good manners hadn't prompted me to give my warmest outerwear to

Sawyer and Macy, leaving me somewhat exposed.

The sky was the kind of dark that only a moonless night in the middle of nowhere could bring. The only lights came from the ship and the stars blinking above us.

The ship was moving, sailing toward Glacier Bay. The turquoise ice the bay was famous for was to have been the backdrop for Andy and Phoebe's wedding tomorrow.

Thanksgiving Day.

It was difficult in that moment to find much for which to be thankful.

"Geez, it's freezing up here," Jane said.

"And dark." Macy's teeth chattered. "Ivy? You up here?"

There was no response.

Xavier pulled a small flashlight out from his inner coat pocket and began shining the light around the deck.

"What are the chances she would've come up here?" I asked, peering over the railing to the helipad below.

"What are the chances *anyone* would've come up here?" Sawyer blew warm breath into his hands and rubbed them together.

"If you prefer to wait in the captain's lounge, I am fine with that." Xavier scanned along the edge of the pool.

"Naw, let's get this over with." Sawyer pulled out his phone, turned on the flashlight, and began walking the perimeter of the sun deck. "There's no way she's out here, so let's make a quick pass and then get back inside where it's warm."

Macy pointed in the opposite direction. "I'm going to look over here."

I pulled out my phone and turned on the flashlight function as well. Xavier walked through what appeared to be stacks of lounge chairs. Jane and I huddled together and shuffled toward the bar area, an alcove off the sundeck. There were no bottles or glasses visible on the shelves, probably put away until the boat arrived in a warmer climate more conducive to hanging out on the deck sipping cocktails.

From behind us, Sawyer shouted, "Whoa!"

"What is it?" I yelled. "Did you find her?"

"No, but look." Sawyer pointed above us.

A broad stripe of neon green had appeared, streaking across the sky like a river flowing through the galaxy.

"It's the northern lights!" Macy squealed from the far side of the sundeck. "I've always wanted to see them. When I was nine, I watched a movie about it in school, and I've been obsessed ever since."

"It kind of reminds me of ghosts escaping a graveyard on an episode of *Scooby-Doo*," Jane whispered, her voice filled with awe. She walked over to the railing.

"It's spectacular," I said. "And it's getting brighter."

I backed up, attempting to take in the full view, when suddenly I tripped. "Oof!"

"Char! Are you okay?" Jane called.

"Yeah, I fell backward. I wasn't looking where I was going." I attempted to sit up but struggled to maneuver over whatever had caused me to stumble. I'd twisted my knee, so it twinged as I awkwardly scrambled to my feet. I shone my phone on the ground to identify the object.

Only it wasn't an object.

I let out the biggest scream of my life.

"Char!" Jane ran toward me.

Xavier, Macy, and Sawyer followed suit.

"What has happened?" Xavier asked. "Why did you scream?"

I was frozen in place, my light illuminating my ghastly discovery.

"*Mon Dieu,*" Xavier said.

"Oh no," Jane breathed.

The five of us gaped in horror at the eyes-wide-open, very-dead face of Ivy Evans.

Chapter Twenty-Two

I ROCKED BACK and forth on the sofa, trying to get warm but still feeling cold to the depths of my inmost being. It was the kind of cold that even the hot tea in my hands and heavy wool blanket wrapped around my shoulders couldn't fully abate, but I had yet to take a sip because it was scalding.

Jane and I were back in our stateroom attempting to recover from the shock of finding Ivy's body. The bloody head wound would live in my nightmares for years.

Windsor was in the kitchen washing dishes. It wasn't his job, but when he'd seen the emotional state that we were in when he brought the tea service, he'd said it was the least he could contribute.

Xavier was still on the scene. Shortly after our discovery, he'd radioed for Irving and Taylor to join him on the Kalispera deck as soon as possible. The other groups came up as well, but Xavier had positioned himself at the elevators to keep anyone from getting close to the body.

Susan had collapsed. A bald man with a ruddy complexion wearing khaki pants and a white polo shirt with a stethoscope hanging around his neck arrived moments later. He introduced himself as Dr. Fraser and then offered Susan a sedative.

Dale had taken a Xanaxed Susan, along with Macy, Sawyer, and Lily, back to the captain's lounge.

Clyde refused to leave while his wife was up there, so Neal offered to stay with him. Xavier agreed as long as they stayed at least twenty feet from the investigation.

"This is beyond a nightmare." Jane lightly sipped her tea. "Poor Ivy."

"Poor Ivy," I parroted. "Who would do this? And why?"

Jane shook her head. "I don't think there's any way to make sense of this."

I bit the inside of my cheek. "I feel responsible."

"Why?"

"Because if I hadn't been so hell-bent on questioning Ivy, she wouldn't have even come to the spa."

"That's ridiculous, Char. We were in a spa on a luxury cruise ship, adrift at sea in the frozen middle of nowhere. In what universe would anyone think that was a dangerous situation unless you're reenacting the *Titanic*?"

She had a point, although, the cruise had become more dangerous by the day. Passengers were dropping like flies.

"Two sisters have been murdered," she continued. "Someone has a grudge, and I'd place money it doesn't have anything to do with us or Andy."

"Of course, it has to do with us, Jane. Someone's trying to frame Andy, and they tried to murder me also."

"Maybe. Or maybe they just wanted you out of the way long enough to lure Ivy from the spa without either of us seeing them. The manager said she didn't see Ivy leave."

I sat up straight. "You're right! And if that's the case, the person knows we'd recognize them."

"So, are we officially ruling out the idea of the unknown stalker being the murderer?"

"Not necessarily. What if the unknown stalker was known to Phoebe?"

"What do you mean?"

"No one knows the identity of Phoebe's stalker, but that doesn't mean the stalker was unknown to the family. It could have been one of the groomsmen or one of her brothers-in-law. And if Phoebe knew them, Ivy probably knew them, too."

"Good point," Jane said. "Except, I thought we ruled out Clyde and Neal."

"I'm not so sure about that. Ivy's death has reopened all possibilities. Other than Ivy, of course."

"So, what if Clyde and Phoebe also had an affair?"

"That would be pretty gross, but I guess it's possible. If she did it with one, she could have done it with the other."

"What I mean is, maybe Neal killed Phoebe out of jealousy over her affair with Clyde."

"Then why kill Ivy? It would make more sense for him to kill Clyde."

"Ehhh, okay, what about this…Phoebe was going to tell Ivy about the affair, so Clyde killed her to keep her quiet?"

"And then he volunteered to help Andy while simultaneously framing him?"

Jane gave me a knowing glance. "What better way to keep a close eye on the investigation? He'd always be one step ahead of the cops."

"They aren't technically cops. So, let me humor you for a moment. If Clyde killed Phoebe to protect his marriage, why would he then turn around and kill his wife?"

She shrugged. "Dunno. I'm just spitballing here. Maybe she found out he killed her sister and was going to tell Mesnier." She tapped her finger on her lips. "Although, I'm still not convinced this isn't all related to Frank's business."

"Hmm." I took a large gulp of my tea and immediately regretted it. "Ow! That's hot."

"What do you mean, *hmm*?"

"What? Oh, it just occurred to me that we always refer to it as Frank's business."

"Right…and?"

"But it's not only Frank's business. It's also Dale's business." I set my teacup down on the table in front of me.

"Sounds like in name only."

"That's how Frank describes it, but that may not be the whole story."

"What are you saying? Are you saying Dale had something to do with his daughters' deaths?"

"No, but Jane, think about it. Setting aside the nefarious stuff Phoebe suspected her uncle had gotten involved with, Dale is a fifty-percent partner in the business. Who stands to inherit Dale's portion?"

"I don't know. Probably Susan."

"Maybe. Or maybe it's the kids."

"Okay."

"And?"

"And what, Char? I'm sorry, I'm exhausted and my brain isn't working. What are you trying to say?"

"There are—were—four Braithwaite kids. That means each one of them were likely due to inherit twenty-five percent of his fifty-percent share."

She squinted. "I don't do math."

"It's roughly twelve and a half percent of the company each."

"Okay?"

"Now that Ivy and Phoebe are gone, Sawyer and Lily are due to inherit twenty-five percent of the company each. That's a significant increase, based on the value of the company from what I've heard."

"Are you saying you think either Sawyer or Lily killed their siblings to get an additional twelve and a half percent of a company they won't inherit until after their father is dead?" She scoffed. "I find that hard to believe."

"Look, I'm not saying it's what happened. I'm just saying we need to look at all angles of this. Money is a compelling motive."

THAT NIGHT I tossed and turned, unable to sleep. I couldn't escape images of Ivy lying dead at my feet or the visual of the blood on the pole Xavier believed was the cause of her head injury.

She'd been outside in the cold night air long enough that tiny icicles had begun to form around her nostrils.

It was that image I struggled with the most. I wasn't an expert, but I was pretty sure that meant Ivy was still breathing for a while after the attack. She'd been left there, incapacitated, to freeze to death. I said a prayer that she hadn't suffered, but the pit in my stomach said it was likely she had.

The next morning, I stumbled into the kitchen to find Jane drinking coffee and staring out the window.

"Morning." My voice sounded froggy.

"Happy Thanksgiving."

"Gah. It's so weird, isn't it?"

"It's awful. That's what it is. This was supposed to be the happiest day of Andy's life. Instead, his bride is dead, her sister is dead, and he's locked in the brig of a ship."

The glass coffeemaker thingamajig sat on the counter, filled with dark brown liquid. A paper towel peeked over the lip. "Did you make coffee?"

"Yeah, I figured we might as well learn how to use this contraption."

I nodded at the kettle on the stove with steam still wafting out of the spout. "That would explain the dream I had about being tied to railroad tracks as a locomotive bore down on me. How did it turn out?"

"Remember that time we were at Sophia Grigoryan's garden party and we didn't know not to drink the sludge at the bottom of the Armenian coffee she served after lunch?"

"Yes. You started talking like an auctioneer and then puked in her rosebush."

Jane's face was somber. "Kinda like that. So, I've got

good news and bad news. Which would you like to hear first?"

This was a game Jane insisted on playing, despite the fact that for more than five decades I'd answered the same way every time. Our grandmother had taught us to always face the tough stuff first so it could be tempered by the positive.

"The bad news. That way, the good news can wash it away."

"The bad news is we missed the Thanksgiving parade. New York is four hours ahead."

"I'll survive. I mean, you've seen one giant floating cartoon character, you've pretty much seen them all. Except that year when it was really windy and two of the balloons broke loose."

Jane laughed. "That was amazing. It looked like the cartoon cat was beating up that giant whiny preschooler."

"So, what's the good news?"

"There's a football game that starts in fifteen minutes."

"That is good news. Maybe we could order room service." It was then I remembered Andy wouldn't be able to watch the game with us because he was being held on suspicion of murder. "It's hard to enjoy any of this knowing Andy's locked up somewhere on the ship. We should take him some food."

Jane's face fell. "I thought about that, too. Do you think Xavier will let us?"

"He'd better. It makes no sense to keep him locked up. He obviously couldn't have killed Ivy."

"He'll probably say, *Just because he could not have mur-*

dered one does not mean he could not have murdered zee other."

"Your French accent is terrible," I said.

"*Sacre bleu!*"

I grabbed the coffee decanter and attempted to pour it into a mug. It moved like lava. "I believe there are actual filters for this thing. They'll probably hold up better than paper towels."

"I couldn't find 'em. At least we'll have all the energy we need to get through this day."

"I'm gonna need a spoon to get through this coffee." I grabbed a napkin and attempted to skim some of the floating grounds from the surface. "Why did you say that, about the coffee maker thing?"

"What do you mean?"

"Earlier. You said, *I figured we might as well learn to use this contraption*. Why did you say that when we're only here for three more nights?"

Jane's left eyebrow arched. "Don't tell me you haven't thought about it. I know it's crossed your mind."

I took a sip and spit several grounds into the napkin. "Thought about what?"

"Staying."

I blinked at her twice. "Staying where?"

"Here." She waved her hand in the air. "This suite. The ship is designed for people to live here full-time if they want."

"You've lost your mind." I snorted.

"You've already paid the bulk of the cost—well, Gabe did—and if you sell the house you won't have to worry about anything."

"You can't be serious. It's a ridiculous idea." A ridiculous idea I'd momentarily considered, but I couldn't tell her that. Besides, I'd already decided against it.

"Why is it ridiculous? You can just float from city to city, exploring and meeting new people all over the world."

"And leave my job, friends, leave Andy? That sounds lonely. It's way too much change. I've had enough change recently, thank you very much."

"You work part-time at a library. I hate to break it to you, but I think they'll survive without you. And you won't be alone. I'll be here." Jane shrugged. "I've been thinking about retiring anyway, while I'm still young and all my joints are working. I can't afford to travel the world on my savings, but we can do it together, here."

"The sea currents must be affecting you. What do they call that? Ocean madness? Scurvy?"

"You know darn well scurvy is a vitamin C deficiency, not a mental health disorder."

"Whatever. You're not thinking straight."

She gave me a resolute smile. "Oh, I'm thinking quite clearly. You. Me. The open seas, the exotic ports of call, the full-time butler."

"Jane—"

"Char, come on, it will be good for you. For us!"

"I don't think—"

"Trust me. This is just what the doctor—"

"Jane, enough!"

It was like the air had been sucked out of the room. Her

face fell.

"Look, I'll promise I'll think about it when Andy's in the clear and I'm on solid ground again. Literally and figuratively."

"No, it's fine."

I could barely hear her over the sound of my pulsing head. "Jane, I—"

"Seriously, Char. Forget I brought it up."

JANE HELD THE door to the security office for me as I carried the tray of food across the threshold. We'd barely exchanged a word since our tiff.

Irving was sitting at his desk, but Taylor's was vacant.

"Morning, ladies. I see you brought me breakfast. So thoughtful of you."

I set the tray on Taylor's desk. "This isn't for you. It's for Andy."

"He's not here."

Jane placed her hands on Irving's desk and leaned toward him. "Lonnie, where is he?"

I'd seen her use this intimidation tactic at the library, but I had little confidence it would be as effective on a grown man as it was to pre-adolescent boys looking at paintings of naked women in Renaissance art books.

They engaged in a minor staring contest. When Irving finally blinked, Jane gave a gasp and stood upright.

Irving sighed. "He's in the library off the captain's quarters. Taylor's watching him."

"Why was he moved?" Jane asked.

Irving became flushed. "You'll have to speak with Xavier."

"And where might he be?" I asked.

"I believe he's not come in yet this morning."

I slanted my head. "He's still in his room? Is that unusual?"

"A little, but I know he had a late night."

Once again, Jane leaned on his desk. "Perhaps you should tell us his room number so we can check on him. Make sure he's okay."

"Wh-why wouldn't he be?"

"Perhaps you haven't noticed, but people seem to be falling like ninepins around here." She used her intimidating voice to go along with her intimidating posture.

I scrunched my face. "Falling like what?"

She bobbed her head. "Ninepins. It's a bowling reference. I learned it from a British friend of mine."

Irving picked up the phone. "I'll just call him."

We waited as he dialed the number. As quickly as the pink had risen up his neck, across Irving's cheeks and up to his forehead, it began to retreat, leaving in its wake a paleness that was rarely seen on a living human.

"M-maybe someone should check on him. It's just, I can't leave my post."

Jane waved off his concerns like a swarm of gnats. "No problem. Like we said, we'll go down and check on him. What did you say his room number was again?"

Chapter Twenty-Three

"HE'S GOING TO kill Irving for giving us his room number. You know that, right?" I balanced the tray and pushed the elevator button for the third level, Marina.

"He'll understand. Irving was just looking out for his best interest," Jane said.

"This feels like an invasion of privacy."

"Char, Mesnier is a big boy. He'll be fine. We've gotta keep our eye on the prize here."

"Which is?"

"Which is finding the real killer so we can exonerate Andy and get him off this floating house of horrors."

I shifted my weight from my left foot to my right. "I have a confession."

She eyed me from beneath an arched brow. "Did you kill Phoebe and Ivy?"

One fight and now she thought I was capable of murder? "Not that kind of confession. This boat…"

"Ship."

"Ship. Whatever. It's kind of growing on me."

"Aha!"

"That doesn't mean I want to give up my life. But I am

enjoying the daily maid service, a butler who brings me coffee in the morning, amazing meals, amazing scenery…"

"Not to mention a handsome Frenchman keeping watch over you."

I made a guffaw combined with a gurgling chortle. "He's not keeping watch over me. He's keeping watch over the ship. And not very well, I might add. The crime rate's pretty high."

"Methinks the lady…" She smirked, not finishing the famous *Hamlet* quote.

Jane's amusement annoyed me to no end, but if I protested any more, she'd never let it drop. I also swallowed my correction of her phrasing of the quote.

The elevator opened, and we walked down the corridor to room 302.

"Who's gonna knock?" Jane asked.

"What difference does it make?"

"I think it should be you. He'll be less annoyed."

"Why?"

Jane clucked. "Come on, Char, you're not that clueless. He's got a soft spot for you."

"I don't see it."

For a brief moment, as we stood in front of that door, I felt a twinge of something I hadn't experienced in a very long time. Anticipation. Butterflies. Nerves.

My marriage to Gabe in many ways had been like a dream. Not a fantasy, more like an out-of-body experience. Detached. Disassociated. Disconnected. Oblivious.

It had hurt to lose him, and it hurt to know he'd been

unfaithful, but if I were completely honest with myself, it was more embarrassing than anything. I'd been going through the motions for a very long time. I couldn't even say for sure when we'd moved from the honeymoon phase into domestic monotony, but that was no excuse for him to take up with someone (or some*ones*) else.

He should have had the courage to tell me he wanted something different. Something more. He owed me that because he'd promised me before God and everyone we knew. I didn't blame him for feeling unfulfilled. I blamed him for taking the easy way out and not giving me the dignity and respect the twenty years I'd spent with him deserved.

As I shifted the tray to my left hand to knock on Xavier's door, I had the fleeting notion I wanted something more as well. Of course, not with the man holding my nephew on suspicion of a murder he hadn't committed, but the spark I felt when I was around him meant that part of me hadn't completely burned out.

My first attempt to rouse him went unanswered. As did the second.

"He must not be here," I said.

"Try once more. He's probably still in bed. Maybe he's a heavy sleeper."

Xavier sleeping in his bed. A wave of goose bumps washed across my arms. I knocked a third time. There was some sort of commotion inside the berth.

Jane's eyes grew wide. "Someone's in there."

From the other side of the door came the sound of the

lock turning. It opened to reveal a haggard-looking Xavier. His curly hair was extra poufed, and his facial scruff was practically a beard. He wore pajama bottoms and no shirt.

He grunted, sighed, and muttered something in French I couldn't understand. "*Bonjour, mesdames.* What can I do for you on this early morning?" He paused for effect. "On my day off, no less."

"How can you take a day off in the middle of a string of murders?" I put my hands on my hips.

"I do not plan to take the whole day, but I had planned to sleep a while longer. I have had many late nights since the Braithwaite-Cobb wedding party boarded this ship." His tone held a hint of derision and accusation.

I attempted to keep my gaze on his face and not his naked torso. "Sorry to disturb you, but Jane and I were hoping to have a word."

"You brought your own food for this meeting?"

"No, it's for Andy." I gave him a pointed look.

"*Bien sûr.* Of course." He sighed again. "May I have a moment to get dressed?"

"Oh, uh, yes. Should we wait for you here in the hall?"

He knit his brows together and squinted at me. "I am not a heathen. Come inside. I will be out shortly." He began to step back and stopped. "How did you find my residence?"

Jane and I exchanged glances. We didn't want to get Irving in trouble with his boss.

"Never mind. *Venez.* Come."

Xavier's cabin was nicer than I expected for a crew member. Unlike his old-world style office, his suite was sleek and modern. Not sparse, but definitely not cluttered with a lot of personal items.

"Not bad." Jane whistled. "He must get the best cabin because of his job. I had a friend who worked on a cruise ship one summer. She'd grown up obsessing over *The Love Boat*, so she signed up to be part of the entertainment corps. I saw the pics. She was jammed into a tiny room with three other girls, sleeping on bunk beds. They didn't even have their own bathroom." She plopped into an armchair.

I set the tray onto the coffee table and sat on the firm gray sofa. "Why did she only do it for one summer?"

"She met a trumpet player from Spain. Eloped at a port-of-call somewhere in the Mediterranean, and he came home with her a couple of weeks later."

"Wow. I can't imagine being that spontaneous. Did it work out?"

"Twenty years later, they've got two daughters and a theme restaurant in Sausalito."

"Good for them."

"Onboard romances are rarely sustainable." Jane said.

Xavier had changed into khaki pants and was pulling on a navy-blue crewneck as he entered the room. I caught a glimpse of his stomach. How did a man of his age stay in such good shape?

Gabe had gained a paunch and sagging jowls by the time he was forty. I hadn't cared, as I had my own gravitational struggles to deal with and he'd never been critical. I'd been grateful for that, believing he accepted me as I was.

Turned out, he'd simply replaced me with a younger

model. Apparently, Gabe's middle-aged body hadn't bothered Kyrie Dawn.

Would he have replaced her someday as well?

"Right, Char?" Jane said.

I turned to her. "What?"

"I said, onboard relationships can be sustained if two people are fated to be together."

"Fate." Xavier scoffed. "There is no such thing."

Jane pursed her lips. "I beg to differ."

I held up my hands in mock surrender. "No need for arguing. We're here to talk about something important."

Xavier sat in the chair opposite Jane and stared her down like she was an opponent. He folded his hands in his lap. "I am listening."

"First, we'd like to say we know you've been working very hard to solve this case," Jane said.

He eyed her skeptically.

"Charlotte and I would like to understand why you are still holding Andy, despite the fact he couldn't have possibly killed Ivy, and that should also rule him out for killing Phoebe."

He blinked three times. "How do you figure?"

"Come on, you can't possibly believe there is more than one murderer on this ship," Jane said.

"In my experience, everyone is capable of murder depending on circumstances."

"*You* said basically the same thing a couple days ago," I reminded her.

She swatted away my words. "I meant that anyone could

have murdered one person. But two murders committed by two separate people? Where the victims are *sisters*? Within days of each other on a ship at sea?" She shook her head. "Not buying it."

Xavier jutted his chin. "I agree it seems unlikely. However, I cannot disregard the vast evidence that points in the direction of your nephew. The fingerprints on the knife. The phone stashed in your sofa. His professional knowledge of technology that enabled him to disable the security cameras."

"Speaking of cameras." I held up a finger. "Wouldn't the cameras have shown what Ivy was doing and who was with her in the time leading up to our discovery of her body?"

"Yes and no. We have video footage of the elevator. She was alone. Nothing on Kalispera. Currently, those cameras are not running since that area is closed for this trip."

"You can disregard all those things you listed anyway. You know, the supposed evidence that points to Andy's guilt," Jane said. "It's all been planted. He's obviously being framed."

Something niggling at the back of my mind finally floated to the surface. "Phoebe's phone was found in our cabin after Andy had come to stay with us."

"*Oui*?"

"So how did it get there?"

He gave me a pitying expression. "How do you think?"

"What I mean is, didn't you check out Andy, looking for signs of a struggle with Phoebe?"

"Dr. Fraser examined him."

"And?"

"Nothing to indicate a struggle."

"And I assume you looked for the knife on his person at that time."

"I believe Officer Taylor searched Monsieur Cobb for weapons."

"But he found no phone?"

Xavier rubbed his chin. "Only his phone."

"Andy was escorted straight to our room after that search and kept there. How could he have picked up her phone from whatever hiding place and when?"

He pressed his lips into a straight line. "You make a point."

"I make a *good* point."

His mouth ticked up at the corner with a slight twitch of a smile. "You make a valid point. However, he was in your apartment shortly after Phoebe's body was discovered and prior to the examination. He could have placed the phone at that time."

"Jane, did he go into the living room?"

Her forehead creased. "I can't remember. He was pacing. Regardless, he was never unattended in our living room."

"Hmm." Xavier sounded unconvinced. "Not even when one of you used the toilet?"

Jane scowled and crossed her arms. "So, you're saying you won't release him?"

"I am sorry. I cannot at this time. I understand your concern, but please trust me that I will do my job well."

"Can we at least take him the food we brought?" she asked.

"I promise you; he is being well fed by our award-winning chef."

The phone rang. Xavier stood and walked over to answer it.

"*Allo*?" He listened for the response. "I had ear plugs. I could not hear the phone." He glanced at Jane and me with a small smirk. "*Oui*, they are here. They had not given away your secret yet." He laughed. "*C'est bon*. It is fine." His eyes widened. "Is that so? Very interesting indeed. Can you forward that information to me in an email?" He looked at us once more and smiled, this time a genuine smile. "*Oui*. I will speak with you later."

He hung up the phone. "We have a development."

Jane and I waited for him to continue. He seemed to enjoy prolonging our eagerness.

"Well?" Jane finally said.

"That was Officer Irving. My contact in Seattle has come through with some interesting news that may pertain to this case."

"Two *interestings* in two minutes." I folded my hands. "Care to share?"

Xavier lowered himself back into the chair. "I do not think that is wise."

"If it's about Andy…" I said.

"It is not."

"Then who? Frank?"

He flinched.

"It is about Frank!" I said.

He tightened his mouth. "You cannot repeat this. To

anyone."

Jane and I both nodded vigorously.

"This morning a raid took place at Braithwaite Industrial Storage."

I sat straight. "A raid?"

He tented his fingers. "It seems the company has been under scrutiny for some time. A joint operation between Homeland Security, the United States Coast Guard, the USDA, local law enforcement, and the FBI, and today they executed a warranted search of the premises."

"And? What did they find?" Jane was practically yelling at him.

"Wait, did you say the USDA, as in the Department of Agriculture?"

"Several international smuggling operations have been using the facilities to traffic in all sorts of things, from stolen antiquities to weapons to, yes, illegal seafood, meats from endangered animals, and rare plants. Some of the items were hidden in Russian dolls."

"Russian dolls!" I said.

Jane pursed her lips. "That's what Phoebe was trying to relay to Ivy." She blew out a breath.

Xavier narrowed his gaze and jutted his chin toward her. "What do you mean?"

"I may have forgotten to mention it in the hubbub of looking for Ivy." I shrugged. "Oops."

"*Oops*?" he repeated. He closed his eyes and pinched the bridge of his nose. "What did you forget to mention?"

"When we were in the quiet room at the spa with Ivy, we

may have questioned her a bit about Frank and why Phoebe was upset with him. Phoebe told Ivy she had to do something important at work, so if she missed the boat, ask Frank about the Russian dolls. We weren't sure if it was code for something or if there were actual, physical dolls."

"There were smuggled items within Russian dolls. The most significant discovery they made, however, and even more odd than the dolls, was a locker full of pangolins and pangolin products."

"What in the world is a pangolin?" Jane asked.

"Isn't that like an armadillo?"

"You are not far off the mark." Xavier pointed to me. "A pangolin is a scaled animal approximately the size of a housecat up to a medium-sized dog. It is quite rare. It is trafficked for its scales, meat, and blood. The meat is considered a delicacy by some, and the scales and blood supposedly have some medicinal properties. They boil the poor creatures to remove the scales."

"I knew Frank was a snake!" Jane slapped the arms of the chair.

"I thought he was a creep, but I didn't think he was some sort of sadistic kingpin."

"Kingpin may be a stretch. Although his crimes appear to be connected to large operations, it does not appear he is the puppeteer. More likely he is the stooge who looks the other way while the big boys do their maneuvering."

Jane's expression became pinched. "You seem to know a whole lot about this sting despite only getting a fifteen-second update just now."

"I have been aware of the investigation since before you boarded this ship in Seattle."

"How can that be?" I asked.

"My job is to keep the passengers and crew safe. That includes background checks on all new owners and on all guests. When you submitted the request, I ran the manifest against all my resources to see if there were any issues of concern. My search triggered one of the systems, and I got a call from one of the investigating officers on the smuggling case. He suggested I allow Monsieur Braithwaite onboard in order for them to execute the warrant without interference."

Jane glared at him. "All this time you knew he was a criminal and you let Andy look like the bad guy?"

"Wait. You investigated me?" My chest tightened at the thought. Then I remembered his look of pity at our introduction. He knew everything about me, and I knew nothing about him.

HERE LIES CHARLOTTE MCLAUGHLIN,
ALWAYS THE LAST TO KNOW.

His gaze locked onto mine and several emotions flashed across his face. Some of them I recognized, but some I did not. Pity was still chief among them, and it infuriated me.

I thrust myself off the sofa and marched toward the door.

"Char, wait, where are you going?"

"Madame McLaughlin, please."

But I kept going. I couldn't take one more consolatory look from anyone. It was starting to affect how I viewed myself, and that felt deeply unfair.

I wasn't dumb. I wasn't pathetic.

I'd be damned if I'd let one more person treat me like I was.

Chapter Twenty-Four

THE ELEVATOR STOPPED on the sixth floor, even though I'd pressed the button for nine and I was alone. I had yet to decide if I was going to eat in the dining room or head straight to Azure Lounge for a mimosa. Better yet, a Bloody Mary.

The doors opened and Dale was standing inside looking like a sad puppy.

No, like a man who'd lost two of his daughters in tragically awful ways within days of each other. The bags under his eyes had bags, and those bags had fanny packs. His gray hair was somehow both frizzy and greasy. His clothes were rumpled, and I was pretty sure he hadn't showered in a while.

"Morning, Char."

I noticed he didn't say *good* morning. "Dale. Did you sleep at all?"

"I haven't slept much since we got on this damn boat."

"Hard to believe today is Thanksgiving."

"Is it? Oh, yeah, I guess it is." His eyes were bloodshot, but I couldn't tell if it was from lack of sleep, the marijuana I smelled on him, or both.

I wanted to ask him if he knew about the raid or what Frank had been up to, but I didn't want to jeopardize that case or Andy's. Instead, I asked the most benign question I could come up with. "You going to breakfast?"

"No, I was hoping to grab something for Susan. She's back in the room."

"How is she?"

His mouth turned so heavily downward his face mimicked a Greek tragedy mask. "She's pretty out of it. Dr. Fraser gave her some strong stuff to get her by."

"Should she be left alone?"

"She's not. Macy's there with her. She's been there all night. I don't know how we'd get through this without her. Sawyer picked a good one."

I couldn't grasp the level of pain Susan was experiencing, but I was surprised to hear Macy wasn't comforting her boyfriend. After all, he'd lost two of his three sisters. "I can't remember. How did they meet?"

He rubbed the back of his neck. "Uh, coffee shop, I'm pretty sure. Macy's a barista at a place near Sawyer's apartment."

"Ah, that's right. Well, I'm glad she's been such a support to you guys. I've felt completely helpless."

The elevator doors opened, and we both exited.

"How is Sawyer holding up?" I asked.

"Sawyer's doing what he always does when life gets hard: he shuts out everyone who cares about him. I'm sure he's holed up in his room smoking pot and pretending none of it is happening."

It was an ironic statement considering the contact high I was getting simply from having ridden in the elevator with Dale.

Dale stared at me for a long moment, his eyes filled with tears. "I need you to do me a favor."

"Anything."

He shifted his jaw back and forth. "I know Andy's your nephew. Hell, he's more than a nephew, you practically raised him. But if you know anything, anything at all, that might shed light on what happened to my girls, please, I'm begging you, don't keep it to yourself to protect him. Let him deal with the consequences of his actions."

"I would never withhold information that would give you closure, even if it meant seeing Andy go to prison. You have my word. But I know that boy better than his own mother. I know what he's capable of and what he isn't. He wouldn't—couldn't—do this."

Dale flared his nostrils. "I hope you're right. And I hope you mean what you say." He turned on his heel and walked away.

I stood there long enough to decide my next move. "Bloody Mary it is."

I wandered into the bar, which was nearly empty. Understandable, considering it wasn't yet lunchtime. A hooded figure was huddled in the corner.

"Sawyer?"

He lifted his head, his eyes bloodshot like his father's.

I indicated the chair across from him. "Mind if I sit?"

He emitted a small grunt and dropped his head back

down, which I took as assent.

He was a good-looking kid, as were all his siblings. His hair was a darker shade of blond than Phoebe and the twins, but it had that bleached tip typical of surfers and skiers. His summer tan, which came from his off-season job leading hikes and mountain bike rides, had nearly faded just in time for the start of the ski season.

In the Cascade Mountain passes, lifts didn't often open until after Thanksgiving, which was one of the reasons Phoebe had selected the date for her wedding, to ensure her brother would be able to attend. It didn't have to be in November, as for the past few years the openings had been pushed back to December due to unseasonably warm autumns–which was likely to be the case again this year–but Phoebe hadn't wanted to take any chances.

"Can I get you anything? Coffee? A drink?"

He sat up and slumped back in the chair, pulling his hood off in the process. "Nah. Thanks, though. You don't look so great yourself."

Ah, the unfiltered honesty of the younger generation. "It's been a lot. Not as much for you, I know, but still, not a fun few days."

Sawyer caught Egan's eye, and he sauntered over.

"Rough night?" Egan asked.

I tried to not take it personally. "You could say that. I thought you worked in the other bar."

"Cortez took today off, so I'm covering. What can I do you for?"

"Can I get a Bloody Mary?"

"Sure. Which one?"

"Which one what?" I blinked at him.

"We've got a variety." He began to tally them on his fingers, his Irish brogue in full effect. "We got yer basic, then we got the shrimpy Mary—that one's got the whole shrimp cocktail vibe goin' on. We got the Greek Maria. She's feta cheese stuffed kalamata olive skewers with some cukes and cherry tomahtoes. The Southern Gentlemary has fried chicken, waffles, and bacon, all smothered in syrup. And then there's the granddaddy of them all."

Sawyer and I both stared at him, awaiting the finale.

"If yer really in the mood for somethin' to take the edge off—you know, hair of the dog that bit you and such—yer gonna wanna go with the Opa."

"I'm afraid to even ask," I said.

He splayed both hands out with palms down like he was showing us his nicely manicured fingers. "Picture this. You've got yer top shelf vodka, yer lemon vodka, yer cucumber vodka. Then we start adding the skewers. Sure, we got yer olives stuffed with cheese, celery, pickled 'sparagus, tomahtoes, cucumbers, but then we're gonna take it up a notch." As he named off each ingredient, he shot his finger like a gun and made the accompanying sound effect. "Onion rings. *Pew.* Corn dogs. *Pew.* Peppered bacon. *Pew.* Beef slider. Chicken wing. Soft salted pretzel. *Pew, pew, pew.*" He raised his hands and mimicked the explosion of fireworks. "*Opa*!"

Even in our somber moods, Sawyer and I couldn't help but applaud.

"So, shall I order one Opa for the table or two?" Egan looked expectant.

If the so-called drink didn't kill me, my doctor would. "As intriguing as that all sounds, I think I'll stick with the classic."

"Aww. So disappointing. Maybe next time. What about you?" he asked Sawyer.

"Sorry, man. I got heartburn just listening to that. I'll have a diet soda."

Egan pouted a bit but didn't argue. He went back to the bar and began working on our orders.

"I just saw your dad in the elevator. He seemed to think you were in your room," I said.

Sawyer ran his fingers through his hair and sighed. "I needed some fresh air."

I didn't argue the point, even though the ship was sealed tight against the cold Alaska air. I glanced out the window to the observation deck. One couple stood taking in the view of Glacier Bay, but they looked miserable. The woman was shivering, and the man was trying to warm her by putting his arm around her, but they were so stiff I thought perhaps they'd started to freeze in place.

The view beyond them was spectacular, though, so I didn't blame them for trying. The skies were a shade of blue I'd never seen before. Just looking at it evoked the feeling of a deep cleansing breath. I supposed it was what the air had looked like before the Industrial Revolution began polluting the atmosphere with particulates. The water, reflecting the sky, was an icy aqua, offset by the glacier at its edge and snow-covered mountains beyond.

There was a serenity that came from seeing something nearly untouched by the grubby hands of mankind.

Perhaps that's what Sawyer meant by *fresh air*.

"Your dad says Macy's been quite supportive."

His gaze was distant, numb. "Yeah, she's been great for them."

There was something unspoken, but I left it alone. "Can you think of any reason why someone would want to hurt your sisters?"

He slowly shook his head, as if mentally sweeping out the cobwebs of grief. "Not even one. Sure, Ivy could be a pain in the ass, but she was a beautiful human. And Phoebe..." His voice broke. "Phoebe always wanted to believe the best in people. She was the queen of second chances. Sometimes even to her detriment."

"How so?"

He leveled his gaze at me. "Things weren't perfect between her and Andy, you know."

The intensity of his stare sent a shiver down my spine. "No relationship is perfect."

"Did you know I almost didn't come on this cruise?"

"I heard something of the sort. I believe Phoebe said you were upset she didn't put Macy in the wedding."

His laugh was without humor. "Of course, she did. I mean, you can't really admit you're making a mistake getting married in the middle of your wedding cruise, can you? Figures she'd put it on Macy."

"Can you elaborate?"

"First, even though they only knew each other a few months, Macy was a better friend to Phoebe in that short amount of time than Nikki has ever been. Mace had a pretty rough upbringing, so she treated Phoebe like the sister she'd always wanted. I do think Pheebs should have put her in the wedding, but I get it. Our relationship was new when she and Andy started planning. For all Phoebe knew, we might not have lasted this long. I haven't had a great track record in terms of long relationships. Macy understood Phoebe's reasoning as well. We were fine with the decision, more so than Lily when she discovered she wasn't a bridesmaid."

I shifted in my seat. How could I have mistaken Lily being upset about Phoebe not including her as a bridesmaid for her knowing her husband had slept with her sister?

"Anyway," he continued, "that most definitely wasn't the reason I was gonna boycott the wedding. Look, I'm not trying to hurt your feelings here, but it was inevitable my sister would come to the conclusion Andy isn't–wasn't–worthy of her. He's a teacher, she was a celebrity with more than a million followers."

"Hard not to be offended. Are you saying teaching children is less important than posting videos of yourself making avocado toast?"

"I'm not saying that, but I knew Phoebe, and I knew how she was. In her mind, she wasn't just making toast. She was an entrepreneur."

"And her product was herself?"

"Yes, her brand that she created from scratch as a kid."

"All of that is admirable, really, but one of the reasons

your sister fell in love with Andy was because he offered her a real life, not a fake one designed for the cameras. She obviously found out how dangerous that could be."

He pursed his lips. "You don't get it. They were never gonna work." He reached into the front pocket of his sweatshirt to pull out his phone. He began scrolling and apparently found what he was looking for, because he shoved the phone in my face.

"What am I looking at?"

"Press play."

I grabbed the phone from him and began to watch the video he'd queued up for me. It was dimly lit and somewhat grainy, made worse by the cracks in the phone screen. It wasn't the quality of the videos Phoebe normally posted to her channel, which were always heavily edited and showed her most flattering angles. I could barely make out Phoebe and Andy's faces, but their voices were unmistakable over the pulsing din of nightclub music.

"Phoebe, it's time to go home," Andy shouted. His face was red, probably from anger, but possibly augmented by the lighting.

"You're not my father!" She stumbled to the side, obviously intoxicated.

"No, unlike your father, I'm actually here for you."

She threw her drink in his face, and he shouted profanity. "You're a jerk!"

He wiped his face with his sleeve. "I'm trying to protect you from yourself."

"I only need protection from you!" She got in his face

until they were nose-to-nose.

"Get out of my face, Phoebe. I'm warning you."

"Or what? You're gonna hit me? I dare you."

Andy pushed her with both hands. I gasped as I watched Phoebe fall backward onto the floor. A figure rushed into view to tend to Phoebe. It was Macy. She shot a scathing look at Andy.

"I hate you!" Phoebe screamed at him, crying.

"Yeah, well, I'm not your biggest fan right now, either." Andy walked toward the camera and put his hand up. "Shut it off, Sawyer. Maybe go deal with your sister."

Although I couldn't see what happened next, I heard a scuffle and then the phone dropped. The video cut at that moment.

"*That's* why I didn't want to come to the wedding."

I handed the phone back to Sawyer. "When was this?"

"Last week. We went out for drinks, the four of us."

"What started the argument?"

"I mean, you pretty much saw it. Phoebe wanted to stay and dance. She'd been drinking quite a bit, probably because of the note—"

"What note?" I interrupted.

"She got another note from her stalker. First time in nearly two years."

"How is that possible? I thought she'd gone to great lengths to hide her contact information."

"She did. I guess it doesn't take a genius to realize Phoebe Braithwaite might have a connection to Braithwaite Industrial Storage."

"She received it at work? What did it say?"

He shrugged. "She didn't say, only that it freaked her out a bit, but she had other, bigger issues. That's why she got so hammered. Andy isn't a big drinker, so the drunker she got, the more upset he got."

"He grew up with a mother who used alcohol and other substances to avoid dealing with the difficulties of her life. That also meant she was numb to the joyful moments as well. He's seen what it does to a person."

"Same with Macy."

"I'm sure Andy was worried about her well-being."

"Sure, but that didn't give him the right to assault her." He held up his hands. "And don't give me any crap about she started it. Did she provoke him? Yep. It still wasn't okay for him to push her."

"I agree, and I won't defend him for that."

Egan set our drinks on the table. We'd been so engrossed in our conversation that I hadn't noticed him approach.

I also hadn't noticed Xavier standing nearby, listening, with his arms crossed. He did not look happy.

"Monsieur Braithwaite, may I please have a look at that video? It seems you have been holding out on me."

Chapter Twenty-Five

"THAT VIDEO ISN'T evidence of Andy's guilt." I rushed to keep up with Xavier as he strode out of the Azure Lounge with Sawyer's phone in his hand.

"I will be the judge of that."

I followed him into the elevator. "Did they have a tempestuous relationship? Sure. Does that mean he's capable of murder? Not in the slightest."

He arched his left brow at me and pressed the button for the seventh and fifth floors without saying a word.

"I know how this looks, but it was an argument with more context than what's on tape."

The elevator doors opened onto the Odyssey level.

"This is your stop."

"Xavier, please…"

He held the door, and it began to squeal. He raised a brow, which I took as a sign he wanted me to get out.

"Oh, before I forget." He reached under his sweater and pulled out a yellow envelope and handed it to me.

I took it from him and glanced at the front. It wasn't labeled. "What is this?"

"You, Madame McLaughlin, have been served."

With that, he allowed the doors to close.

I stared at the elevator in a stupor and then at the envelope in my hand.

I'd been served? What did that mean? Like in a court proceeding? Was this part of the investigation into the murders? If he wanted me to answer questions, all he had to do was ask. No need for official paperwork.

I began to open the envelope as I headed for my cabin. Inside, there were legal-sized papers. At the top of the first page, it read:

IN THE SUPERIOR COURT OF
THE STATE OF WASHINGTON
IN AND FOR THE COUNTY OF KING

And in the upper left-hand corner:

KYRIE DAWN WUMPENHAUER; AND
QUINTON GABRIEL MCLAUGHLIN,
PLAINTIFFS,
V.
CHARLOTTE ANNE COBB MCLAUGHLIN,
DEFENDANT.

I stopped dead in my tracks outside suite 702.

"What in the world?" I pulled the papers all the way out of the envelope.

Next to the names, in bold caps, were the words COMPLAINT FOR MONETARY DAMAGES.

"You've got to be kidding me!"

Jane opened the door to our cabin. "Char? What's going

on?"

I marched past her into the living room. "I cannot believe the nerve of that woman!"

"What woman? Slow down and tell me what's going on."

I closed my eyes. When I reopened them, I pored over the papers to make sure I hadn't misread.

Nope.

"She's suing me."

"Who's suing you?"

"Kyrie Dawn."

"What? That's ridiculous! She wouldn't dare after everything she's put you through. She couldn't!"

I held up the paper. "Oh, but she is. Listen to this. *Comes now the plaintiffs Kyrie Dawn Wumpenhauer*"—

"Wumpen-what?"

"Wumpenhauer. Apparently, that's her real last name."

"No wonder she went by only her first and middle names."

"*Comes now the plaintiffs, Kyrie Dawn Wumpenhauer and also on behalf of her minor child Quinton Gabriel McLaughlin, by and through their attorneys of record, Rodenbusch Murawski LLC, and brings this action against the above-named defendant in order to rectify financial disparities in the distribution of assets for the estate of Gabriel Patrick McLaughlin, deceased.*"

"What does that mean? Financial disparities? She thinks she didn't get her fair cut? She already got twenty-five percent of the pot, not a small amount. They weren't married. What more could she want?"

I scanned the document. "She wants the suite."

"The suite," she repeated. "The one in which we're standing right this moment?"

"Uh-huh. Says here it was her idea to buy it, she decorated it, he never came here without her—poor, delusional child—and she claims the baby has a strong attachment to it because he spent so much time bonding with his father here. She needs it so her son has something other than money to remember Gabe."

Jane rolled her eyes. "She is a real piece of work."

"What if I lose this lawsuit?"

"You won't. Any reasonable judge will see this for what it is. A disgusting money grab." She squinted at me. "How in the heck did you get these, anyway? We're anchored next to a glacier, miles from any port, and we haven't docked once."

I set the papers down. "I don't know. Maybe a mail boat or something. Maybe at Icy Strait. I can tell you how I got them, though. I was served by Xavier Mesnier."

"Oof. That had to hurt."

"Oh, that wasn't even the worst part. He gave them to me right after confiscating Sawyer's phone."

"Why did he do that?"

"Because he happened upon Sawyer showing me a video he'd recorded of a nasty fight between Andy and Phoebe from last week."

"Oh, that's not good."

"Jane, Andy pushed Phoebe to the ground. It looks really bad. His face was practically unrecognizable, he was so upset with her."

"What are you trying to say? You're not saying you think

he's capable of murder."

"I don't know what I'm saying. There are a lot of things I didn't think people in my life were capable of doing, but I was wrong. Maybe I'm just a terrible reader of people I care about."

"Stop that. Gabe was not everyone. He was one lying piece of—" She stopped herself. "I don't know who convinced you along the way that you couldn't trust your gut, but it's not true."

"My life tells a different story." I waved my hand dismissively. "It doesn't matter. All that matters now is helping Andy."

Jane touched her temples with her fingertips. "Every time I feel like we're making progress on exonerating him, something happens to set our efforts way back."

"We've got to do more. It's crisis time. We'll be back in Seattle in less than seventy-two hours. If we don't solve this thing by then, Andy will be escorted off this ship in handcuffs and into the waiting arms of Port of Seattle Police officers."

"What did you have in mind?"

"I don't know. I need to take a shower. I'm overdue for a hair wash, and the hair on my legs could use some attention, too. As soon as I'm out, we can plot out our next steps." I sighed. "Maybe I should just give it to her."

"What?"

"This place." I waved the papers.

Jane snatched them from my hand. "Absolutely not! This is your place. It was purchased with your communal finances, and it is your community property. This chick needs to learn she doesn't just get to claim things as her own simply because she wants them. She's an invader and a squatter, and someone needs to teach her a lesson."

"So, what? You're saying I teach her a lesson by selling the place so she can't have it?"

"No! I'm saying live here! Full-time. This could be our act three, our renaissance, our rebirth into a new existence."

I scoffed. "We already talked about this. Be reasonable, Jane."

"I've been reasonable my whole life, and so have you. I'm going to be sixty years old in three years. You're not that far behind me. I'm done being reasonable. I think it's time you set yourself free to live the life you never believed you could have. But you can. *We* can. It's at our fingertips."

"Maybe I don't want to sail around the world with you. Did you ever consider that?"

Her mouth snapped shut. I knew that look. She was on the verge of tears, a rare occurrence for Jane. Part of me wanted to give in just so she wouldn't be upset. The rest of me wanted to dig in my heels as far as they would go.

For too long I'd been a bystander in my own life. No more.

"I'm sorry, Jane, but I'm kind of enjoying my new life of solitude."

She handed the papers back to me. "You keep telling yourself that."

SOMETIMES IT FELT like I could wash away my troubles in the shower. As the steaming water cascaded over my face, across my shoulders, and down my back, I could feel the tension of the past several days begin to release. I washed my hair—twice—and then stood under the spray for several minutes as the conditioner softened it. By the time I'd rinsed, shaved, and loofahed my whole body, my skin was pink and my toes were wrinkled.

I stepped onto the mat and wrapped myself in a towel. I grabbed a smaller towel and twisted it around my hair, creating a turban on top of my head. As I pulled on the robe hanging on the hook next to the shower and dropped the towel onto the floor, I thought I heard the doorbell.

"Jane?" I called. "Is that the door?"

I strained to hear her open it, but instead the bell rang again.

"Jane! Get the door! I think it's your food!"

I tied the robe closed and opened the bathroom door. The bell rang a third time.

"Jane!"

Oh, for the love of—

Maybe she was in the bathroom and couldn't hear it. Wonderful. Nothing like answering the door in a bathrobe. I grabbed my phone from the counter and shoved it in my pocket. I shuffled out of the bathroom and around the corner as the person gave up ringing and began pounding.

"For goodness' sake," I muttered as I made my way to the entryway. "Don't order food and then not be around to—" I gasped. "Oh my gawd! Jane!"

She was crumpled in front of the door with her eyes closed. She appeared to be sleeping, which was ridiculous. No one fell asleep in the middle of the day in front of the door.

I might have thought she'd fainted, too.

That was, of course, if it weren't for the blood streaming from the wound on her head.

Chapter Twenty-Six

I RUSHED TO Jane's side, her motionless body blocking the door. She was still warm, which was a relief.

The insistent knocking continued.

"Help! I need help!"

"Then open the door!" The voice, female, was somewhat familiar, but I couldn't place it.

"She's blocking the door. I can't open it. Please, go get help. My sister seems to have fallen and she's injured."

"I will go get the doctor."

"Hurry! And get Xavier Mesnier as well."

I placed two fingers on Jane's throat and felt a faint pulse. I caressed her cheeks and ran my hand across the part of her head that wasn't bleeding.

"Stay with me, Janie. It's gonna be okay."

It must have only been a few minutes, but it felt like forever by the time Xavier's voice boomed in the hallway.

"Charlotte, please open the door."

"I'm afraid to move her. She's really hurt."

"I cannot help if you do not let me inside. Do you know what happened?"

"No, I came out of the shower and she was lying here

unconscious and bleeding."

"Do you believe it was an accident?"

"I can't tell."

"Okay, Charlotte, listen to me. First, take photos of her in that position. We need to know exactly how she is lying to determine what happened. Then, carefully pull her away from the door. It does not have to be much, only a foot or two."

I grabbed my phone from my robe pocket and took the picture. She was gonna be furious when she saw the unflattering angle, but that was of little consequence in that moment.

Next, I pulled her away from the door, only able to move her a couple of feet. She didn't even whimper, which scared me even more.

Finally, I reached up and pulled the handle to open the door a crack. "I don't know if I moved her enough. She's heavier than she looks. Don't tell her I said that."

"I won't." Xavier's large hands reached in, and he gently lifted Jane a smidge farther so that he could fully enter the suite by sliding through the narrow opening. I scooted backward to get out of his way.

Behind him I could see Haimi Dara, the server assigned to our table every night for dinner. Haimi paced back and forth in the hallway mumbling to herself, her gaze darting around under thick, furrowed brows. She was still holding the tray with chrome lids protecting Jane's order. The sight of her distress nearly broke me.

"Haimi, you can put the tray down. No one will be eating anytime soon."

Dr. Fraser came out of nowhere—probably the hallway—and kneeled next to Jane.

He glanced at me. "Ian Fraser. I'm the onboard physician." He had either a Scottish or Northern English accent.

"I know. I saw you up on Kalispera. I was the one who found Ivy Evans. I'm Charlotte McLaughlin. This is my sister, Jane Cobb. Thank you for coming so quickly."

"This group is certainly making me earn my keep." He felt for her pulse and pulled the stethoscope from his neck. He listened to her heartbeat for a minute and then examined the wound. "Let's get her to the infirmary so that I may examine her more thoroughly and treat her."

"Is it safe to move her?" I asked.

"Carefully, yes. We have a gurney in the hallway."

I wanted to follow them to the infirmary, but I was still in my robe, so I told them I'd meet them there as soon as I was dressed. I watched as the three of them accompanied Jane down the hallway toward the elevator. My breath caught in my chest, and a tear slid down my cheek. I wiped it away and shut the door.

I stood in the entryway, staring at the floor where my sister had been lying in a heap with blood dripping down her left temple, lightheaded and a little nauseated. I rested against the wall for support.

I didn't know if it was stress or sympathy pain, but my head hurt so much it might explode. I stumbled into the kitchen and filled a glass with water. From my purse, which hung from the back of one of the barstools, I took a bottle of pain reliever and popped the top. After swallowing the pills and swigging the water, I leaned against the counter.

Just a few months ago, I'd been living in blissful ignorance. Andy was in a promising new relationship. He seemed happy. Gabe was still alive, and as far as I was concerned our marriage was solid. I had a life I was okay with. Maybe it wasn't a dream life, but as far as being awake, it served its purpose.

I had no idea about Kyrie Dawn, her baby, her lawsuit against me. Heck, I didn't even know about the boat, much less this suite I technically owned. Phoebe was alive, Andy wasn't facing twenty-to-life for her murder, Ivy was alive, and Jane wasn't lying unconscious with a head injury.

What I wouldn't do to take back my last words to her. My knees buckled at the thought. What if those were the very last words we ever exchanged? What if I had to live the rest of my life knowing the last thing that I said to my sister was I didn't want her around? How did people reconcile that? How would I ever get over it?

I clasped my hands together and closed my eyes. "Oh, God, please let her be okay. I can't do all this without her. If Andy goes to prison and Jane doesn't make it, I don't know what I'll do. They're my people, God. They're all that matters to me in this world." I opened my eyes. "They're all I've got."

I'd never felt so alone in my entire life, even after everyone had departed Gabe's wake and I was by myself in that big house.

I inhaled a deep breath and stared out the window. The

glacier looked back at me in its formidable glacialness.

One summer, when the Pacific Northwest was experiencing an unusual hot spell, I put together what I called ice camp at the library. I'd invited kids to come learn about glaciers and snow, so we watched movies about sled dogs, we ate sno-cones, and I jacked the air conditioning down to an icy sixty-five degrees.

Of course, in order to teach about glaciers, I had to learn about glaciers. We tended to think of glaciers as monoliths, one large block of ice, but actually, they're a composite of several singular irregular-shaped crystals. They interlock, working together to form a massive, imposing structure over time, but it starts with small, individual structures.

The glacier is nourished and grows stronger when more crystals bond, often from snowfall events, and it weakens by erosion and part of the whole breaking away.

At the time, I used the glacier as an analogy for how families and communities need each other.

Before I had headed in for my shower, I'd told Jane I didn't want to live with her or anyone else. The truth was, I needed her. I'd taken her for granted, and I was on the verge of losing her and Andy.

I threw off my robe and ran into the bedroom to get dressed. I didn't even bother with brushing my hair. I grabbed my purse, room key, and my phone, and rushed out of the suite. The door locked automatically behind me.

By the time I got to the infirmary, Haimi was pacing in the lobby and Jane was hooked up to an IV and an oxygen mask, with Xavier and Dr. Fraser hovering over her. Even when she slept, she made little noises, but in this moment she was placid. Not peaceful, but quiet and still.

Dr. Fraser glanced up when I entered the room. "She's stable."

"Will she be okay? Will she wake up?"

"I don't have all the answers you want. Time will tell on some of this. We must be patient and allow her body to heal itself."

"Wait, aren't you going to heal her?"

"Now that I know her vitals are steady, I can clean the wound and suture it shut, but her being awake or asleep, that's going to be up to her."

"This is scary."

"I imagine so." He gave me a tepid smile. "Have faith."

This wasn't reassuring. I turned on Xavier. "Now are you willing to admit Andy didn't kill Phoebe? There's a maniac roaming this ship. Meanwhile, you've got Andy under twenty-four-hour watch."

"Did it occur to you perhaps I am protecting him and the investigation?"

My attempts to read him were futile. If only I knew him better, maybe I'd feel more reassured. "I hope that's true."

"Can you show me the photos you took?"

I unlocked my phone and handed it to him. He examined the photos, enlarging them and moving his focus from one part of the scene to another. He handed the phone to Dr. Fraser, who silently viewed them himself.

"What do you know about her injuries and how she got them?" Dr. Fraser asked.

My voice came out stronger than I expected, considering how weak I felt, as though I might pass out at any moment. "Very little. I went to take a shower…"

"What time?" Xavier interjected.

"Uh, I don't know. I took a really long shower. Longer than usual. I know she said the second game was about to start and she ordered food." I called out to the lobby. "Hey, Haimi, what time did Jane's food order come in?"

She stopped pacing. "Approximately twelve fifteen."

Xavier looked at his wristwatch and then at me. "A bit past thirteen hundred hours. That was a very long shower."

Despite the circumstances, the intensity of his gaze created a sensation of heat that rose from my chest, up my throat, and into my cheeks.

"Yes, well, uh, she probably called right around the time the game started."

"Game?" Xavier said, his focus still squarely on my ever-warming face.

"Football." I blinked at him. "It's Thanksgiving. Turkey. Parade. Football."

"Ah, yes, American football."

I blew out a breath. "Anyway, when I got out of the shower, I heard the doorbell ring several times."

"That was me," piped in Haimi, holding up her index finger. She continued to walk the length of the infirmary.

Xavier merely nodded.

"I figured Jane must have been in her bathroom. That's when I found her. I guess she slipped and hit her head when Haimi rang the doorbell. Although, I didn't hear her fall or scream, but it was probably right before I turned the water off. Plus, I had the fan running."

"No." Haimi stopped pacing. "I heard no fall, no scream. No noise at all. I believe she fell before I went to the room."

The doctor said, "I'd have to agree. This wound, the position in which she was lying, looking around at the area, I'd be hard pressed to say it was simply a fall." He continued to examine Jane's head.

"What are you suggesting?" I asked. "Someone did this to her? How is that even possible? She was blocking the door."

Xavier held up my phone. "In looking at the photos, it would seem possible she answered the door for her attacker, believing it was Haimi with her food order. Perhaps the assailant reached in and hit her with something and then shut the door. She would have then fallen where she stood."

"This is all my fault."

Xavier tilted his head. "Why do you say these things?"

"Because I've been snooping around, trying to solve these murders and exonerate Andy. I put her smack dab in harm's way. Literally."

"You have been trying to seek truth to help someone you love. Also, I did not see Madame Cobb resisting to investigate with you."

"I should have just left it up to you. Maybe then she wouldn't be lying here unconscious."

"I am going to say something to you, but if you repeat it to anyone, I will deny it. *D'accord*?"

Dr. Fraser cleared his throat.

"You as well, Ian."

Dr. Fraser gave a wry smile.

"What is it?" I asked.

"I have been grateful for your help, Charlotte. You have a—*je ne sais pas,* how do you say—a knickknack for these types of investigations."

Despite the circumstances, I had to laugh. "I think you mean knack, not knickknack." I crossed my heart. "I will tell no one. And thank you. I appreciate the compliment."

"Aha!"

We both turned to look at Dr. Fraser.

He held up his tweezers, and in them was a bright orange sliver of wood. "You find what this belongs to, you will find your weapon."

I squinted at it and gasped.

Xavier and I exchanged a wide-eyed glance and at the same time said, "The paddles."

"How many are there?" I asked.

"Twenty total, but most of the rafts have plastic paddles, only a few have wooden."

"Which levels have them?"

"Mykonos, Aegean, and Capri."

I groaned. "Numbers, please."

He pursed his mouth. "Nine, six, and five."

"We can't do this all on our own. It's time to enlist some help and get all hands on deck."

"Ship pun?"

"Sorry, couldn't help it."

Chapter Twenty-Seven

"MAYBE I SHOULD'VE stayed with Jane and let you handle it," I said.

Xavier gave me a sidelong glance. "She is in good hands with Dr. Fraser. There is nothing that you can do sitting at her bedside worrying over her."

He was right, but I still felt unsettled.

We'd gathered what remained of the Braithwaite-Cobb wedding party in the captain's lounge. Even Rhonda had managed to get dressed and make an appearance.

We'd told them to bring coats, hats, and scarves, and most had complied. Those who hadn't would soon regret it.

I scanned the room one by one. Were any of them responsible for what had happened to Phoebe, Ivy, and Jane?

Neal Alcorn's hair was mussed, likely having spent the last twenty-four hours pleading for his marriage and comforting his wife upon the death of her second sister. He'd had an affair with Phoebe, which could have been motive, but he'd admitted it to Lily prior to Ivy's death. If one assumed a single perpetrator of all three attacks, I felt reasonably comfortable ruling out Neal.

Lily's face had an edge to it I'd never seen before. It made me sad to think her trusting heart had been broken. I knew firsthand how that felt. Lily's reaction to the news of Neal's infidelity had been genuine. She hadn't known until that moment I'd dropped it in her lap by accident. Perhaps she'd noticed an unease in her spirit, some warning signs she'd dismissed, but I was confident she hadn't killed Phoebe over the affair, because she had no clue it had happened. And even with the increased inheritance and recognizing how greed could be a strong influencer of bad behavior, I didn't believe Lily would kill her sisters for money.

Clyde, also a disheveled mess, was either a man in agonizing grief or he was giving an award-winning performance. I'd seen enough theater to spot both good and bad actors, and Clyde's raw pain rang true to me.

Dale and Susan had no motive at all, so I didn't even consider them. Susan was so heavily medicated she could barely sit upright in the chair. Dale was supporting her weight as she leaned against him.

Speaking of sedated parents, Rhonda stared back at me with an equally blank expression to Susan. It was the perfect example of *the lights are on, but nobody's home.* I made a mental note to look for a treatment center for her as soon as this nightmare was over. She'd lost too many years and a relationship with her son because of her inability to cope with the loss of my brother, but it wasn't too late to salvage what time she had left on the planet. Eventually, Andy would fall in love again, and at some point, there would probably be grandchildren. I wasn't Rhonda's biggest fan, but for everyone's sake, a present and functioning Rhonda was better than the alternative.

Sawyer had once again pulled his hood tightly over his head like the Unabomber mixed with a boy bander. Macy sat on the other side of Rhonda, next to Susan and away from Sawyer.

Sawyer had said Macy grew up in a tough household, so it made sense to me that she would feel compelled to take care of his parents, but he needed her comfort as well. Sometimes crises brought people closer together, but that didn't appear to be the case in this situation.

My morning with Sawyer had eliminated any minuscule suspicion about his involvement with the murders. As with Lily, money as a motive didn't seem plausible.

Then there was Frank and Elaine. I'd pretty much ruled out Elaine, for the simple fact that she was too much of a birdbrain to be a criminal mastermind. The only way for her to inherit Phoebe and Ivy's shares of Braithwaite Industrial was if she knocked over that entire branch of the family tree and then her own husband. From everything I'd heard, Elaine wasn't involved at all with the business and didn't have any interest in doing so. She spent her days shopping, brunching, and pampering herself at various spas. Other than financial reasons, any other motive she might have had was much less clear than Frank's.

Frank remained my number one suspect. In addition to his general ick factor, he was running a criminal enterprise out of the family business, or at the very least, was looking the other way. Phoebe had discovered the operation and was starting to make trouble for him. I didn't know what she'd told Dale, and I couldn't ask him without tipping off Frank that the authorities were onto him, but I did know she'd confronted Frank about whatever she'd seen and heard.

As for Ivy, perhaps Phoebe had shared her theories with her sister and after Phoebe had been killed, Ivy had confronted Frank with what she knew. Andy was a convenient patsy. Everything Phoebe had told him about her suspicions of Frank's nefarious dealings would be discounted if Andy were framed for her murder. There was a good chance that after our arrival at the Port of Seattle, when Frank would likely be arrested for the smuggling operation at his facilities, he'd also be investigated for the murders. It was a comforting thought.

As for the friends of the bride and groom, there hadn't been a lot of red flags to delve further into their relationships with Phoebe and/or Andy, and I'd seen no indication of motive to kill Ivy.

Vance appeared tough, with his tattoos and piercings, but nothing about his demeanor struck me as violent. Quite the opposite, actually.

I didn't particularly like Duncan. He was sleazy with a heavy side of misogyny, so I hadn't completely ruled him out, but my instinct said he was all bark and no bite. He had the type of personality that came from deep insecurities masking as swagger, and I didn't really think there was a lot of substance to him. Didn't mean he wasn't capable of mustering ill intent under the right circumstances—I just hadn't seen much from him that led me to think serial killer.

Nikki wasn't my favorite, either. She was gorgeous but

also rude, a tad narcissistic, and I'd heard she hadn't always been the most loyal friend to Phoebe. That was Andy's take on it, at least, after he'd argued with Phoebe about making her the maid of honor. He'd hated to admit it out loud at the time, but he said it made him wonder if Phoebe was vainer than he thought and that was why she'd chosen Nikki to be her maid of honor.

Admittedly, most of my misgivings about Nikki had to do with her attitude and my own insecurities. I reminded myself that being unlikeable didn't make a person a murderer. After all, how many news interviews with neighbors of *nice guys* who turned out to be monsters proved that point? When true-crime author Ann Rule discovered that her coworker, *nice guy* Ted Bundy, was a serial killer, she was shocked.

Still, I settled on putting Nikki by herself in the *probably not guilty* column, halfway between *maybe* and *all-clear*.

Last, but not least, was Serena. She was looking down at her hands in her lap, fiddling with her fingers. Occasionally, her right index finger darted to her left wrist and scratched. It was the first time I'd seen her without her bracelet.

At that moment, she lifted her head and made direct eye contact with me. She smiled, but it didn't reach her narrowed eyes.

I had yet to put Serena in any category. Prior to the cruise, she would have been firmly in the *no way-not possible-couldn't be* column. She'd been friends with Andy for quite a while, and he was close enough to her to talk his fiancée into making her a bridesmaid.

But I didn't blame Phoebe for not being thrilled with the idea initially. Asking his fiancée to allow his female friend in their wedding in the first place was a pretty big ask. Not to mention, she'd wanted another friend to join Nikki as one of her attendants. If Phoebe had her way, Serena would have been merely a guest.

I could only imagine Andy had been quite convincing to talk the strong-willed Phoebe into making the switch. From everything I knew of their relationship, Phoebe got her way ninety-nine percent of the time. Perhaps Phoebe hadn't felt threatened by Andy's friendship with Serena. After all, Phoebe was a former celebrity and Serena was just a mousy teacher. But Serena hadn't looked like a mousy teacher two nights earlier. She was a head-turning bombshell. This alternate side to her personality caused me to question everything I thought I knew about her.

Did having a heretofore unknown sexy side make her more likely to be a killer? Not necessarily. What it told me, though, was there was more to Serena than met the eye, and she wasn't to be underestimated. I also had witnessed emotions in her directed toward Andy that indicated she didn't view their relationship as strictly platonic. Unrequited love or obsession was a common motive for crimes of passion.

Of course, that didn't explain Ivy's death.

Nothing explained Ivy's death, really, other than that Ivy must have known something about the killer and had to be silenced. It was the only thing that made sense to me.

I scanned the room once more. How could any of them

be killers? Maybe I was barking up the wrong tree or whatever the nautical phrase was for situations like this. Running the sail up the wrong pole? Following a broken compass? Rowing with the wrong oar?

Speaking of oars…

Xavier stood at the front of the room, holding one of the orange wooden oars he'd grabbed from a locked storage room. His legs were spread apart in a power stance. Xavier stood with his hands on his hips, fingers splayed. I stood on his left; he had a pale band of skin around his fourth finger where a ring had once been.

He'd been married. And not that long ago, either. Maybe he still was but had removed the ring for some reason.

I ran my left thumb along the inside of my finger where the indent remained from the ring I'd removed only a few weeks ago. I still hadn't gotten used to it being bare after two decades.

He cleared his throat. "I need your help."

"Is the boat sinking? Are we going to have to row our way over to the glacier until help arrives?" Lily asked.

"No, this is not about the ship sinking. It is regarding the two murder investigations, along with the most recent incident."

"What incident?" Lily's lower lip trembled as she scanned the room. "Who isn't here? Is someone else dead?"

"No one else is dead, but—" I began.

"Jane's not here. Where's Jane?" Frank bellowed. "Is Jane dead?"

Was his bluster an act? Maybe he was hoping Jane was

dead, which meant he'd been successful in his attack. "No, like I said, no one's dead, Frank."

"However, Madame Cobb—"

"Me?" Rhonda looked at Xavier like he'd said the magic words to awaken her from her daydream.

"No. The other Madame Cobb. Jane. This is why I have gathered you all here, to expedite the search for—"

Frank interrupted with that haughty, booming voice of his. "Oh, you need us to do your job for you now?" His sour, smirking expression was accompanied by an obnoxious chuckle as he took a bite of an ice cream sandwich. I wanted to shove it down his throat.

"I'll be sure to mention your cooperation—or lack thereof—in finding whoever killed Phoebe to the authorities when we dock back in Seattle."

Frank stopped chewing and shot me a glare.

"The same person who attacked Jane," I added.

"Jane was attacked?" Frank swallowed his bite. "I'm sorry, I didn't know."

Or did he? The verdict was still out.

"That's awful. Is she okay?" Sawyer peeked out from his hoodie.

"No, she's not," I said. "We won't know for a bit whether she'll wake up."

"What can we do?" Lily asked.

"We have a theory about the weapon used to harm Madame Cobb. We hope discovering it will also reveal information leading to the killer of Madame Braithwaite and Madame Evans." Xavier held up the oar.

Susan emitted a mewl. Dale patted her hand in what I thought was one of the least effective ways to comfort a person.

Xavier continued, still holding the oar aloft. "The evidence suggests one of the ship's wooden oars like this one was used in the latest assault. These are located near the lifeboats and preservers on the Mykonos, Aegean, and Capri decks."

"That's five, six, and nine," I clarified.

"You want us to look for oars?" Clyde's face was pinched and his voice was incredulous. "My wife is dead, and you think searching for oars will somehow magically reveal who killed her?"

"I appreciate your frustration, and if you would like to sit out, I understand. We need to find the weapon so we can further the investigation. The crime was committed on Odyssey deck." Before I could interject again, Xavier added, "Level seven. There are no rafts located on that level, therefore, it must have been brought up from one of the lower levels or down from two levels above."

"Doesn't it make the most sense it would be level six, since that's the closest?" Sawyer asked.

"Very possibly. However, we cannot be certain until we locate the oar and the location from which it is missing. Because of the large area to cover, we would like to enlist the help of whomever is willing, as with the search for Madame Evans."

"Are they all orange and white like that one?" Macy asked.

"They are," Xavier said, "but not all of them are wood. Some are plastic. We are only looking for the wooden ones."

"Of course, I will help." Clyde seemed to be able to set most of his anger aside for the greater purpose. "I need to know who did this to Ivy."

"I should stay here with my wife," Dale said. He looked over at Rhonda. "And that one. Someone's got to stay with the zombies."

"I could stay with them," Macy offered. "If you want to be part of the search party."

Dale gave her a warm smile. "That's very kind of you, but I'd rather have the young and spry out there looking." He nodded toward Frank. "Us old geezers can hang here and wait for word."

Frank grunted. "Speak for yourself, old geezer. I'd like to find the bastard who killed my nieces. Count me in."

Elaine's mouth twisted into an awkward grimace. "I think I'll wait here. It's really cold out there."

"Charlotte and I are headed to the ninth level. Who would like to join us?" Xavier asked.

"Sawyer and I can check up on Kalispera," Macy volunteered. "You never know if the guy stashed the paddle up there."

"That level is still closed. It is a crime scene."

"Okay, well then, I guess we'll join you and Charlotte."

Sawyer played with his hoodie string.

She elbowed him. "Alright, babe?"

"Huh? Yeah. Sure."

Duncan and Vance said they'd take the sixth. Clyde,

Nikki, and Serena would scour the fifth.

That left Lily and Neal.

"Let's go with Clyde." Neal attempted to steer Lily by the arm toward the fifth-floor group.

Lily jerked her arm away from his grasp. "Then the teams would be uneven. I'll go with these guys."

She walked over to Duncan, who had a broad smile on his face.

"Welcome to the cool team." He swung an arm around her shoulder, and his friendly smile transformed into a lascivious one.

I wasn't sure Lily understood that she'd just walked into the lion's den, but she'd soon learn.

Neal's cheeks reddened and his mouth drooped into a sullen pout. His shoulders slumped as he joined the fifth-floor group. He shot daggers toward Duncan, but Duncan appeared unfazed.

Nikki looped her arm through Neal's, which caused him to perk up a bit. He stole a glance at Lily, who pressed her lips together.

Making your wife jealous when trying to get back into her good graces following the reveal of an affair didn't seem like the smartest strategy to me, but it wasn't my responsibility to fix their marriage.

Sawyer watched the scene with furrowed brows. Macy looped her arm through his, and he smiled down at her.

Xavier handed a walkie-talkie to Neal. "You will be in charge of communication for your group."

Neal regained some of his posture—probably why Xavier

chose him. We needed everyone to be focused on the mission, not consumed with their own problems.

Xavier gave the other walkie-talkie to Lily. Duncan began to take it from her, and Xavier held up his hand.

"No. Madame Alcorn will be reporting back to me."

Duncan held up his hands in mock surrender.

It became clear that Xavier had a secondary motive: he was forcing Lily and Neal to communicate. A tickle of admiration fluttered inside my chest.

"*D'accord.* Do you all understand what you are to do?"

Everyone nodded.

"If you find anything, please alert us right away."

With that, we dispersed in three groups of four.

The sixth-floor group, Aegean, left first. Duncan attempted to place his hand on the small of Lily's back, but she shrugged him off. Vance smacked Duncan up the backside of his head and gave him a warning look.

Behind them in the fifth-floor group, Capri, I caught Neal giving a smug smile. Clyde had on his game face. Serena and Nikki exchanged wide-eyed looks. I didn't blame them. Both women had opted for fashionable rather than practical.

It was a balmy thirty-five degrees outside, with a windchill of twenty-five.

Chapter Twenty-Eight

SINCE MY GROUP—SAWYER, Macy, Xavier, and me—needed to go up only one level, we skipped the elevator and headed for the stairs. Macy volunteered her and Sawyer to take portside, while Xavier and I would examine the starboard side.

As we stepped onto the deck at the bow, we were immediately assaulted by arctic winds. Even my heavy coat wasn't enough to protect me from the bone-chilling cold. If I had to wager, Nikki and Serena were going to last less than a minute in their skimpy outfits before they went scurrying back indoors.

The scenery, however, was totally worth the frostbite. We were near the highest point of the ship, and our view of the bay and the glacier were unobstructed.

I walked to the edge to take it all in. The water was like mirrored glass, the craggy mountains loomed around us, and the turquoise ice glowed against the backdrop of fresh snow. My breath caught in my chest.

The extraordinary landscape was supposed to be the backdrop for Andy and Phoebe's wedding, and it was heartbreaking to think about what could have been. What *should* have been.

"She would have been a beautiful bride. Like a snow queen from a fairy tale."

I hadn't realized Macy had sidled up next to me until she spoke.

"I was just thinking the same thing."

"It's a shame for it to go to waste." She clucked. "Maybe I can talk Sawyer into getting married today."

I turned to look at her. "What?"

"I'm kidding. Obviously, that would be super tacky." She turned away from the railing and looked up at the Kalispera deck. "Maybe I should check up on the tenth level. You never know if the guy stashed the paddle up there."

"Um, I think we should just stick to the plan for now."

"You sure? It wouldn't take me long."

"Mace." Sawyer waved at her.

She smiled at him. "Coming." She turned back to me. "Guess I'm going this way." She bounded over to him and grabbed his hand. "C'mon. We've got the other side. Charlotte and Mr. Mesnier can check around here."

She attempted to pull away from him, but he drew her back and kissed her on the forehead like a father would a child. She gave him a coy smile.

She was so young. I hadn't really noticed it before. Sawyer was in his early thirties, and I was pretty sure Macy was barely of legal age. Twenty-two or twenty-three at most.

The age gap itself wasn't that big of a deal. After all, my own husband was twelve years older than me, but perhaps that was why it bothered me. I was in my early twenties and

Gabe had been in his late thirties when we'd married, and he'd taken advantage of my naiveté.

The strange thing was that despite their nearly ten-year age difference, Sawyer and Macy appeared to be at about the same maturity level. Maybe it was because of the things Macy had been through in her young life, while Sawyer had everything handed to him. They'd managed to meet in the middle.

Whatever. If they were happy, I was happy for them. If they weren't happy, well, time would take care of that.

"I've missed you." Sawyer searched her eyes.

"I've missed you, too."

"You've been so busy with my parents..."

"I just feel so bad for them. I'm sorry if you've been feeling neglected." She stood on her tiptoes and kissed him. "I'll do better. Promise."

She broke free of him and scampered around the corner.

Sawyer ambled behind her. "Wait for me!"

"No, you need to pick up the pace," she called from the port side, her voice nearly swallowed by the wind.

Xavier came up beside me. "Ah, the energy of young love. It will keep them warm."

"For now." My fingers were beginning to go numb. I clasped my hands together and blew on them.

"May I?" Xavier took my hands in his and rubbed them to create friction.

I glanced at his face, but thankfully he was concentrating on his task. I wasn't sure how I would handle full eye contact. I began to pull back and he released my hands.

"Thank you."

"Everything okay?" he asked.

"Yeah. No, nothing's okay. This is wrong. Everything's wrong. I need to go be with Jane."

He took a step back. "Of course. I understand."

Well, shoot. He probably thought I meant him warming up my hands was wrong.

"Xavier, I—Thanks. For everything. Let me know what you guys find."

"I will."

I hurried away as fast as my near-frozen toes would take me. Eventually, I'd need to clarify to him what I meant, but my number one priority was getting back to my sister.

"YOU'RE BACK SOONER than expected," Dr. Fraser said. "Any luck?"

"I bailed on the expedition. It didn't feel right not being here."

"Understandable."

"How is she?"

"Pretty much the same. She's stable. I'd expect her to wake up soon."

"And if she doesn't?"

I sat on the stool next to Jane's bed and grabbed her hand. She'd painted her nails neon yellow for '80s night. "Yikes. These are atrocious."

If she were awake, Jane would have made some sort of

snarky comment like *I've seen salad better dressed than you* or *if you joined the Spice Girls, you'd be Vanilla Spice.*

"C'mon, Jane. Time to wake up. You've made your point. Joke's not funny anymore."

She stirred, but her eyes didn't open.

"I'm sorry I said those things. I didn't mean them. I think traveling the world with you would be lots of fun. It's just been so much, and that letter from Kyrie Dawn was the final straw. I snapped. I need a moment to process everything and not be pushed into it. There's something about this tidal wave of change coming at me without warning that makes me wanna stick my head in the sand until it all calms down, you know?"

I grabbed a tissue and blew my nose.

"My whole life I've tried to go with the flow. You know this. Make things easy for everyone. Show up first to help set up and be the last to leave in order to help tear down. Never ask too much. Never make a fuss. Don't ask too many questions. Don't need too much, because everyone else has needs, and I'll tend to mine if there's any time or energy left over. It was so easy for you to leave. No one expected anything of you. They all knew you were gonna do whatever you wanted. I didn't have that luxury. Someone had to stay and pick up the mess. Someone had to fill in the gap for Andy.

"And I was happy to do it. Most of the time. He was dealt a crappy hand, and he's tried to make the most of it. He wasn't perfect, and he got himself into trouble a few times, but for the most part he's a good kid and he tries hard.

I just don't know that I can get him out of this jam. Not this time."

"If anyone can, you can." Jane's voice sounded like it had been through a shredder. Her eyes fluttered.

"Oh my gosh! You're awake!"

"Are you sure? I still feel like I'm asleep. Oof. My head is killing me. Why are you in my bedroom?"

"I'm not. We're in the infirmary. Do you remember what happened?"

She squinted at me. "Um. I have no idea what you're talking about." She touched her head and encountered the bandage. "What the—" She started to pull at it.

"Don't touch that!"

"Why? What is it?"

Dr. Fraser came in the room. "Well, look who's decided to rejoin us. Did you have a nice nap?"

"I'm not sure. What's going on?"

"You really don't remember anything?" I asked.

"You keep saying that. Dr. Fraser, tell it to me straight. Do I have amnesia?"

"Perhaps you may have a touch of retrograde amnesia. Can you tell me your name?"

"Jane Robertson Cobb."

"Do you remember anything that happened prior to you coming in here with a head injury?"

"Other than an argument with my sister? No."

Dr. Fraser looked at me. "Did you hit your sister over the head in anger?"

"What? No! I was in the shower!"

"Mrs. Cobb, do you believe your sister may have inflicted this injury on you?"

"Absolutely not. Are you saying someone bonked me on the head?"

"With a wooden oar," I said.

"Ouch. Literally."

"And you don't remember seeing anyone? Did anyone knock on the door?"

Jane's face was pinched with concentration. "Argh! I wish I could remember. I've got nothing."

There was a knock on the door, and Xavier poked his head inside. He first looked at me, his expression unreadable, and then he caught sight of Jane. "You are awake! This is great news!"

"Thanks. I'm like a soap opera character. I've got amnesia." She fluffed the pillow behind her.

"Congratulations. Not good for our case, though."

"Any luck with the search?" I asked.

He gave us a rundown. After I left, Xavier, Macy, and Sawyer spent thirty minutes systematically checking every boat and every paddle. They also looked around the helipad and examined the three rows of kayaks, stacked four-high. They never came across anything that appeared disturbed, much less broken. Each seemed to be present and accounted for.

Lily was in charge of the walkie-talkie for her group, and she radioed Xavier to tell him they'd found the location of the missing oar—not the oar itself, but the spot where it was supposed to be—on the Aegean level.

The three groups had reconvened inside the doors leading to the Aegean deck, minus Serena and Nikki. Apparently, they'd noped out after ten minutes and scurried back to the captain's lounge to sit in front of the fire.

Lily led everyone to the port side of the ship. The door to the stairs was nearby, making for an easy escape with the stolen oar, according to Xavier. Most residents used the elevators, even when traveling up or down one level.

At the aft of the ship, she came to an abrupt halt and pointed to a life preserver on the wall. Above the preserver was one orange and white wooden oar, mounted at an angle. Only a metal bracket remained where the other oar had hung. They said they radioed as soon as they located it, and no one had touched any of the surrounding area, so Xavier had texted Irving to bring a forensic kit.

In the meantime, he warned the gathered passengers, they needed to stay vigilant, keeping their eyes open and staying aware of their surroundings at all times.

"Lily brought up the reception dinner, which is still scheduled for five P.M." He checked his watch. "Which is in approximately forty minutes. She said since it is Thanksgiving and the food was already paid for, you might as well eat it together. Safety in numbers and all that."

"Char, you should go." Jane tried to sit up.

"No, I'll stay with you."

"I need my rest and you need to eat. You should go. Plus, you might hear something useful."

"Are you sure?"

"One hundred percent."

"Okay. I'll be back after dinner. Want me to bring you a plate?"

Jane tipped her head toward Dr. Fraser. "Is that okay?"

"Fine by me."

Xavier escorted me into the hallway.

"Are you going to dinner?" I asked.

He raised his eyebrows. "Why would I be included? It is a family event."

"I mean, it's Thanksgiving. No one should eat alone on Thanksgiving."

"I am not American. We do not celebrate this holiday in France."

"I understand that, obviously, but growing up in my house it was always an open-door policy on major holidays. We even had friends and neighbors from other parts of the world celebrate the Fourth of July with us."

"I would not feel comfortable infiltrating a family dinner."

"You make it sound like going undercover to sneak across enemy lines."

He gave me a pointed look. "I may not be perceived as an enemy, but I doubt I am perceived as a friend, either."

"Are you talking about them or me?"

He tilted his head. "I cannot imagine I am your favorite person, considering I have your nephew in custody."

I pressed my lips together. "I believe you're trying to solve these crimes, and I trust that when all is said and done, you will release Andy because he's been proven innocent. Not everything is as it appears, right?"

He arched his brow. "You seem to have much faith in me, having only met me a few days ago."

"Well, then, don't let me down."

Chapter Twenty-Nine

THE MOOD IN the private dining hall when I arrived at five could only have been described as odd. That had been the recurring theme of the trip.

It was to be expected, considering the original purpose of the dinner was to celebrate the wedding of Phoebe (murder victim) to Andy (prime suspect). Not to mention, two of the guests with the loudest and most boisterous personalities–Ivy (murdered) and Jane (bludgeoned)–were noticeably absent.

Neal arrived right after me.

"This is weird, huh?" Neal said. "Thanksgiving under these circumstances?"

Lily joined us. "Look, I know it's not ideal. We've got to just suck it up. We'll find something to be thankful for if it's the last thing we—" Lily stopped herself. "There's always something to be grateful for."

Neal gave her a contrite and hopeful smile. She sighed.

"C'mon, Neal. I guess we should stay together. For the time being, at least."

"I'll take it," he said.

I'd worn my aunt of the groom outfit because I'd packed exactly what I needed based on the scheduled itinerary. I hadn't brought a secondary *the wedding's off because the bride is dead and the groom is in the brig* outfit just in case.

My dress was silk with an embroidered lace and tulle overlay in a hue somewhere between mauve and dusty aubergine with what the saleswoman at the bridal store had called an illusion neckline. I kept calling it a V-neck, and she got a bit huffy about that. *It's a gown*, she'd scowled, *not a T-shirt from Abercrombie*. Whatever the neckline was called, it had a scalloped edge. The gown was a floor-length mermaid style, but I'd bought it two sizes larger than I needed so that it wasn't too contoured to my body.

Still, Frank's eyes nearly bugged out of his head at the sight of me. He leaned away from the table and gave a low whistle. Elaine dug her elbow into his side.

He fidgeted with his ill-fitting gray suit, overly starched white dress shirt, and orange tie. The shirt buttons were doing their very best to stay where they belonged, but it was clearly only a matter of time before one of them collapsed under the strain of his paunch. Frank wasn't heavy, he just carried more weight in the areas of his body where alcohol tended to congregate, like his second chin and his stomach.

His expression was more sour than usual, and I didn't think it was only about being chastised by his wife. He swigged his scotch on the rocks and waved Haimi over to refill his glass.

Elaine had opted for cosmos and already had two empty martini glasses in front of her and one half full. She brought a larger selection of clothes than I did, because I couldn't imagine her dress was intended to be worn at the wedding.

The leopard print bodice of the mini dress featured a low-cut princess sweetheart neckline. The sleeves were sheer black lace, as was the entire back of the dress all the way to her hips. Her hair had been teased, but she'd missed a spot in the back that was flat, and her makeup application seemed haphazard. Either she and Frank had taken a quick roll in the hay prior to dinner, or she'd been rushed and distracted while getting ready.

Elaine reached for her drink, and in the process knocked over one of the empty glasses into Macy's lap.

It turned out it wasn't completely empty.

"Elaine!" Macy jumped up and began urgently dabbing at her dress with her dinner napkin while muttering expletives under her breath.

A shade of rich, mossy green that deepened the brown in her distressed eyes until they almost looked black, the dress was a simple but elegant style, with a thin bow tied at the hollow of her throat and tiny brass buttons all the way down the front. She wore her brown hair in a tight bun at the nape of her neck. Her makeup was subtle and flawless, but her expression was distraught.

"I'm so sorry, Macy," Elaine slurred. "Here, come with me to the powder room and I'll help you get cleaned up."

Macy flung the napkin on the table and followed Elaine out of the room.

"Your girlfriend has a temper," Frank said to Sawyer.

"Your wife spilled her drink on her dress. She doesn't have a lot of money, and she saved up to buy it especially for the wedding." Sawyer glared at his uncle. "Speaking of tempers, what's got you so cranky tonight?"

Frank shifted his jaw. "I got some bad news today. Not sure how it's all gonna play out."

Dale guffawed. "Bad news? You call a raid at our storage facility bad news? It's not *bad news*, Frank. It's apocalyptic."

Whoa. Had Dale known what Frank was up to after all? I'd always assumed he was the ignorant silent partner. Maybe he'd wanted everyone to believe that. Or maybe he'd chosen not to see things he didn't want to acknowledge or have to deal with.

Might Dale and I have been similar in that respect? On some level, had I been purposely blind to Gabe's words, actions, and character in order to claim plausible deniability of the shortcomings in my marriage so that when it all crumbled around me, I could play victim? Deep down, I'd been aware. I wasn't dumb. All the signs had been there, but I'd looked past them.

Maybe I simply didn't want to know my life was a lie. Willful obtuseness.

Speaking of oblivious, Susan shifted in her seat next to Dale. Her beaded peach silk dress screamed mother of the bride, but her sedated grief-stricken face told the tale of a woman drowning under the weight of significant loss.

Susan didn't even glance at Dale or Frank despite the exchange.

"What do you mean there was a raid at the warehouse?" Clyde asked Dale. "You didn't think that was something worth bringing up to your son-in-law, the corporate attorney?"

"I've got plenty of attorneys," Frank interjected. "In my business, you need sharks. You're a minnow."

Clyde pushed his chair back and stood. "I don't need to take this. I'm not even technically part of this family anymore."

He marched out of the dining room.

"Daddy, is the business in trouble?" Lily asked.

Dale sighed. "I don't know, Lilibet. It's not good. Seems your uncle Frank here has been allowing shenanigans on the property. I haven't had a chance to discuss our legal exposure with the lawyers, but I'm guessing when the US government shows up, it's never a good sign."

Frank made a dismissive gesture. "It'll all work out."

"You could go to jail. Hell, we both could go to jail."

"Jail?" Lily's lip quivered.

Dale turned to Frank. "What the hell's a pangolin, anyway?"

"Do you mean penguin?" Nikki asked.

"I wish it were a penguin." Dale said.

"I know what it is," Serena offered. "A pangolin is like an anteater. Some people say they look like mini dinosaurs. We learned about them during our science lesson about threatened species."

Sawyer scrunched his brows together. "You were keeping exotic pets in the storage lockers, Uncle Frank?"

Dale scowled. "It's worse than that. Apparently, they found boots made from pangolin and skin cream made from protected sea turtle shells. As for the live pangolins, let's just say they weren't smuggling them to be pets."

His words hung in the air.

Serena burst into tears. "You monster!" she shouted at Frank and ran out of the room.

Rhonda, who hadn't said a word all evening, peered around the table like she'd just awoken from a deep slumber. "I don't want to be here anymore. Char, tell Andy I said good night."

She clumsily got out of the chair and slowly walked across the room and through the doorway.

"They're dropping like flies," Frank said and then shrugged. "More turkey for me."

"Oh, Uncle Frank." Lily groaned. She got up and left the room as well.

Neal, recognizing an opportunity to get back into his wife's good graces, followed her.

The remaining diners—Frank, Dale, Sawyer, Nikki, Vance, Duncan, and I—looked at each other, unsure what to do next. Except for Susan, of course, whose focus was on the condensation dripping down her water glass.

"Happy Thanksgiving," Sawyer muttered.

AFTER DINNER I went back to the medical center to check on Jane. Dr. Fraser was gone, but a woman was sitting in the reception area.

"How is she?"

"You must be Charlotte." The woman smiled. I guessed her to be in her forties, but only because of a few gray hairs at her temples and crow's feet around her brown eyes that appeared when she smiled. "I'm Becca Fraser. I'm the resident nurse and Ian's wife. He asked me to stay with her tonight. She's resting. Her vitals are all good. I think she's going to be just fine."

"That's a huge relief. Can I see her?"

"Of course, but just peek your head in. He wants her to get as much rest as possible. When we land in Victoria Saturday morning, he'd like a former colleague of his who specializes in head injuries to come onboard and examine her."

"That would be great."

I opened the door as quietly as I could. Jane was snoring. I took that as a good sign. I gently closed the door.

"Did she remember anything about who attacked her?" I asked Becca.

Becca shook her head. "Not that I'm aware."

"Shoot. I was hoping she could shed light on who's behind all this. Let me know if anything changes. I'm in room 701."

Becca smiled. "Will do. Have a great night. Try not to stress about her."

I chuckled. "I'll try."

The doors to the elevator were halfway closed, but I managed to push the button just in time. I was surprised to see Macy in the car. Her wide-open mouth and eyes said she was equally surprised to see me.

"Oh, hey, Charlotte."

"Hi, Macy." I stepped inside and pressed the keypad for

seven as the doors closed. No other buttons were lit. "Are you going back to your room?"

She furrowed her brows. "Huh?"

I indicated the keypad.

"Oh." She pressed six. "Shoot, I was spaced out. Forgot to press it."

"Where were you coming from?"

She rubbed two fingers at the hollow of her throat. "I went down to the casino on four. I played the slots for a bit."

The doors opened on six. I stood with my back to them to keep them from shutting. "Any luck?"

She stepped forward. "Not even a little."

"Bummer. Well, I'm glad I saved you from having to ride the elevators up and down."

She gave a forced laugh and stepped out of the car. "Yeah, thanks. I need to get my head out of the clouds." She slapped her palm to her forehead a couple times. "Good night."

I said, "Good night," and let the doors shut.

A few moments later, the elevator opened to the seventh floor.

Once again, I was surprised to see someone on the other side. This time, it was Serena.

"Oh, Charlotte." She touched her fingers to her chest and inhaled. "You startled me."

I noticed her wrist was still bare. "No luck finding your bracelet?"

"Oh, it's not lost. I just took it off because it was irritating my wrist."

I'd held the doors open long enough that they'd started screaming at me. "Ah. I have sensitive skin, too. Was that a gift from Andy? He has one that is quite similar."

"Actually, I gave it to him for his birthday last year."

"How nice. I'm curious. What were you doing on this floor?"

Her cheeks reddened. "I was hoping maybe Andy would be in your room. I figured with everything that's happened, Mr. Mesnier would know he couldn't have killed Phoebe and released him."

"You'd think, but no."

She stepped into the elevator. "We should probably let this thing close before we wake up the whole floor."

"Where are you headed now?"

"I think I'll go up to Azure Lounge and grab myself a drink."

"Okay, well, have fun. If I see him, I'll let Andy know you came by."

"Thanks," she said as the doors closed.

I was nearly back to my stateroom when I got a text from an unknown number.

"Hi Char, it's Elaine. I was wondering if we could meet later to talk about what happened today at Braithwaite Storage. I'm freaking out and I don't know who else to speak to about it."

Elaine chose me of all people? But I understood why everyone else might be too close to the situation. It was 7:45 P.M.

"Of course, Elaine. Would you like to come by my room at

eight to chat?"

The reply came lightning fast.

"Let's do 8:30. I have something I've got to do first. And can we meet on the ninth level on the observation deck? Afterward we can grab a drink."

"Perfect, I'll see you then."

Inside my suite, I headed for the bedroom. I kicked off my heels, pulled off my dress, and grabbed a pair of jeans, a sweater, and some tennis shoes from the closet. I could switch the shoes out for my steel-toed boots for warmth, but I ultimately stuck with the sneakers. They had an extra-cushy insert that made it like walking on a cloud, while my boots were heavy and tended to give me blisters on my baby toes.

Within ten minutes, I was ready for action. I grabbed Xavier's business card from the counter and my coat from the hall closet on my way out the door. As I walked to the elevator, I texted Xavier.

"If you don't hear from me by 8:45, come looking for me on the observation deck."

His response came as I got into the elevator and pressed nine.

"Who is this?"

"Charlotte McLaughlin"

"What are you doing?"

I decided not to answer his question, for fear he might stop me. Things had started to come together in my mind. It had taken me longer than it should have, but I was pretty certain I knew who had killed Phoebe and Ivy and who had attacked Jane.

My phone buzzed once more in my pocket as the elevator doors opened, but I ignored it. If I didn't read his message, I wasn't bound by its content, likely a cease-and-desist order.

Plausible deniability.

Chapter Thirty

THE DINING ROOM was still in full swing for dinner service, and the Azure Lounge was ablaze with flashing lights, live music, and the din of conversation. I zipped my coat and braced myself for the cold as I walked through the double glass doors and out to the observation terrace.

Once the doors shut behind me, the noise became muted. The ship was anchored in place, so the engines were at rest. Waves lapped against the hull, and I could hear seagulls squawking overhead, even though I couldn't see them.

There was one couple on the observation deck huddled together, looking up into the clear night sky. A pale band of green signaled the coming light show of the aurora borealis. The woman was shivering. I suspected she wasn't enjoying the experience but didn't want her companion to know it. They lasted only a few more minutes before returning to the warmth of Azure Lounge.

Even with my thick coat, my bones ached from the cold. It was below freezing by at least a few degrees. Also, I'd forgotten how useless jeans were in frigid temperatures. Thankfully, the wind was minimal.

Elaine was nowhere to be seen. I checked my phone.

8:07. I wasn't due to meet her for another twenty-three minutes. I ignored the notification of the three texts from Xavier.

There were very few lights on the Kalispera level above me. Every once in a while, though, I saw a flash of light bounce off the darkness above.

Someone was up there.

I crept over to the outer stairs. They were metal with teeth for traction, narrower than the interior stairs, probably used mostly by crew members. It wouldn't be good to slip and fall to the deck below. It did not look like a forgiving surface.

I put one toe on the first step. Thankfully, it made no sound. I mentally patted myself on the back for choosing to wear the tennis shoes with soft rubber soles rather than my boots.

I took another step, but this time the metal creaked below my foot. I froze in place. I was still in the shadows of the eaves, so when the light from above shone down, I felt confident I was hidden.

I held my breath and waited for the light to disappear. I couldn't hear footsteps on the deck above me, but I could see by the way the light flickered, the person behind it had moved away from the railing.

I took a tentative step and then another. Soon, I was able to peek over the edge to get a glimpse of the Kalispera deck.

A hooded figure dressed all in black was hunched over near the bar area where I'd tripped over Ivy's corpse. They seemed to be rooting around, using the flashlight on their phone to cast light on the ground. They scraped one of the lounge chairs across the deck and lifted one side to scour underneath it.

What was my next move? I couldn't text anyone; the glow from my phone would alert them that I was there. I didn't think I could climb much farther without making my presence known, and I didn't feel great about holding my own in a physical altercation. I hadn't worked out since Gabe's funeral, and even before that, I hadn't been in the best shape.

They had their back to me, so I climbed a couple more steps and shimmied onto the deck, doing my best to stay low.

I duck-walked a few feet and crouched behind a lounge chair. After about thirty seconds, my knees and hips were screaming for mercy, so I schlumped into a position Andy liked to call crisscross applesauce. I was pretty sure it was technically called the lotus in yoga, but my form definitely wasn't textbook. Also, not the greatest position for readiness to defend myself.

The dark form stumbled. fell to its knees, and emitted a grunt. They crawled around for a few moments, and then suddenly, they stopped. As their flashlight moved, I caught a glimpse of something shiny.

I knew without a doubt it was the missing piece of jewelry.

I thought the person muttered, "Oh, thank God," although the wind had begun to pick up and it made it difficult to make out the words.

The engines began to rumble below me. The ship's anchor clanged as it was pulled from the bottom of Glacier Bay.

The figure got to their feet and shoved the item in their coat pocket, swaying a bit with the ship's movement. They pulled out their phone and glanced at the screen before tucking it into their pocket.

I still couldn't see their face, although I was pretty sure I knew who was hidden under that hood. I suspected she was checking the time to make sure she wouldn't be late for our meeting.

She began to walk toward me with her head down. I hadn't thought about the fact I was smack dab in the way of the exit. She was about twenty feet away when the aurora thrust a bright ribbon of lime green across the sky.

She gasped at the colorful display.

Being right didn't feel as good as I thought it would. All I felt was sad. Sad for what had happened, for the lives that had been lost for no good reason, sad for the Braithwaites and what this would mean for them, and sad for what was to come. It was all so tragic and unnecessary.

The face, swathed in a glowing green, was that of Macy Keeling.

Her youth was on full display under the northern lights. I imagined nine-year-old Macy longing for beauty in her life amid the ugly she experienced every day.

None of her personal struggles justified her actions, but I felt empathy for the deprivation she'd endured that led to the desperation I believed had fueled them.

Unfortunately, in the same way the aurora had cast a glow on Macy's face, it also illuminated mine. She turned to leave and caught sight of me. She stood rooted to the spot and stared at me for a moment, calculating her options.

There was no way for me to escape. She was younger, more fit, and nimble. By the time I could clamber to my feet, she'd be there.

My phone buzzed in my pocket, but I didn't dare pull it out. Hopefully, it was getting close to eight thirty. I said a quick prayer that Xavier would know where to come looking for me when I wasn't on the observation deck and didn't respond to any of his texts.

"You're early for our meeting." Macy's voice was monotone.

"Yes." I slowly slid my legs to the side like a mermaid perched on a rock.

"Did you know it wasn't Elaine texting you?"

"I suspected as much."

"How?"

"The spelling and grammar were too good. Plus, I remembered Elaine mentioned she always used a ton of emoji in every text. Yours had none."

She pursed her lips. "Ah. I didn't know that. Oh well."

"Was that text actually from her phone number?"

"Of course. It had to be in case anyone checked later. I grabbed it from her purse when she followed me to the bathroom after spilling her drink on me. Easy. So, how did you know I'd be up here? We were supposed to meet downstairs."

"I didn't know. I saw the light from your phone. That's when I realized there must have been something left behind during the assault on Ivy." I pointed at her jacket. "I take it you found your locket."

She pulled it out and held it up so that the silver shimmered under the light of the aurora. "I didn't notice Ivy had pulled it off in our struggle. The chain broke. By the time I realized it was gone, the area was cordoned off." She shoved it back into her pocket.

"I can't understand why you hurt Ivy."

"I didn't want to hurt her, not initially, at least. I wanted to be sisters. I texted her that morning, asked if she wanted to go to lunch together. I didn't hear back, so I went to talk to her at her room. Clyde said she was at the spa with you and Jane. I told him I was hoping to take her to lunch, and she must have missed my text. He laughed and told me she got my message." Her face hardened.

"That must not have felt very good."

"She ignored me. She didn't even respond. So rude. It's not okay to treat people like that."

"Macy, if you didn't intend to kill her, why did you lock me in the sauna?"

"Look, I didn't plan to kill her, but I also knew if my back was against the wall and I had no other choice, I'd do what I had to do—like with Phoebe—and I didn't need you sticking your nose into it."

"Tell me what happened."

She blew hair out of her face. "I came down to the spa. No one was at the check-in desk, so I peeked in the book to see where Ivy was scheduled to be. I saw you go into the sauna, and I decided I would keep you there. I know how you like to be in everyone's business."

"How'd you get her out of the spa and up here?"

"I signed into a texting app with Sawyer's account and asked her to meet me up here ASAP."

"What did she do when she saw it was you instead of Sawyer?"

"She was pissed. I told her I just needed to know why she ignored my texts. She said I was a psycho, and she didn't know what Sawyer saw in me. She told me I was too clingy, first with Phoebe and then with Mom. I lost it. I can't even really tell you what happened next because I kind of blacked out. When I realized what had happened, Ivy was lying on the ground with a head wound, not moving. There was blood on the pole next to me like I conked her head against it. I don't remember." She shrugged.

"Mom?"

She squinted at me. "Huh?"

"You said she told you that you were too clingy with *Mom*."

Her smile was pained. "Oh, uh, Susan."

"I bet that really hurt your feelings."

"Everything I've done was to be part of that family. None of those kids appreciate having a mom like Susan. They're all spoiled brats. And then to be annoyed with me for trying to care for Susan, it just made me so..." She growled in frustration.

"Hurt?" I supplied.

"And angry. Really angry."

I watched as she fought an internal battle.

"Sometimes it's hard to know what to do with all that rage," I said.

Her lip quivered. "My mom was a rager. Not all the time. Sometimes we had a lot of fun together. On Sunday nights we'd watch rom-coms and eat popcorn with chili powder and lime juice sprinkled on top. She thought she invented it. I didn't have the heart to tell her about Tajin." She shifted her jaw. "But then she'd get dumped by one of her loser boyfriends. She'd get drunk and gamble away our rent money."

"That's why you don't drink or gamble. You told me in the elevator you were at the casino."

Her mouth formed an O. "I didn't realize you knew that." She chuckled. "Oops. Yeah, those are disgusting habits for weak people like my mom. And Frank." She practically spit his name. "At fourteen I was cleaning toilets for our landlord. I think my mom made up the difference...if you know what I mean."

I didn't want to think about it. "Sounds like you had to carry a heavy load of responsibility at a young age."

"Not to hear my mom tell it. She made me feel like I was a two-ton weight around her neck. She'd say, *Marcella, if it weren't for you, I'd be living the good life. None of these guys want to date a single mother. And the ones that do? Well, they have bad intentions.*" Macy wagged her finger. "She'd wag her finger at me and say, *Do you know how many times I've had to give up a man because of you?* Like it was my fault they were creeps."

Marcella. Macy. Cellaphane. It was all starting to make sense.

"It wasn't your fault, Macy. You were a child."

She snapped at me, "I know that. You think I don't know that? You don't think every therapist and psychiatrist I've seen since I was nine and got sent to foster care for the first time, hasn't said the same thing?"

"What happened to your mom?"

"I turned eighteen. That's what happened. She kicked me out. I had nothing. I couch-surfed, and I did a few things I'm not proud of, but I survived. I met some people who taught me how to be a gamer. I was good at it. I even joined some tournaments and won. That helped get me off the streets. I even started going to school to be a coder."

Ah, the computer tech savvy required to shut off part of the security system. That had gotten lost in all the chaos of the past several days.

"How does Phoebe fit in? I assume you were her stalker."

Her face flushed. "I wasn't a stalker. I was her friend! I was the first to comment on every video, and she responded, too. Maybe not every time but a lot of times. And I battled her trolls. People could be so nasty. One time I hacked a guy's email and found out he'd been cheating on his wife. I made an example of him." She jutted her chin with pride.

"Seems like Phoebe became important to you."

"We were important to each other. Her videos were everything to me. They gave me a glimpse of a life I didn't know existed. I started to believe that maybe it was possible for me, too." A single tear rolled down her face, along with a streak of black from her eye makeup. "I just wanted her to know how much she meant to me."

Her expression became clouded. "Then she started acting like I was scaring her. I loved her! How could she think that?"

My phone buzzed again. If I could keep her talking, Xavier would find me in time.

"When she shut down her accounts, I was devastated. I got so depressed. That's when I realized I could get close to her another way."

"Sawyer."

"Yeah. He's not the brightest, and it turns out, I'm pretty good at getting people to trust me."

"If you cared so much about Phoebe, why did you kill her?"

She lifted her chin in defiance. "It's not like I didn't give her a chance. Lots of chances, as a matter of fact. It turned out that in real life, she wasn't as nice as in her videos. She didn't appreciate the life I aspired to have. So, I decided to take it for myself."

"But that only worked if she was out of the picture. And Andy, too, I guess."

She shrugged. "He was an easy target. After Phoebe stormed out of dinner that first night, Andy followed her. Sawyer and I came over to take their spots at the table, and I realized Andy's fingerprints were all over his steak knife. Who uses a steak knife to butter their bread?" She rolled her eyes. "Lucky for me, I guess. Anyway, I wrapped it in my napkin and slipped it into my purse. I didn't plan to use it that night, but then they had that big fight and it felt like an early Christmas gift."

I shuddered at her cavalier discussion of plotting a murder and framing an innocent man. "So how did you get her down to the fourth level to meet you?"

"I texted her to meet me on the VIP deck because I had evidence of her relationship with Neal."

"I thought you only found out about that after Phoebe's death."

Macy's laugh sounded hollow. "That's the thing! I was bluffing. I mean, I'd seen a couple glances between them. One night when I was outside her house, he was there for a long time so I suspected something had happened between them, but I didn't know for sure about the affair until she texted me back. She was freaking out, begging me not to tell Andy or Lily. That's another thing. She slept with her sister's husband. And not even the hot one. The boring beige one." She made a retching sound. "She didn't deserve to be part of that family."

"That's not how families work, Macy. It's not about deserving anything."

"You would say that. Your sister is your best friend."

"Yes, and you nearly killed her, too."

"I needed you two to stop investigating. You were starting to get too close to the truth." She laughed. "I didn't care who I took out of commission. She opened the door, so she's the one who got cracked." She shrugged. It reeked of *I don't make the rules.*

I felt three buzzes in a row from my phone. I was sure it was Xavier letting me know he was nearby. I'd keep her distracted and talking. "So, you got Phoebe to the VIP deck and then what?"

"Oh, you know, suddenly Miss Perfect knew her whole persona was about to be exposed as a lie, and she was pleading with me. It was pathetic really."

"You didn't have to kill her."

"No. But then she crossed the line."

"How?"

"When she realized the begging wasn't getting her anywhere and I didn't want a payoff, she got really mean. She said I was jealous. Jealous of her life. She said Sawyer had hooked up with Nikki the night before the cruise and he was going to dump me when this was all over."

"That had to hurt."

She shrugged. "Ehh. Not really. I mean, I've been using him. I was hoping to marry him, though. Not because I wanted to be with him." She made a disgusted face. "I just wanted to have the Braithwaite name. I wanted to be official." Her expression morphed into a scowl. "She said her mother would never accept me. That she barely tolerated me. That she felt sorry for me." She shook her head. "I can't stand people feeling sorry for me."

"I get that. Believe me. So, you snapped."

"I didn't snap! I'm not crazy!" She inhaled a deep breath and lowered her voice. "I'm not crazy."

"You killed two people, Macy. That's not okay."

She tsked. "You make it sound like I was out of control.

Phoebe made me angry, no doubt. All that did was validate that she was toxic for this family. I did Dale and Susan a favor. I cut out the cancer. Same with Ivy. They were both spoiled brats." She jerked her head a couple times. "Some people just don't know how good they have it."

I shifted to my knees and attempted to stand.

"Nope," she said.

Macy was holding a carving knife.

"These cabins are really well-stocked. They've got everything. *En garde*!" She lunged at me like a fencer and giggled.

A bright light shone on her face, temporarily blinding her. She shielded her eyes.

"Macy, release the weapon!" Xavier called from behind me.

I didn't hesitate. I rolled to my right, out of her range.

Macy squinted past the light and into the darkness. "Oh, hey there, Pepe le Pew Pew! I see you finally caught up with Charlotte and me. Pretty embarrassing to be outsmarted by a couple of girls, huh?"

"You are clever, I will give you that."

She thrust her knife in his direction. "You're not giving me anything! I'm taking it. Isn't it just like a man to take credit for a woman's work, Char? Charlotte?"

I hunched behind another lounge chair and tried not to breathe.

"Aw, come on, Charlotte. I thought we were in this together."

"Macy, I am ordering you to drop the knife."

"I am ordering you to drop zee knife." She mimicked

him with an abysmal French accent. "How about no? How about we do things my way for once?"

"What is it you want?"

I suspected he was placating her, but I didn't care as long as it deescalated the situation.

"I want a helicopter, ten million dollars, and I want Charlotte to come with me so no one tries any funny business."

"She is not going anywhere with you." His tone was firm. He wasn't going to let anything bad happen to me on his watch. "You have no leverage here."

"Is that so?" Macy's gaze, still alight from the flashlight and aglow from the aurora, darted around without landing anywhere. "I don't think so. I'm in charge of my life now. I'm done with people trying to control me." A small smirk twitched at the corner of her mouth. "Somebody tell that witch Nikki she can have Sawyer. He's a terrible kisser anyway."

With that, she ran full speed toward the edge. Xavier yelled for her to stop, but she leaped onto the railing and vaulted herself over the side. There was a whoop, followed by a splash.

"Oh my gosh!" I ran to the edge and peeked into the dark frigid waters below.

The next several minutes were a blur. Xavier got on his radio and called for the captain to halt the ship and send up flares. He directed nearby crewmembers, who ran to release one of the rescue vessels, shining spotlights across the water, and yelling for Macy.

I stood in shocked silence, unable to move. Xavier wrapped a wool blanket around my shoulders. Irving was with him.

"Charlotte, go with Lonnie. He will take you someplace safe and warm. I will come see you when I can."

My teeth chattered, both from the cold and from the adrenaline running through my body. Irving guided me to the service elevator. The ship's horn sounded, and two red flares shot into the air, swirling with the green bands of the aurora.

"Isn't it crazy?" Irving said.

"What?"

"It's exactly one month until Christmas."

Chapter Thirty-One

"I CAN'T BELIEVE it." Sawyer held his head in his hands. "I just can't believe it."

Nikki hovered over him, rubbing his back. "You couldn't have known."

The girl moved quickly. I gave her that.

"Let me get this straight," Frank said. "That little mousy thing killed two people and then tried to take out Jane *and* Charlotte?"

He looked to me for confirmation. I just stared back.

Once more, we'd gathered in the captain's lounge. Xavier had radioed Irving to let him know he'd be in shortly to update all of us. Irving stood watch by the door, despite the threat having been…resolved.

Susan rocked back and forth, verging on catatonic. Rhonda sat next to her looking the more stable and lucid of the two. Actually, Rhonda appeared the most well-rested of the whole group, but she'd also been sleeping every time we'd knocked on her door.

Dale's face sagged and his gray hair frizzed out of his ponytail. There was a strong possibility he hadn't slept in four days, and it showed. He'd aged about ten years just this week alone.

"So, what now?" Lily asked. "There won't even be a trial. It's like the nightmare is over but we can't wake up."

Neal attempted to move closer with his arm stretched toward her, but her scowl stopped him mid-hug. He had a long, arduous road back to her good graces. I wasn't sure he had it in him.

The somber mood was broken when Andy burst into the room. Irving reacted the way any well-trained officer would, grabbing Andy and thrusting him onto the ground with his right arm wrenched behind his back.

"Hey!" my nephew yelped.

"Andy?" I rushed over. "Irving, let him go."

"Oh, Sorry, Mrs. McLaughlin. Instinct kicked in." He helped Andy to his feet. "Sorry, man."

Andy grabbed his right wrist. "No worries, I get it. Everybody's been on edge."

I leaped at him and threw my arms around him. Tears flowed down my cheeks.

He laughed and hugged me back. "It's okay, Auntie Char. I'm okay."

I released him and put my hands on both sides of his face. "Is it over?"

"It's over. Well, this part of it, anyway. Now I've gotta come to terms with everything that's happened." He held me at arm's length and then glanced over at Dale and Susan. He gave me a sad smile, and I returned the gesture.

Andy approached Susan and kneeled in front of her, his eyes red. "Susan, I'm so sorry. I'm sorry I didn't do a better job of protecting your baby girl."

She blinked at him a couple times until her internal light switch flipped and she appeared to see him for the first time. "Oh, Andy, I know you loved her. She was a comet. She just burned too bright and too fast for this world." She stared at the ceiling. "She's with the stars now. She'll be okay."

Dale nodded solemnly. "You'll always be important to us, son."

Xavier entered the room. Andy stood and wiped tears from his eyes with the back of his hand. He gave Xavier a quick head bob, and Xavier returned it in kind.

"I wanted to let you all know we have recovered the body of Macy Keeling."

A murmur washed across the room. People exchanged glances, but no one seemed to know what to say.

"I cannot begin to comprehend how difficult these past few days have been for all of you. You came on this ship expecting to celebrate, but instead you are mourning two members of your family. While I am relieved that we have identified the perpetrator of these crimes, I imagine the discovery that it was one of your own must bring added sadness and confusion."

Sawyer lifted his head and made eye contact with Xavier.

"Monsieur Braithwaite, this revelation must be especially painful for you. I want to reassure you that all of us were fooled by Madame Keeling's carefully crafted persona. You are a victim here, not complicit."

"I appreciate you saying that, but it's gonna take some time before I could even consider the possibility this isn't my fault. I brought that woman into my family, and she destroyed it from within!"

"Sawyer." Dale rose and took a seat next to his son. Nikki made room so that he could put his arm around Sawyer.

"I'm sorry, Dad." Sawyer broke down.

Dale hugged him tighter. "I promise you; this isn't your fault. We considered her to be a family member. We chose to get close to her. She exploited the dysfunction in our family and showed where we all need to improve."

Frank grunted. "I always thought there was something off about that girl."

"Oh, Frank, shut up!"

Ooh, he did not expect that from Elaine.

"Don't you talk to me that way."

"Somebody needs to," she snapped.

Frank sat back in stunned silence. I suspected it was the first time Elaine had ever stood up to him. I enjoyed the moment, a taste of what was to come when the authorities met Frank at the docks when we landed at the Port of Seattle.

Xavier raised his left eyebrow, and I caught a glimpse of a smile forming.

"We will sail all night tonight and tomorrow, landing early Saturday morning in Victoria. Then we will go on to Seattle, where we will disembark early Sunday. At that time, I will need you all to meet with local investigators and answer any questions they may have. The three bodies will be transported to the King County medical examiner's office for autopsies. After that is complete, Monsieur and Madame

Braithwaite, you will be able to take custody of your daughters for whatever arrangements you'd like to make."

"A funeral and burial, of course," Susan said.

"Mom," Lily said. "Macy may have been a psycho, but she knew everything about Phoebe from studying her videos. That's why all the gifts she sent anonymously to the house were Phoebe's favorite things. I think we should consider the possibility Phoebe really wanted her ashes spread in the Montlake Cut."

"We can discuss this later as a family in private," Dale said. "Thank you, Mr. Mesnier. For all you've done. You've probably never had to deal with something like this before. I bet you'll be glad to see us get off this ship."

"I wish I could have discovered the killer of Phoebe before she took another life." Xavier glanced at me. "Truthfully, despite the circumstances, it has been a pleasure to meet you all." He held out his hand to Andy. "I wish you the best. I hope you understand I was simply doing my job."

Andy shook Xavier's hand. "I know. She did a pretty good job of making me look like a killer."

Xavier turned to me. "I was told your sister is awake and asking for you. Would you like me to accompany you to the medical?"

"I'd appreciate that, thank you. Are you coming, Andy?"

He jerked his head toward Serena, who was hovering nearby. "I'll be there in a bit. I need to talk to Serena first."

Xavier and I walked to the elevator without saying a word, and yet the air between us felt heavy and charged. His jaw clenched and released.

The elevator ride was similarly tense and awkward. We made no eye contact, choosing instead to watch the numbers as they went down to five.

Becca Fraser glanced up from her desk when we walked in.

"How is she?" I asked.

"She's awake. Groggy, but she's been cracking jokes." Becca smiled. "She's a lively one."

"Yes, she is. Can I go in to see her?"

"Yes, of course."

I turned to Xavier. "Thank you. For everything."

He pressed his lips together and ducked his chin. "*Mon plaisir*. Truly." He gave a half bow to Becca, turned his back on us, and walked out of the medical office.

I carefully opened the door, but it creaked, and Jane's eyelids fluttered open.

"Hey."

"You don't have to whisper," she said in a raspy voice. "I'm awake. Did I hear Frenchy out there?"

"Yes, he brought me down here. He's gone now."

"I heard what happened. Nurse Becca filled me in. Are you okay?"

I sat on the chair next to her bed. "I am now that Andy's released and I know you're going to be okay."

"Other people get to take care of you sometimes, too, Char."

"We can talk about that once you're no longer lying in this bed."

Jane sighed and rolled her eyes. "So, how did she do it?"

I filled Jane in on everything I knew. How Macy had become obsessed with Phoebe's videos to escape her difficult home life, how she'd felt spurned by Phoebe, and how she infiltrated the family through Sawyer. I told her about Macy luring Phoebe to the VIP deck with a text threatening to reveal her affair with Neal.

"What about Ivy?"

"She said she was upset that Ivy was ignoring her texts. She logged into Sawyer's texting app to get Ivy up to the Kalispera deck, and when Ivy saw it was Macy, she just got mean. Macy claimed she blacked out and bonked Ivy's head against the pole."

"Speaking of bonking heads, did they ever find the oar she hit me with?"

"Not yet. I'm sure Xavier and his team with be scouring the ship to find it. He says they'll be passing the investigation over to local authorities when we dock...along with the bodies. Also, Frank will have his welcome wagon."

Jane gave a feeble smile. "I'm looking forward to that. Does that make me a bad person?"

"If it does, then the same applies to me."

"You're a good person, Char, and a wonderful sister. You deserve better than the hand you've been dealt."

I sniffed. "I've been thinking about that a lot over the past few days. I'm starting to realize that I played a role in my own bamboozlement. Is that a word?"

"It is now."

"Anyway, I've decided it's time I take a more active role in my own life. I'm not a passenger. I'm the driver."

"I hope that means what I think it means."

"What do you think it means?"

"Hopefully that you're about to tell me to give notice at my apartment because the Cobb sisters are hitting the open seas."

I laughed. "I'm a McLaughlin, not a Cobb."

"I don't care what you call yourself as long as it's preceded by *ahoy there*."

Chapter Thirty-Two

"HERE'S TO NEW beginnings." Jane hoisted her champagne flute in the air.

I held up my glass. "To new beginnings."

We both took a sip.

"Any word on Frank?" She raised her voice to be heard over the bubbling jets of the hot tub.

"Nope. Still in the wind."

When we'd docked in Victoria, British Columbia, Canada, Frank and Elaine had gotten off the ship, along with several of the other passengers. After the horns sounded our departure, Frank was nowhere to be found. Elaine said they'd gone to the Empress Hotel for tea, but when she'd turned around to ask if he wanted a scone with jam, he was gone. One of his accomplices in the smuggling ring had not only tipped him off about the raid but also his impending arrest once we docked in Seattle, so he decided to hide out in Canada instead of facing the music.

"Xavier says they've frozen all Frank's accounts, so all he's got is the cash he had on him. Eventually, he'll have to try to get back into the US and when he does, they'll nab him. Elaine's already filed for divorce," I said.

"I have to ask. How are you feeling now the house has finally closed? Has it sunk in?"

"It's a little sad but also a relief. I'm not sure I've completely processed that chapter of my life closing yet." I sipped my champagne. "I have no doubt the people who bought it will enjoy it more than Gabe and I did."

"You had good times there, didn't you?"

"I did. *We* did. It's just hard to remember what that felt like. Everything I've discovered since Gabe's death has tarnished those memories and I find myself wondering if any of it was real. I was there, I lived the experiences, but looking back on them through the lens of his betrayal, they're no longer canon in my story. It's unsettling that I can't rely on my own memories to inform my identity."

"What Gabe did or didn't do has nothing to do with your identity, you know."

"I'm starting to believe that, but for twenty years my identity was wrapped up in being Gabe's wife, so it's gonna take some time to figure out who I am aside from living in that house and playing that role. Moving onboard and buying the Seattle condo are the first steps."

"I love that it's so close to Pike Place Market, and it'll be nice to have somewhere to stay when we're in town. I doubt Andy and Serena will want us barging in on them at their new place."

"I'm one hundred percent sure of that." I laughed.

"How worried are you that Kyrie Dawn will win her lawsuit and we'll have to give all this up?"

"I talked to the attorney this morning. He says choosing

to live here full-time will help our standing. Possession is nine-tenths of the law, and all that."

"I'll bet she was furious when she found out."

I shrugged. "I try not to think about her if I can help it. Now that the dust has settled and you've said your good-byes, do you think you'll miss your job at the library and all your friends in Turlock?"

"Nah. It was time to move on. I've spent my life reading about the adventures of others. It's time I experience some things for myself." She smiled at me. "I'm glad I get to go on these adventures with you, my sister and best friend."

"Me too. Although, we haven't lived together since the eighties. You think we're gonna drive each other crazy?"

"Probably. Although, probably not as much as we're gonna drive poor old Frenchy crazy. Speak of the devil..." She crooked her head in the direction of the bar.

I followed her line of sight and locked gazes with Xavier. He gave me a slight nod and a slighter smile.

I raised my glass in salute.

As I set it on the edge of the hot tub, I caught my smiling reflection in the glass, aglow from the setting sun as it sunk beneath the Pacific Ocean.

I could get used to this.

The End

If you enjoyed *Until Depths Do Us Part*,
you'll love the next book in…

The Cruising Sisters Mystery

Book 1: *Until Depths Do Us Part*

Book 2: *A Matter of Life and Depths*

Book 3: *Frightened to Depths*

Acknowledgments

First, I want to thank my family for being good sports about the chaos my renaissance has brought into our lives. I appreciate all the patience, love, and encouragement.

To my agency siblings, I'm so grateful to be part of the BRLA family.

To my agent, Dawn Dowdle, who barely batted an eye when I said I wanted to try something new. I hope I've made you proud.

Thank you as always to my extended family and friends, especially my writing sisters.

Lastly, thank you to my editor Julie from Tule Publishing, who saw a vision for this book and series and is guiding me to new and exciting things in my writing.

About the Author

Kate B Jackson (KB Jackson) is an author of mystery novels for grownups and mystery/adventure novels for kids. She lives in the Pacific NW with her husband and at least one of her four grown children at any given time. Her debut middle grade release is "The Sasquatch of Hawthorne Elementary" (Reycraft Books) about a twelve-year-old boy hired by the most popular girl at his new school to investigate what she saw in the nearby woods. Book one in the Chattertowne Mysteries series, "Secrets Don't Sink," (Level Best Books July 2023) introduces Audrey O'Connell, a small town feature reporter who, when her former boyfriend's body is found floating in the local marina, uncovers the depths to which some will go to keep secrets submerged.

Thank you for reading

Until Depths Do Us Part

If you enjoyed this book, you can find more from all our great authors at TulePublishing.com, or from your favorite online retailer.

www.ingramcontent.com/pod-product-compliance
Lightning Source LLC
LaVergne TN
LVHW041108080826
845145LV00007B/1729

* 9 7 8 1 9 6 4 7 0 3 6 8 8 *